Amy turned to face him and leaned against the trunk of the maple.

"One of the main reasons I chose to come back to Heartache now is to support my sister when Heather testifies against the guy who tried to kidnap her." She drew a deep breath. "So I promise you, I am committed to seeing Jeremy Covington behind bars, too. I may have been absent from this family for ten years, but I'm still a Finley, and hearing how that creep threw her into the back of a van with another girl that he'd tied up..." She shook her head, unable to finish the thought. "I am here to see justice done, Sam. But I am not here to testify."

An interesting distinction, Sam thought. Especially considering no one had asked her to testify when she claimed not to know anything.

The more she resisted, the more he wanted to record her statement. As a cop, he had a naturally suspicious nature, but his instincts told him she knew more than she was letting on. But those same instincts warned him if he pushed Amy too hard, she would shut down altogether...

Dear Reader,

The idea of "going home" holds unique memories for all of us. Some of them are warm and wonderful as we remember happy Thanksgiving dinners gathered around a table laden with food or long summers playing in the backyard with friends. But for people who have experienced a trauma, going home can be riddled with lots of unpleasant memories, too.

For Amy Finley, returning to Heartache means a mix of emotions. I am inspired by her strength and determination even as I understand why she needed to stay away from her family for so long. The payoff of returning—a possible healing of old relationships—is dangerously enticing for a woman with so much history in Heartache, Tennessee.

I welcome you back to town with open arms and hope you enjoy Amy's return as much as I did. A whole lot has changed since she left, but the new town sheriff is as appealing as he was as a teen. Maybe some things never change...

Happy reading,

Joanne Rock

JOANNE ROCK

Whispers Under a Southern Sky

HARLEQUIN®SUPERROMANCE®

ISBN-13: 978-0-373-61001-3

Whispers Under a Southern Sky

Printed in U.S.A.

Three-time RITA® Award nominee **Joanne Rock** has penned over seventy stories for Harlequin. An optimist by nature and perpetual seeker of silver linings, Joanne finds romance fits her life outlook perfectly—love is worth fighting for. A former Golden Heart® Award recipient, she has won numerous awards for her stories. Learn more about Joanne's imaginative Muse by visiting her website, joannerock.com, or following @JoanneRock6 on Twitter.

Books by Joanne Rock

HARLEQUIN SUPERROMANCE

Heartache, TN

Promises Under the Peach Tree
Nights Under the Tennessee Stars
Dances Under the Harvest Moon

HARLEQUIN DESIRE

Bayou Billionaires

His Secretary's Surprise Fiancé
Secret Baby Scandal

Visit the Author Profile page at Harlequin.com, or joannerock.com, for more titles.

To Mom and Dad with so much love.

CHAPTER ONE

RUNNING ON FUMES, Amy Finley coasted into the driveway of her temporary home shortly before midnight. Even after ten years away from Heartache, Tennessee, she'd remembered how to get to her father's old hunting cabin. It was one of the only places in her hometown where she'd actually made a few happy memories.

Now, shoving out of the passenger side of her car—the driver's door was broken—Amy stepped onto the pine-needle-covered ground in the woodsy hills east of where she'd grown up.

Her sisters figured no one had been in the cabin in the last six years. Their father had died four years ago, but even before then he'd abandoned his old habit of coming up here in the fall as he'd gotten more involved in his career as mayor of Heartache.

Erin, the older of Amy's two sisters, had promised Amy the electricity and water would be turned on this week, so the property would be slightly more livable for Amy's return.

She found the key to the front door by sliding a hand beneath a windowsill around the side of the building. Same place it had always been, inside a hollowed-out knot in the pinewood. It was a miracle no rodents had made off with the key in all these years, although she hadn't been worried. She would find her way inside the rustic cabin one way or another. Security wasn't tight around here.

Something she planned to address as soon as possible if she wanted to feel safe.

At the thought, a shiver tripped over her skin despite the mild fall weather. Tucking deeper into her pale blue hoodie, she refused to think about The Incident. The night that had driven her from Heartache for an entire decade, making her miss her father's funeral. Her sister's wedding. Her mother's alleged recovery from severe bipolar disorder.

She'd believe *that* when she saw it. If she ever worked up the nerve to face her mom again, anyway.

For now she told herself to take her return one step at a time. Her first step was moving into the cabin and starting renovations. She would need the distraction of a project to get her through the other tasks she'd set for herself. She was here to make amends with her family—her siblings if not her mother. And, perhaps more important, she'd come home to support her sister as Heather prepared to testify against a local criminal awaiting his trial.

Amy had her own reasons for needing to see the man behind bars, but no one in her family knew about those, and she planned to keep it that way.

One step at a time.

Turning the rusted, thin key in the lock, she used her shoulder to nudge open the door. Instead of smelling the must and mildew she expected, however, the clean scent of lemon polish drifted past her nose. *What on earth?*

The door creaked open on stiff hinges and a floorboard groaned under her tread-worn tennis shoes as she stepped inside. Flicking on the lights in the small space, she saw the pine-plank floors had been swept clean. One of the single-pane windows had also been opened, and a set of calico curtains hung on the wrought iron rods above the windows.

Her sisters co-owned a consignment shop in the small downtown area. They must have brought some finds from their business up here to give Amy a warm welcome. An antique glass milk jug held a vase of wildflowers on the tiny counter next to the white porcelain kitchen sink. A green plaid place mat held a bottle of wine, a corkscrew, one clean glass and a pan of brownies visible through a layer of plastic wrap.

She dropped the duffel bag from her shoulder and closed the front door behind her, drawn to the brownie pan despite the chilly breeze blowing through the whole house from the open window. A crisp yellow notecard sat atop the treats.

Welcome home, Sis. Can't wait to see you when you're ready. Love, Heather and Erin

It was the kind of thoughtful gesture a normal sister should love.

Except that it had taken her ten long years to face her siblings after that hellish week when she'd been seventeen and her world had fallen apart.

This hunting cabin was still fifteen miles from the home where she'd grown up, but it was the closest she could bring herself to seeing any of the Finleys even now.

She didn't know if she'd ever really be ready to face any of them again.

Setting the card back on the brownie pan,

she moved around the small cabin, closing the window so she could warm up the place.

Not much had changed besides the curtains. A common area with a fireplace made of river stones dominated the cabin. Off to the side of the living space was the tiny kitchen, including a few cupboards and a refrigerator, but no stove or oven. Back when she'd come here with her father, they'd used an outdoor grill or a campfire for all the cooking. Two small bedrooms held built-in bunk beds that were little more than plywood planks anchored to the rough log walls. There was no furniture besides a small table in the kitchen with two ladder-back chairs. Thankfully, her sisters had left a box labeled "memory foam mattress topper" on one of the plywood bunks.

Amy had brought a bedroll, but considering the cabin's level of rustic simplicity, the memory foam was a bonus she wouldn't refuse. With no central heat or air, she'd have to build a fire, but she'd brought her own supplies to do just that.

She wasn't sure how she felt about her sisters coming up here to prep the place for her. She'd been adamant when she agreed to come home that she'd only see them on her own terms. When she felt ready for that.

For tonight, just being back in Tennessee,

back in this tiny town, was enough for her to handle. After digging a flashlight out of her duffel, she flicked it on and stalked out to the car to retrieve her boxes.

It would be hours before she prepped the place enough for it to be comfortable, even with the freshly hung calico curtains and sleeping bag. Or maybe because of them.

Her chest tightened, and it wasn't from the strain of carrying in the heavy load of firewood. She'd become a loner. Practically a recluse. When she'd left here, she'd moved to Atlanta and become a waitress, eventually putting herself through college since she refused to take a nickel from her family. Even her father.

Funny to think how a person could become so isolated even in a big city, but it was easy. Amy was an expert at being by herself. What she wasn't good at was family.

Community.

Trust of any kind.

She hadn't gotten where she was today because of those things. She now had an accounting degree and a potential start-up business in spite of all of them. Maybe that was why, after she got a fire going in the big hearth, she ignored her sisters' gifts and unrolled a sleeping bag in the living area. Just like she used to do with her father when they would tell stories late into the night.

Disregarding the growl of her empty stomach, Amy hoped tomorrow she'd be stronger. Because tonight, all she wanted to do was to get in her car again and drive to Atlanta. Back to a place where she didn't have to work so hard to fix relationships that had failed her.

THREE CUPS OF coffee into his day, Sheriff Samuel Reyes struggled to keep his tired eyes focused on the map in front of him. He hated this kind of research even on a good day—the boring-as-snot part of police work that kept him behind a desk. Today he was trying to make pieces of a resistant puzzle fall into some kind of meaningful order. He'd been over and over the map of Heartache's quarry, trying to find a pattern or a clue in the pins that marked places where the sheriff's department had discovered evidence in his current case.

The pins were old school, as was the paper map. But for him, there was no substitute for working with his hands and seeing the physical images.

Today, however, his brain was failing to connect any dots. Part of it was because he'd reviewed the same map a hundred times. But it was mostly because he'd spent the majority of last night pacing the floors with his infant son. A baby he hadn't even known existed until three weeks ago. A baby his ex-girlfriend had handed him on his doorstep along with the news that she had grown weary and needed a break from the two-month-old she hadn't seen fit to tell him he'd fathered.

So he'd been parenting the infant alone for the last three weeks. Nothing like trial by fire.

"Any luck?" Heartache's mayor, Zach Chance, walked into the town-hall conference room that served as Sam's office most days.

With his patrician features and perfectly pressed collared shirt, Zach looked the part of a slick politician even though he was a fairly normal dude. For a tech-company millionaire.

Zach had cleaned up in the digital security market before returning to Heartache from the West Coast two years prior. He still managed his virtual company from Heartache, but he was now the mayor. He'd also been the one who'd twisted Sam's arm into leaving San Jose to become Heartache's sheriff. Both men had grown up in Heartache, so it hadn't been that big of a sacrifice to come back.

Sam liked small-town living more as an adult than he had as a kid, even if some days he couldn't keep his eyes open while working.

"Nothing yet." He gripped his empty cup

of coffee and pitched the paper container in the trash can. "We need more evidence before Jeremy Covington goes to trial, but I'll be damned if I know where we can get it."

His eyes felt like sandpaper when he blinked. Hell, he'd barely managed to find a clean shirt this morning, and he wouldn't be surprised if he'd slept in the pants he was wearing.

"I've gone over and over Heather's statement, too. And I'll be damned if I can find anything that helps connect what she saw to Jeremy's previous crimes." Zach dropped into a chair at the opposite end of the conference table.

He'd recently gotten engaged to Heather Finley, daughter of Heartache's previous mayor who'd died while in office.

Heather had been the victim of an attempted kidnapping last fall, and Sam had arrested Covington, a former member of the town council, and his son on a number of charges, including sexual assault and stalking. But since then he'd been having trouble building a strong enough case to ensure both Covingtons served serious jail time.

Both Zach and Sam were convinced that Covington had stalked and assaulted many other victims—including Zach's own sister, Gabriella, ten years ago. Sam had followed Gabriella that night, worried because she had seemed depressed and secretive. He'd found her desperately fighting off an attacker. Sam had managed to keep Gabby from being hurt and chased the guy away. But her attacker had been wearing a stocking mask and it had been pitch-black in the woods around the quarry road, so he sure as hell couldn't identify him and neither could Zach's sister.

Now that they'd caught Covington, Sam and Zach's family finally had an opportunity to see justice done after an event that had altered all their lives.

"I dug out the notes I made about what happened to Gabriella, and me, too. I wish we'd gone to the police." Sam drummed his fingers on the conference table, thinking back to that long-ago summer.

"You were a foster kid who'd had your own run-ins with the sheriff," Zach reminded him, letting him off the hook. "And Gabby had just wanted to get out of town."

Sam, Gabriella and Zach had moved to the West Coast. Sam got a GED and took college courses, eventually enrolling in the police academy. Zach went to college and started his tech company. They'd both looked after Gabriella, who had needed intensive counseling. These days, she ran a support group for victims of cyberstalking and assault.

"And your notes are all admissible as evidence, thanks to you," Zach continued.

Sam had written a report about that night and mailed it to himself, as well as local police, as soon as he'd turned eighteen.

He'd kept his own copy—unopened but postmarked—and given it to a superior officer at the police academy along with his application. The cop had filed it with his records, helping preserve the evidence so it was still admissible in the case against Covington.

"Not that my notes help much to connect that incident to him." Sam had berated himself a million times for not pulling the mask off the guy's face instead of running after Gabriella to make sure she was safe.

"We'll find something." Zach pounded a fist on the table, making Sam's map jump. "We're going to find more victims, and one of them is going to have the piece of evidence that ties it all together to nail Covington's ass."

Sam had thought so at first, but months into this case with little progress, he was starting to wonder. Shoving back from the table, he headed over to the pull-up bar he'd installed in an archway between the conference room and the kitchenette.

The chin-ups at least got his blood flowing when his brain shut off. Reaching for it now, he began to haul his body upward until his chin was parallel with the bar. Then he lowered himself slowly and repeated the motion.

"Why don't people come forward to prosecute scumbags?" He didn't understand why anyone would remain under the thumb of someone who hurt them.

"You have to ask? We had reasons for not going to the cops as kids." Zach reached for a bowl of peanuts on the conference table. They were left over from a retirement party they'd given one of the women in the clerk's office.

He tossed a nut in the air and caught it in his mouth while Sam kept pounding out pull-ups.

"Yeah, child services could have separated you and Gabriella once they realized your mom wasn't taking care of you. I was afraid the cops would find out I'd beaten the guy up and send me to juvie since Gabriella didn't want to tell anyone what really happened." Sam had gone over and over their options in his head and knew they'd done the best they could at the time.

"Right. And everyone else who avoids talking to cops feels like they have good reasons, too." Zach tossed another nut and centered his head beneath it so it fell straight onto his tongue before he chomped it.

Sam raised and lowered himself. Raised and lowered.

"They don't, though. I went to the high school this week to talk to the kids, since the bastard tends to target teen girls. But all that most of the kids cared about was that their parents would take their phones away if they found out they were texting late at night. I don't call that a good reason for not stepping up to do your civic duty."

It was damn lazy and self-centered, in fact. He'd had a tough time responding to those kinds of concerns from the kids who'd partic-ipated in the discussion after his talk.

At their age, he didn't have a *home*, let alone a cell phone. And even as a teen he would have done anything and everything to protect the people he called friends. He had, in fact.

So he couldn't understand kids who closed their eyes when they saw their peers in trouble.

"But scaring them off isn't going to help our cause," Zach said as he pulled the map of the quarry closer to examine it. "We need those kids to think of us as their friends, dude."

"Then you should have been the one to talk to them." Sam released the bar and dropped to his feet, grateful that the rush of blood through his veins was chasing off some of the sluggish-ness. "I'm a walking zombie lately. No sleep isn't exactly enhancing my public face."

"Which was already so warm and fuzzy." Zach never looked up from the map.

"I didn't become a cop to play guidance counselor to a bunch of teenagers."

"Well, this is Heartache." Zach finally glanced up. "It's not the kind of town that needs a lot of policing, so as long as you're here, you're going to have to do some public outreach."

"Or I can deputize the guidance counselor." Sam scooped his keys off the desk, wanting to get away from the office and air out his brain. "But right now, I need a plan to unearth more witnesses."

He headed for the door that led into the town hall. Normally he'd be inside for the biweekly court session. Sam liked to be there so he could clarify any of his reports for the judge or argue with defendants who wanted to dispute arrests or citations. But this week, the docket was light. Probably because he'd been too deep in the Covington case to spend much time on anything else.

Stepping out into the parking lot, he was striding toward his pickup when a familiar silver sedan slipped into a spot next to his.

Heather Finley, Zach's fiancée. Sam lifted a hand in greeting. He had old history with the Finley family since he'd dated Heather's younger sister, Amy, back in high school. But she'd left Heartache not long after Sam, and her otherwise close-knit family didn't mention her much.

"Sam." Heather flagged him down before he could pass her, waving at him as she opened the driver's-side door. "Do you have a minute?"

Honestly, if he could have come up with an excuse to avoid social chitchat, he would have. He liked Heather just fine. She was a kind and talented woman, volunteering with the town's rec department to teach music to local kids whenever she wasn't building her own following as a country-music performer.

And while Sam admired Heather for understanding her civic duty and testifying in the Covington trial, small talk had never been his strong suit.

Especially with the Finley family. He'd never forgotten the way they'd alienated one of their own.

"Zach's inside," he said, halting his pace. "Conference room."

"Great." She gave him a lopsided smile, her long red curls covering the shoulders of her bright green trench coat. "I owe him lunch after he drove me to Nashville last weekend. But I wanted to check in with you first." She hit the key fob to lock her car doors. "Are you still living on Partridge Hill Road near the town line?"

"I rent a place up there, yeah." Having some space between him and the rest of Heartache made the longer drive to work well worth it.

"My sister is moving into our old hunting cabin off one of the dirt roads at the top of the hill—"

"I thought Erin and Remy liked being close to your family?"

"Not Erin." Her pause seemed to stretch out for minutes. Hours. "Amy."

"Amy?" Sam hadn't allowed himself to think about Amy Finley in years. Well, except when she sneaked into an occasional dream.

She'd been his high school girlfriend. A relationship they'd kept quiet at her insistence because of her mother's instability. A relationship he'd been forced to walk away from to help Zach's sister. They'd left town in a hurry, scared that Gabby's stalker would try to attack her again. They'd agreed Gabriella would be safest if no one knew where they were going. He hadn't even said goodbye to Amy. Weeks later he'd sent a message to tell her he'd had to leave to help a friend, but she hadn't responded.

And now, after ten years of silence, she was back. *Holy hell.*

"Yes. It took a long time, but Erin and I finally convinced her to come home to Heartache, at least temporarily. She's going to renovate my father's hunting cabin into a real home so we can put it on the market. I'm hoping she'll stay for my wedding." Heather tucked a strand of hair behind one ear. "I thought maybe, if you knew she was up there, you could keep an eye on her."

No.

The reaction was strong and immediate. He wasn't going to put himself anywhere near Amy Finley. Didn't matter that their relationship had died a cruel death a decade ago. He didn't need any more trouble with women than he already had.

"She'd be...what? Twenty-seven years old by now?" He rubbed the back of his neck, where his exhaustion was turning into a knot of tension. "She won't want a watchdog."

He tried to temper the refusal with a grin, but he had the feeling it came across more of a grimace.

"I'm sure she doesn't." Heather surprised him by agreeing. "But it's a remote cabin, and the access is limited. I just thought you'd want to know someone is living up there for at least a few months. If you see anything suspicious, keep in mind she's all alone on that hill."

Guilt crowded away the bout of selfishness.

"Of course." He nodded, accepting the responsibility that he suspected would only stir up trouble. "I never consider myself off duty, anyhow. I'll know if anyone goes up or down that road."

Zach's fiancée beamed. She didn't look much like Amy, who he remembered as rail thin and tall with skin so pale he could spot veins beneath its surface in bright sunlight. But there was a radiance in Heather's eyes that was similar to her younger sister's, a happiness so joyous a person would have to lack a pulse not to smile back.

Sam did just that.

"Thank you. I feel better knowing you'll check on her since I'm not sure when she'll be ready to see any of her family." Heather bit her lip for a moment before continuing. "For now, I'm just happy she's home for however long she's here." She reached to give his forearm a gentle squeeze before she brushed by him to enter town hall, her suede pumps tapping a purposeful rhythm while Sam tried to recover from her news.

Amy Finley. Back in Heartache.

He had no business feeling one way or the other about that, given how they'd parted. But that didn't prevent an old memory from drifting through his mind—Amy riding shotgun in his pickup truck on a hot summer day, promising she knew the perfect spot for skinny-dipping. He'd been seventeen and crazy about her, and even though he was supposed to be driving them both to work, he'd ended up following her directions to a private spot in the woods, where a bend in the creek made a shady pool.

She'd slid off her shorts too fast for him to see much—and he didn't want her to catch him drooling over her—but he'd never forgotten the way she'd darted through the green trees, laughing and teasing him the whole time.

No doubt a woman like that had moved on. Family. Kids. He hadn't looked her up online and hadn't asked about her, even though his best friend was now engaged to her sister.

She'd never gotten along with her family. She'd even told him once that he was the only reason she could stand to stay in Heartache…

Damn.

Shutting down the old regrets, he moved toward his truck again. He didn't need this kind of distraction now. His personal life had gotten about a thousand times more complicated this year, for one thing. And for another? He wanted all his professional focus on solidifying the case against Jeremy Covington. He'd given up Amy ten years ago to put this guy behind bars.

He would make damn sure the sacrifice had been worth it.

CHAPTER TWO

RETURNING FROM THE grocery store, Amy took the Partridge Hill Road slowly, climbing the sharp incline at a respectful speed. The tarmac looked like the town had been ignoring it for decades, and she was wary of the potholes and cavernous cracks.

Her car was on its last leg—to be expected since she'd snagged it on eBay for next to nothing after her previous vehicle had died. A gray sedan built for efficiency and not comfort, the car was held together with duct tape, furnace cement, a few well-placed zip ties and a whole lot of YouTube video knowledge on DIY mechanics. She was proud she'd kept the thing running this long, but she wasn't about to risk her luck on one of those black holes.

Even if that meant she couldn't zip past the house where Sam Reyes lived.

She kept her eyes on the road so as not to risk any accidental sightings. Not that she wasn't curious, of course. Her long-ago boyfriend had been hot when other teenage boys were still gangly and awkward. Her imagination could quite nicely envision him as a man full grown. She didn't need that visual confirmed, though. Especially not after they'd had the world's most awkward non-breakup.

He just up and disappeared. Vanished into thin air with Gabriella Chance, a particularly adorable majorette who probably would have been homecoming queen. If she hadn't left school to run away with Sam. His mysterious email—weeks later—claiming that he'd left to "help a friend" hadn't exactly eased her anger.

Thump!

The car dipped down into a rut she hadn't seen. The passenger-side tire scraped something sharp, a grating noise against the wheel. She hit the gas on instinct since her vehicle was prone to stalling.

And yet, of course, her sedan died right there.

"Unacceptable." She closed her eyes. Willed the vehicle to life. "If not for me, you would be in a scrap heap."

Sadly, it wasn't her first dialogue with the vehicle. But for the first time the cursed thing seemed to listen because it fired up again with a cough and a splutter.

"Yes!" She hit the gas hard, desperate to get

out of sight from the last house on Partridge Hill Road.

She wasn't a woman who enjoyed being rescued, and, thankfully, her closest neighbor wouldn't be obliged to fill that role today. Racing up the rest of the hill, she dodged the remaining pits and crevices, flush with victory and the knowledge she had enough supplies to last her for the next two weeks. She wouldn't need to worry about seeing anyone until she felt well settled in, and—

Oh. Crap.

A large man stood on the porch of the hunting cabin.

Dressed in black and wearing dark sunglasses, the figure stood with his back to her, his large shoulders bent over something he seemed to be examining on the front-porch swing. A hit man deciding which weapon to use? Her brain churned out a whole series of crazy possibilities when he did not turn toward her as she slowed the car.

Fear crawled up her throat since no one should be here. Her sisters had promised her—*promised*—that they would let her decide when she wanted to see the family. No one else knew she was here. And the guy on the porch sure didn't look like he was selling something. Or trying to convert her.

Why hadn't the man noticed her yet? She debated backing down the road again. She could just slide it into Neutral and she'd be at the bottom of Partridge Hill in moments. Then suddenly, even with her heart beating hard and the car's heater blowing on high, she realized she could hear the wail of an infant.

Even as she told herself that made no sense, the man on the porch straightened. He held a baby in his arms.

But that wasn't nearly the most shocking thing about her uninvited guest.

Because the man in front of her was Samuel Reyes.

Seeing her, he raised his hand. A greeting? A warning?

She mimicked the movement as she sat in the driver's seat, staring at him as if she'd seen a ghost.

So much for getting past his house unnoticed.

Shutting off the engine as he walked toward the car, she wondered about the etiquette for this situation. How did a woman act when confronting a man who'd broken her heart and run off with another girl? Did she go with a breezy, blasé manner like none of it mattered? Pretend she didn't recognize him?

He was more handsome than she'd imagined he would be, and her imaginings had been plenty favorable to start with. He looked like a man who took his job seriously, and trained hard enough he'd be able to capture Olympian sprinters while on foot. Even in his dark pants and jacket, the muscles in his limbs were evident.

His features were more sculpted, too, his jaw and cheekbones more angular somehow, his gray eyes more hooded. Or was it that his expression was less open, his gaze more calculating? Sliding across the seat to the working passenger-side door, she reminded herself to breathe.

He was at the car door sooner than she was, opening it and holding out a hand to help her out.

Her heart beat faster for no good reason.

"Looking for someone?" she asked, ignoring his hand to step out onto the patch of gravel that counted as a driveway.

Her gaze skittered over the wriggling baby wrapped in a blue blanket in his arms. The infant couldn't be more than eight weeks old. Round-cheeked and red-faced, the baby lay tucked into one of Sam's arms and stared at Amy with wide blue eyes. The child had quit crying for the moment, making the sound of the silence all the more awkward.

"I came up here to see you. Hello, Amy." Sam reached past her to retrieve her shopping bags from the car, following her example. "Let me give you a hand."

He smelled good. Like spicy aftershave and wood smoke, as if he'd spent the afternoon near a campfire.

"I can manage," she assured him. "And you appear to have your hands full." She wondered why her sisters hadn't mentioned Sam had a kid. It struck her as highly relevant. "Congratulations."

She brushed past him to enter the cabin, needing to escape from a confrontation she wasn't ready to have. In theory, she'd understood he lived close to the cabin. Her sister Heather, ever the family peacemaker, had warned Amy of his proximity in a letter. But she hadn't counted on him seeking her out and trying to talk to her.

Then again, he couldn't know she'd lost the skill of idle chitchat. Since she'd left Heartache, she no longer bothered making small talk with strangers or pretending a level of social comfort she'd never developed. While waitressing, she'd taken orders, delivered food and kept coffee cups filled. Occasionally, a chatty trucker would remind her of her father and slide past her guard, roping her into conversation about something besides the weather and how he'd like his eggs cooked. But for the most part, she kept to herself.

Besides, Sam was holding a baby.

A healthy, beautiful swaddled bundle that only reminded her of the pregnancy she'd lost a year ago. She'd faced the miscarriage alone since she'd scared off the father within weeks of discovering they were going to be parents. Amy hadn't mourned the loss of the stockbroker boyfriend. But the baby?

The hurt of it yawned like a hole that would never close.

She was opening the front door of the cabin with the key when Sam caught up with her. She sensed his movement behind her, heard the rustle of plastic shopping bags.

"You're in luck," he said as she shoved open the thin pine front door. "Turns out I can carry a baby and a few bags, too."

He followed her inside, not waiting for an invitation—or maybe guessing she wouldn't give one. As he dropped the bags on the floor beside the ones she'd deposited there, she was reminded of the first time he'd spoken to her.

"Do you remember when we got paired to set up the archery stands in gym?" She shared the thought, protecting herself from having to ask him about the infant or himself just yet.

"You told me you'd manage just fine on your own." Sam leaned a hip against the tiny kitchen counter, making the cabin look smaller just by being inside it. "Surly then. Surly now." He grinned. "It's good to see you haven't changed."

She felt herself smile before she realized how fast he'd put her at ease. But then, was there any point in putting up walls with this man who was her only neighbor for miles? This man who had a baby with another woman and couldn't possibly disappoint her more than he already had?

She forced herself to relax.

"You, too. I didn't recognize you on the porch, and I got rattled." After reaching into one of the grocery bags, she tossed some soy milk and a bag of mixed greens into the refrigerator.

"That's a relief. I was afraid you'd gotten rattled *because* you recognized me." He shuffled the baby from one arm to the other, using his free hand to empty the contents of one of the bags and set everything on the countertop while she tried not to stare at the child with a tuft of fluffy brown hair.

Part of her longed to offer to hold the squirming bundle, but she didn't know if she could keep it together. Her miscarriage had been traumatic—a turning point in her decision to reconnect with her family. After the worst of the initial grief faded, she had decided she wouldn't ever have a family of her own now, but she did want to salvage some kind of relationship with her siblings.

"So what's his name?" She reached toward one of the baby's small feet, guessing it must be a boy by the blue blanket and onesie. She tucked the blanket around the kicking leg.

Then, realizing how close that had put her to Sam, she scuttled back a step and returned to loading the small cupboards with food supplies. She also shoved the police scanner she'd bought to the rear of the counter, not wanting to reveal the full depths of her personal paranoia.

"Aiden." Sam held the child at arm's length and studied him. The baby stopped pedaling his legs long enough to stare at his dad as thoroughly as his father examined him.

She noticed Sam's ring finger remained bare.

"Nice. Is that a family name?" She realized suddenly that he may not know much about his real family and kicked herself for asking. Sam had been in foster care when they'd dated.

"I don't know. I didn't choose it." He tucked the baby back against his chest and swiftly changed subjects. "I didn't mean to intrude, and I can see you're busy. But Heather told me you were here, and I wanted to make sure you were okay out here alone."

He was already heading for the door, which she told herself was probably just as well. The chapter of her life with Sam's name on it was long over. Even if he hadn't ditched her without a word, there was still the matter of that tiny boy nestled in the crook of one strong arm.

"Yes, I'm fine, thanks. I'm up here for a couple of months to renovate this place into a year-round home so I can sell it and split the profits with my siblings." Besides bringing her closer to her family, she needed the money to set up her accounting business. A business that would let her work from home and focus her energies on numbers and data as opposed to people. "I'm doing a lot of the work myself, but there will be a few contractors here, too, so don't be surprised if there is more noise and trucks going in and out."

"Sure thing." He nodded. Frowned. "Amy, you were friends with Gabriella Chance back in school, weren't you?"

"Gabriella?" The girl he'd left her for? Amy was floored by the bluntness of the question.

Funny, she'd always thought of herself as the socially awkward one. Maybe Sam had her beat.

"Zach's sister," he reminded her. "She was in your grade."

She gripped a box of pasta so tightly it started to cave in.

"Right." She shoved the box in the cabinet and closed the door with a satisfying bang. "Up until she left town, that is. But, yes, we were friends before that."

Before Gabriella took away the most important person in Amy's world.

"I'm building a case against a man I believe stalked Gabriella during high school, but I need more evidence to connect him to her."

She grabbed the kitchen counter, suddenly feeling like the floor was giving way beneath her. She couldn't speak. How much did Sam know about that part of her past? About the night she'd followed him to Gabriella's house? Her throat convulsed reflexively until she had to find a glass in the cupboard and pour herself a drink of water.

Sam watched her, but he didn't seem to notice the effect his words were having. She couldn't talk about this with him.

"It's imperative I put this man behind bars for a long time, but he's been smart about covering his tracks," he continued, his forehead furrowed and his jaw flexing. The tension and frustration of the case were obvious.

"I don't know anything about that." Which was true. She'd had no idea the man had been there for Gabby. Setting aside her glass, she turned from him and lifted a bag from the hardware store. Her hands shook as she withdrew Sheetrock screws, joint compound and tape.

She concentrated on the task, needing a physical distraction to keep herself from thinking about the past.

"You might know something and not realize it." He sounded certain. "Would you mind if I came back sometime when you have a couple of hours to talk? I'd like to ask you a few questions about that summer."

The summer of The Incident had been the darkest of her life until her miscarriage. She couldn't discuss it with him for even a few minutes, let alone hours.

"I'm not sure about that." She shook her head, not looking at him.

"I'm sure you must have your own questions. You deserve more of an explanation about why I left than I gave you."

"I did have plenty of questions about that summer and your *friendship* with Gabriella, too. Not that I need answers. It's been ten years, Sam. I've put it behind me."

Silence met her comment, tempting her to turn and gauge his expression. Just when she couldn't stand the drawn-out tension any longer, Aiden burst into a prolonged cry that filled the cabin. She did face Sam then. He was repositioning the baby on his shoulder and whispering something into the boy's ear.

To her, he said, "We really have to talk. I'm

trying to find a regular sitter for Aiden, and as soon as I do, I'll be back."

She wanted to tell him absolutely not. She didn't need the frustration, the hurt, the temptation or the reminders of all she didn't have in her life by seeing him again. And she sure didn't need to relive an episode she'd struggled to put behind her for years.

But Sam and his child were already gone. Aiden's cry grew smaller and quieter as Sam walked away from the cabin. She watched him out the kitchen window, his broad shoulders retreating.

For now.

She believed him when he said he'd be back. He wanted answers for his case. Or for Gabby.

Damn it.

Shoving the rest of the groceries and building supplies into their proper places, Amy hurried to make a list of the tasks she could complete on the cabin renovation right away. Today. The sooner she finished this project, the sooner she could leave Heartache and all those questions about the past behind.

"I HAVE A seven-page paper to research for AP English, a take-home test in calculus to complete and a slew of college application essays to write." Bailey McCord thumbed through the pages of her purple daily planner, where she made notes about her homework assignments. She sat in the passenger seat of her car after begging her best friend—her only friend these days—to do the driving. "Tell me again why I am interviewing for a job I don't have time for and that I'll never get in a million years?"

Her friend Megan Bryer was steady at the wheel of the used Volvo Bailey's dad had bought her just last week. Bailey was grateful for the gift, even if she'd come to think of the car as her consolation prize for her mother going to jail. That definitely took off some of the sheen of new wheels.

"Don't be so hard on yourself." Megan turned down the radio as she steered out of the Crestwood High School parking lot. "I read an article last week that suggested we feel really uncomfortable around confident, self-accepting women. Doesn't that describe our whole high school? Let's not be the girls who bond over talks about how fat we are or how our math scores suck."

As they passed the girls gathering for dance-team tryouts on the football field, Bailey could kind of see her point. She knew for a fact that a couple of them had agonized for weeks over whether or not to try out because they had "back fat" that the formfitting costumes would show off.

But Bailey was having her own crisis today, and it was a little more substantial than imagining back fat that didn't exist. "If I could talk to my friend and not feminism's newest crusader right now, I'd be so grateful. I've been panicking about this since sixth-period lunch."

"Right. Okay." Megan tightened her grip on the wheel. "Maybe I have been dying to share that quote. But I also wanted you to know you have as good of a shot at this job as anyone else. Have confidence."

"Meg, I'm not the kind of girl to undersell myself. I'm writing college application essays that make me sound like a child prodigy. But I have mega-valid reasons to worry about applying for a job with the man who arrested my mother. The sheriff is…" She couldn't think how to describe him, but he wasn't exactly warm and encouraging. Even if he hadn't arrested her mom for harassment last month, instantly turning Bailey into a high school pariah, she would have thought he was sort of scary. "…the sheriff," she finished lamely.

Her mother had had an affair with Jeremy Covington, a guy now accused of stalking girls online for the last decade. Bailey's mom had covered up the affair by convincing Bailey to date Jeremy's son, J.D., who'd been as much of a jerk as his father. Little did Bailey know her mother was simultaneously helping her new boyfriend by cyberstalking Megan. Jeremy and Tiffany McCord were both on the town council, and they'd thought they could scare Megan into convincing her father—also on the council—to move away from Heartache. Apparently, Jeremy and Tiffany had seen Megan's dad as their chief competition for the mayor's job next year. It was all so convoluted, petty and sickening. Bailey's dad had sent all his wife's things to a storage facility last week, half emptying the house in the process. It was like living in a ghost town. And through it all, Bailey felt so angry at her mom for betraying her in every way. Bad enough she'd cheated on Dad. But she'd also destroyed Bailey's trust.

As if high school wasn't already hard enough.

"He may be the sheriff, but he's also just a guy who needs help with a baby." Megan kept her eyes on the road, but she used one hand to straighten the pendant on her necklace, a present from her new boyfriend, Wade. The pendant was a tiny saltshaker, which apparently symbolized how they met—they both worked at the Owl's Roost diner and had their best talks over refilling the shakers.

It was kind of cute, Bailey had to admit.

And sort of unheard of to be with a guy who listened to you. But then, Bailey's last boyfriend had gone to jail around the same time as her mom for also helping Jeremy stalk girls, so, clearly, she attracted the wrong sort.

"I do like babies," Bailey admitted, double-checking Sheriff Reyes's address in her phone. She'd always wanted a sibling, but she'd never gotten closer than the occasional new baby doll as a kid. "But I can only work so many hours this semester."

She'd looked into graduating early after her family became the town's most talked-about scandal, but she would have had to file the paperwork back in August. Now she was putting all her efforts into loading up on AP classes in the spring to cram as many credits onto her transcript as possible.

"So tell him that." Megan reached over to give Bailey's arm a quick squeeze. "He'd be lucky to have you."

She took comfort from her friend's easy confidence in her.

"I'm so glad we're friends again." Bailey hated that she was Ms. Mushy lately, crying every time she turned around. But it was the truth, and Meg deserved to hear it. "Hanging out with you is the only good thing about me not being able to graduate early."

"We can have a fun senior year even if no one else wants to hang out with us." Megan was used to being more of an outcast, and she seemed comfortable enough in her own skin that it didn't bother her. An unabashed gamer who took quirky to a whole new level, Meg couldn't get through a day without recounting an idea for the fantasy video game she wanted to create. She also played guitar and composed music that sounded like a sound track to a steampunk novel—electronica meets baroque.

"Fun?" Bailey laughed. "I'd be happy just to know what that word means again."

The last few months had well and truly sucked. Because watching her mother go to jail and knowing Tiffany had harassed Bailey's best friend wasn't the worst of it. She'd also dealt with the fact that J.D. had hit her.

She still hadn't told anyone about the worst parts of their relationship, and she really needed to. How disappointed would Megan be in her if she found out Bailey was that big of a coward? She'd told the cops he'd shoved her and that had been enough to get a restraining order. But she hadn't been able to share the rest of it. Maybe that was one of the reasons she'd felt compelled to answer Sheriff Reyes's ad for a babysitter. Surely she'd work up the courage to talk to him about it if she saw him every day?

"Fun is our new mission, then." Megan drove onto Partridge Hill Road and slowed the car to look for the house. "We're not going to let a few bad breaks keep us down. Let's hear it for girl power!"

She hooted and hollered, pumping a fist out the window. Bailey did the same, needing to yell as an outlet for the nervous energy building up inside her.

She wasn't ready to face the sheriff yet. And she sure as hell wasn't ready for the world to know she'd turned into a doormat the moment a bad-tempered guy had taken out his anger on her. How weak did that make her?

For today at least, it felt easier to pretend she was someone else. Someone strong and smart. Someone who didn't have a secret eating her up inside.

CHAPTER THREE

I need background checks on every candidate.

TWO DAYS AFTER his visit to Amy, Sam sat at the long wooden table on his deck and sent the text to Zach. He'd thought long and hard about where to conduct interviews for a sitter for his son, mindful that it could be problematic for a single man to hire an underage girl. He hoped like hell he got some applicants who were grandmothers. In any case, he'd decided to hold the interviews outdoors, in full view of the road in case nervous parents wanted to oversee the proceedings. He didn't begrudge any parents the urge to supervise their kids. God knew he wasn't letting Aiden out of his sight until he was twenty-one.

Which was why he'd called for the background checks on the applicants. To keep Aiden safe. Zach's digital security firm could unearth even more information than Sam's police computers. It was a sad commentary on the tools available to a public servant these days, but knowing how important this mission was, Sam wanted the best possible intelligence on the four women he was interviewing today.

Background checks on high school girls?

The text flashed across his phone screen, delivering all the snark that Zach would have given the question in person.

Do I need to remind you J. D. Covington was in high school?

Sam typed with one hand and draped a blanket over the playpen with the other. He'd brought Aiden outside for the interviews, wanting to see how the potential sitters might interact with him. Not that ease with a baby was his number one criterion. Sam himself had possessed zero sense of how to handle a kid when his ex-girlfriend had handed Aiden over to him. But Sam had learned fast.

It still floored him that he had a son. The past month had changed his life so drastically that he didn't even recognize his house with all the baby gear. Plus he walked through his days like a zombie.

But for the privilege of raising his own child? So worth it. He was just glad his ex-girlfriend had brought the boy to him when she was struggling, or he might not have ever known about his existence. His ex was a traveling nurse, and she'd left town without telling him she was pregnant.

She might have had a tough time with it, but for Sam, who'd been raised in foster homes and had little memory of his real parents, being a dad ranked as the most important thing in his world.

Something he never could have predicted after all the years where catching Gabriella's stalker had been the priority.

Point taken, Zach texted back. Send names when you're ready.

Sam was inputting the information when an old white Volvo sedan slowed to a stop on Partridge Hill. He could see the vehicle clearly since his backyard ran parallel to the road. For the last two years, he'd been the only one on this end of the rural county route, but now Amy Finley was living in the woods north of his place. He'd thought about her often since they'd spoken.

Her reaction to his questions had accelerated his timetable for finding a sitter for Aiden, in fact. In his own hurt at leaving her that long-ago summer, he'd overlooked her as a potential witness. Something he would remedy as soon as he secured help watching his son. His foster mother had been helping him out while he was working, so he couldn't ask her to pinch-hit other times.

"Back here." Sam raised his voice to be heard across the expanse of lawn separating him from the two girls exiting the Volvo. "You can cut across the grass."

He recognized both of them. Megan Bryer had almost been one of Jeremy's victims, and her friend Bailey McCord had the misfortune of dating the younger Covington, J.D., who'd acted as his father's accomplice. Bailey's mother was also in jail for her role in harassing Megan, although Tiffany's expensive attorney wouldn't let her languish there much longer. The request for a bail hearing had been filed last week.

Sam had never thought much of the pushy town councilwoman, although her husband seemed like a decent guy.

"Hello, Sheriff Reyes," the girls greeted him in unison, voices matching in pitch and cadence.

He tried not to wince. Had he ever been that young?

"Thanks for coming. Which one of you is looking for some extra work?"

"I am." Bailey McCord stepped forward. Blonde and blue-eyed, she was a pretty girl who—unlike a lot of the teens he saw around town—didn't rush to flaunt it. She carried a purple binder with a matching pen that had a feather cap.

"Great." He pointed to the chair at the long wooden table he'd built himself last fall. "Have a seat, and I'll tell you about the job."

"Is it okay if Megan stays?" The pink in her cheeks suggested she was nervous.

He knew he had that effect on people, but he'd never developed much of a knack for fixing it.

"I'd be grateful if she did." A thought occurred to him. "For that matter, I wouldn't mind hiring you as a team to babysit my son. An eight-week-old is a lot of work."

He planned to have Aiden watched at his foster mother's house since she was at home all day and would be nearby if there were any problems. While she'd offered to watch Aiden full-time herself, Sam worried that would be too much for her since she kept the books for the family's pizza shop and still supervised two foster sons. But he would rest easier knowing there would be someone else in the house.

Bailey frowned. Megan looked interested, though.

"Really?" Megan took a seat beside her friend.

Her hands were covered in henna tattoos and...
was that a saltshaker around her neck?

"I'd up the pay accordingly." His savings
were fairly substantial, as he'd invested all his
early earnings in Zach's digital security firm,
which had gone on to be extremely successful.
"Plus, if you shared the duties sometimes and
split them other times, it would ensure I'd have
at least one of you available more often." He
liked the idea more and more with a big case
to investigate and limited hours to devote to it.

Bailey looked interested now, too; the girls
exchanged sidelong glances while Sam explained his schedule and Aiden's.

Something about the silent give-and-take between the girls brought back a memory from
his last summer in Heartache. When he'd asked
Amy to ditch the last day of school with him,
she'd been in the school parking lot with Gabriella. Amy had met Gabby's eyes. Later, he'd
learned that look had meant that Gabby would
cover for her with the teachers. Who knew so
much could be communicated in a glance?

Lifting the blanket shading one side of the
playpen, he showed off his son and took a moment's satisfaction out of seeing how quickly
the boy sealed the deal. The girls were smit-
ten. But then, that only led him to wonder why

his son's mother couldn't have been equally charmed. He hated that for Aiden.

"This all sounds good, Mr. Reyes." Bailey straightened from the playpen and bit her lip. "But before you make any decisions, I want to be sure you know that my mother is Tiffany McCord." She folded her arms tightly, meeting his gaze. "Just in case, you know, that's a problem."

Her honesty about something that was obviously painful to admit notched his opinion of her higher.

"It's not. I could have never become a cop if the mistakes of my birth family were held against me." He flipped the cover back over the baby's makeshift bed. "My foster family has taken in a lot of kids over the years, and the first thing they tried to knock into our heads was not to make judgments of each other based on anything other than our actions. Everyone deserves to earn their own reputation."

"I like that." Bailey smiled.

"Very cool," Megan agreed.

He wished he'd won over the other kids at Crestwood High as easily when he'd spoken to the student body last week. Maybe having more interactions with teens would help him figure out how to talk to them. Any one of them might be a potential witness, and he wasn't going to overlook the chance for evidence again.

Besides, having Megan Bryer and Bailey McCord nearby held appeal for his case. He'd interviewed Megan about the attempted kidnapping last month, but she hadn't been able to give him many details since her captors hadn't shown their faces.

Bailey, meanwhile, was someone he'd hoped would come forward with information because she'd dated J.D. But so far she hadn't offered any insider knowledge about her ex-boyfriend or his jailbird father.

Since Megan had already given her deposition and Bailey seemed not to have any relevant info, he was comfortable employing them. His first priority was Aiden. Heartache wasn't exactly a thriving metropolis with lots of options for caregivers.

"I'm going to check these references." He slid the folded sheet of paper Bailey had given him into the breast pocket of his jacket. "Megan, you're welcome to submit some if you are still interested."

He watched them do more of the ESP thing, their gazes connecting.

"I am." Her ponytail bobbed as she nodded. "I can email them to you when I get home."

"Fair enough." He reached to shake hands with each of them. "Thank you for stopping by. I'll get back to you this week."

As they turned to leave, Sam retrieved his phone to check his messages. He added Megan and Bailey to the list of people for Zach's background checks, typing their names into an email.

Before he finished, a message flashed across the screen from an app he'd never used before, a program he didn't recall downloading.

Stop asking for victims to come forward. Your son's safety is at stake.

He read the message twice, his hand reaching for the top rail of the playpen instinctively. His blood chilled.

What. The. Hell.

Emotions surged, fear and fury leading the charge.

But before he could forward it to Zach for analysis, the message vanished.

Searching every conceivable screen and folder on the phone, Sam used his landline to call Zach.

He picked up right away. "Chance."

"I just received a threat to Aiden on my cell. The message disappeared after I read it."

Zach swore. "Don't touch anything on the phone. I'll see if I can find it. Want me to pick it up, or are you coming into town?"

"I'll bring it to you." He made up his mind as he pocketed the device. "I was going to drop off Aiden at my mother's, but first I'm going to assign someone to watch her place. I'm not taking any chances with him."

"Of course. I'll meet you at the town hall?"

"Yes." Sam clenched his fist to try to hold back the fury boiling just under his skin.

That was his son they were talking about. A defenseless kid.

He needed to speak to Amy Finley, and sooner rather than later. She might have reasons for keeping the past secret, but nothing was more important than this. Sam was going to learn the truth.

THE PAN OF brownies called to her. Again. Okay, for the fourth time.

Amy set down her sledgehammer and swiped a hand under her hard hat to mop the dampness from her forehead. She'd removed her first wall in the hunting cabin today, merging two small sleeping spaces into one normal-size bedroom.

Soon she'd work on tearing down the metaphorical walls in her life—the ones that kept her from reuniting with her family. But for now, she felt good to have tackled the literal variety. Plus she hadn't turned the police scanner on again after a quick listen in the morning. Surely that meant she was getting her feet back under her in this town again.

Besides, eating the brownies her sisters had made didn't mean she'd forgiven them for leaving her alone with her mother more times than she could count as a teenager. It just meant she liked chocolate and homemade sweets.

Period.

Standing the sledgehammer in one corner of the living room, she brought the pan out onto the small front porch to escape the demolition dust. Outdoors, it smelled like pine and dried leaves, a heady autumn fragrance that she breathed in deeply.

She missed the country only for moments like this—the proximity to nature that had been her best reprieve from the stress of living under the microscope in a small town. She'd always loved the sound of cicadas in late summer or the sight of peach orchards in bloom each spring, turning half the town pink. But fall was her favorite season with the wealth of pumpkins and Indian corn decorating entryways, and the rich, earthy scent of drying leaves.

She took a seat on the swing to devour her

treat and enjoy the quiet. She hadn't eaten two bites when her only neighbor appeared on the hill below the house. Sam Reyes charged toward her with purposeful steps. For a moment, she was able to observe him unaware. Dressed in dark pants and a gray button-down shirt with the sleeves rolled up, he looked more like a Fed than a local sheriff today. He walked fast, his posture rigid and his gaze downcast.

He was a handsome man. Prominent cheekbones and the straight blade of his nose gave his face character. A full lower lip and moody gray eyes were romantic touches that would make women notice him. He'd definitely turned her head as a teen. And now?

He caught her staring.

"Amy." He gave a brief nod. No smile. No other greeting.

Had she thought those gray eyes were romantic? Today they had the crystalline sharpness of ice chips. How crazy that she could tell he was upset when she hadn't seen him in a decade.

"You caught me." She swallowed her first bite of brownie. "I was just thinking these are so good it's a crime, and out of the blue, the sheriff appears." She held out the tray. "Would you consider a bribe?"

"No. Thank you." Stepping up on the porch, he settled against the wooden railing. "I need to ask you a few questions."

She lost her appetite. Setting the pan aside, she stood.

"Would you mind if we took a walk?" She hoped the movement would hide her nervousness. "I've been cooped up inside since I got here, except for my one outing to the stores a few days ago."

And, frankly, she didn't feel comfortable walking through the woods alone. But with Sam, she could at least enjoy the sights and scents while he questioned her. Nerves fluttered as she steeled herself for the conversation she did not want to have.

"Sure." Nodding, he waited for her to precede him, then followed her onto an overgrown path behind the cabin. Their footsteps crunched pleasantly through dried leaves as they trekked uphill. "I've thought a lot about what you said the last time I was here. About you having questions regarding my friendship with Gabriella and the way we left."

The statement caught her off guard. She'd been bracing for him to start quizzing her about that summer. She hadn't been expecting answers.

"You left without a word to me." Her voice sounded brittle, the memory a dull ache.

"I regretted that. But let me explain. A few days before I left, I was at Zach's house, waiting for him to get home from that nursing home where he worked. He'd had to stay late because one of the patients had fallen ill."

She remembered. Before Zach Chance became mayor of Heartache, he'd grown up in the town, the son of a wealthy, white-collar criminal who'd scammed millions of people in a pyramid scheme. Zach had done everything he could to separate himself from his crooked parents, taking a job at a senior center where he'd volunteered countless hours.

"Zach was a teenage mayor before he became the real mayor." When Amy had heard he'd taken over after her father passed away, she thought it made sense.

"Right." Sam lifted a low branch for her to walk under, his boots a steady thrum of vibration beside her. "He was worried about his sister that summer because she hadn't taken it well when their father went to jail. I was trying to help keep an eye on her."

"That was kind of you." She hopped over a rotted log.

He made the relationship sound more innocent than what she'd imagined. But he sure didn't need to run away with the Chances to help Zach watch over his sister. He must have had good reason for wanting to leave town with them.

"I owed Zach. He made school bearable for me as a foster kid. Ensured I had friends and wasn't just the freak of the week from the local foster group home."

"I didn't know." She'd certainly never viewed him that way. But then again, she was younger than him and hadn't been aware of him until she'd started attending high school.

"Anyway, I was at their house when Gabby told me she was leaving to meet a friend." He shook his head, eyes on a distant point ahead, lost in a long-ago moment. "And if they'd had normal parents, she probably wouldn't have been allowed out of the house at that hour on her own. But her dad was in jail, and their mom was grieving like the guy was dead."

"I'm convinced there's no such thing as normal parents." It had been a common refrain between them at one time. "Except you, now that you're a father, of course."

He didn't crack a smile at the playful jab. A bird flew low over her head, landing on a nearby branch.

"Of course. And I had to be the responsible one then, too."

"You told Gabriella she couldn't meet her friend?" she guessed, watching the blue jay hop from a maple tree into an evergreen.

"No. I followed her." Something in his voice changed.

"What happened?" Amy slowed her pace as they neared a rushing stream, not wanting to miss anything.

"She stopped the car on the quarry road and got out like she was going to…" He halted at the water's edge. "I thought at first she might jump off a cliff or something. It was so deserted out there."

"She didn't see you?" Amy hugged her arms around herself, warding off a chill despite the warmth of the late afternoon sun.

"I cut the lights of my own car and parked well behind her, then sprinted through the dark toward her." He seemed lost in the past, his gaze unfocused. For a long moment, he paused. When he continued, his voice was hard. "But some other guy got to her first."

"A boyfriend?"

"I think that's what she expected. I found out later she was meeting a guy she'd been talking to online. He must have been stalking her for some time, looking for the right moment to set up a meeting. But this guy was no teenager—he was masked, but I could tell he was older than we were." Sam's hands fisted even now. "He had her on the ground and was on top of her before I could even get close to where they were."

She gasped, connecting the dots to her own trauma that night. "He hurt her?"

"He tried his damnedest." His eyes cleared, focusing on her. "But I got there before he could do much physical damage. I lunged at him, but he was bigger than me, and he started to get the upper hand until I got my hands on a log about the size of a baseball bat."

"A weapon," she half whispered, knowing she couldn't change the outcome of a story that was long over, but she still found herself breathless from hoping Sam and Gabby got away.

"I hit him so hard I thought I killed him." He leaned down to scrape his hand along a scraggly cattail growing near the creek bed. The movement released a cloud of fluffy white into the air. "Gabby had run off, and I left the guy to search for her. Another car came along, and I debated calling for help when it stopped, but I couldn't see well enough, so I hid instead. When Gabby was safely in my car, I went back to where the body should have been, but it was gone."

"Meaning he got up and went in the other car?"

"Or else a friend came and took the body away." He shrugged. "I couldn't be sure, and I was too scared of getting kicked out of my foster family's house to go to the cops. Besides, Gabby wanted no part of talking to police. She was hysterical."

Pieces of the past fell into place, slowly making sense.

"So Zach wanted to take his sister away from a cyberstalker who might still be after her. And you needed to get away from the guy, too, or else not be in Heartache when someone discovered him dead."

"That's why I left." He pointed to a flat rock near the stream, and she followed the unspoken suggestion, taking a seat. He dropped down a few inches away, a strong, masculine presence that tripped a whole chain of sensations inside her she had no business feeling.

She hugged her knees to her chest.

"You didn't breathe a word to anyone, including me, because you couldn't afford for anyone to link you to the stalker." His reasons for leaving—and keeping quiet about it— were so different from what she'd imagined. But Sam had possessed a strong sense of right and wrong even as a teen. Of course he'd made the choice to be noble at all costs.

"Gabriella's mother didn't even protest when Zach said he was taking her out to the West Coast when he started college. Hell, I'm not sure Mrs. Chance realized Zach hadn't even graduated high school yet. She just gave him some money and told him good luck."

"It definitely helps to have cash when you're starting over in a new city." She'd refused all help from her family after she'd left town, not realizing how difficult it would be to make ends meet on her own. "I told my dad I was going to file the paperwork to become an emancipated minor when I left, but he said not to bother. They wouldn't fight me."

Or fight *for* her.

When it came down to it, her parents hadn't blinked at her departure any more than Mrs. Chance had protested her daughter's.

"I heard you moved to Atlanta." He sifted through some tall grasses and pulled up a flat stone. "Zach kept tabs on news from Heartache, always keeping an eye out for info on the man who jumped Gabriella."

"And now you think Jeremy Covington was the man who lured Gabriella out and assaulted her?" But Gabby wasn't the only one he'd hurt. This case was bigger than she'd realized.

And while she understood why Sam took this case personally, she would not be able to help. She had her own reasons for needing to stay far away from the man who hurt Gabriella. She wasn't any more ready to share those reasons now than she had been a decade ago.

"I do. And I want to see his ass in jail for more reasons than I can count." He whipped the stone side-arm to send it skipping along the water's surface. "I've been working overtime to find more leads and be sure Jeremy Covington is put away for life. But yesterday I got a message on my phone that threatened Aiden if I keep searching for witnesses."

Amy felt a weight land squarely on her chest. A vision of Aiden's blue eyes and happy, kicking foot clutched at her.

"How could he have threatened you from jail? Do you worry you have the wrong man?"

"Never." He reached to touch her, laying one big, broad palm over the whole of her forearm.

Even as one anxiety eased, another emotion took its place. A sharp awareness of Sam Reyes.

She knew he wanted answers about that summer that had changed both their lives forever. But right now, with a new attraction stirring inside her faster than her usual instincts for self-preservation, Amy blurted the most important question.

"Are you married?"

CHAPTER FOUR

LIKE A BUCKET of water to the face, the mention of marriage had him surging to his feet.

"Married?" He could have sworn they'd been talking about his case. Stalkers. Jail time. But a wife? "Hell no."

From another woman, he might have considered the question a signal of interest. Except Amy was staring at him like he was a bug under a microscope, with none of the old warmth and happiness he recalled from when they were dating. She'd changed a lot over the years. Sure, she'd always been aloof and more standoffish than the other Finleys. But when you got to know her privately, there had been a wry sense of humor and a sweetness about her that had drawn him.

Now? Her wary body language and restless green gaze suggested she didn't let anyone close to her anymore.

He started walking and she stood to follow him, her footsteps on the fallen leaves surprisingly quiet while the sun glinted off auburn highlights in her brown hair.

"You didn't mention Aiden's mother the first time we met and I wondered." She pointed to a deer downstream, a young doe watching them intently. "Then today, when you said your son had been threatened, it made me curious who was watching him for you."

The doe didn't hold his interest nearly as long as the woman did. He found it interesting that her thoughts had lingered on his son and the threat to the boy.

"Lorelei. My foster mother." He studied Amy's face while she watched the deer. Her pale skin and delicate features were the same as he remembered. She still looked as if a stiff wind might blow her down, but he knew that wouldn't be the case if she was toughing out a winter in that hunting cabin with no stove and no heat. "She and her husband still take in kids. The house is right in town and always full of activity. No one will get close to Aiden there."

"Good." She nodded, a smudge of dirt on her cheek calling to his fingers. "I didn't mean to pry." She hugged thin arms around her waist and turned to glance up at him. "You may find it hard to believe, but I've actually become a *worse* conversationalist as an adult than I was at seventeen."

"You weren't prying." He leaned down to the rushing stream to grab a handful of cold water and splashed it on his face, appreciating the stinging chill on his perpetually tired eyes. "I'm just a bit shell-shocked trying to get used to single fatherhood."

He wasn't the kind of guy who ever felt the need to explain himself. Except right now, with Amy Finley, he found himself wanting to. And he would have. But she chose right then to clutch his arm in a tight grip.

"What is that?" she asked quietly, her eyes wide, her whole body rigid.

Straightening, he followed her gaze.

A full-grown wild boar steamed hot breath into the cool fall air, staring directly at them.

He tensed. Took her hand. Kept his eye on the animal.

"Let's call it a pig," he said softly, trying not to startle the beast. "As long as we're not between it and any piglets, we're going to be just fine."

Gently, he tugged Amy behind him, grateful as hell for her quiet footfall. No chance of her startling the thing; that much was certain. Her hand trembled in his, though.

Behind the boar and on the other side of the stream, the doe fled. The steaming hulk of pig did not spare a glance in its direction. Chances were good the animal would take off soon, too, but every now and then, the things turned vicious. Sam had a weapon on him, but he had no inclination to be stuck eating gamy pork all winter.

"We're going to back up a step, okay?" he told her, reaching an arm behind him to find her. His hand collided with a gently curved hip.

She was close. Very close.

He gave her hip a squeeze, and Sam told himself the gesture was a normal human instinct to offer comfort and reassurance. Somehow his brain didn't account for the fact that what he actually clutched was the curve of her ass. The top of her thigh.

The sudden lightning strike of sexual response was as inappropriate as it probably was inevitable.

He let her go fast, cursing himself for being ten kinds of idiot.

"If that thing charges," he continued quietly, "you run in whatever direction I don't. Understand?"

She made an inarticulate sound he took for agreement as he backed up and she followed suit.

The boar surged forward, scaring the living hell out of him for about two seconds until it peeled off to the west at a dead run, disappearing into the brush. Soon the thundering hooves and crackle of branches and underbrush grew fainter.

Sam stared after it, certain it had taken off for good, but wanting an extra second for the realization to soothe his hammering pulse. Behind him, Amy's forehead brushed the back of his shoulder for a fleeting moment, her reaction so fast he might have imagined it.

"Are you okay?" He turned to her in the unnatural quiet left behind in the wake of the two-hundred-pound beast.

"Fine." She gave a clipped nod, her posture brittle, spine ramrod straight. But her head was dipped ever so slightly, confirming that brief bit of contact that still scorched his shoulder. "Although I've probably had my fill of fresh air for today." Then her head straightened; her lips quirked. "I'm ready to head back if you are."

So cool. Composed.

Had she felt that moment of heated attraction? Or was he the only one to dream up the shared lust?

Sleep deprivation. Surely he had to be suffering from lack of a solid eight uninterrupted hours of rest. Well, and too many months of no sex.

Best not to think about sex.

Nodding, he couldn't restrain the impulse to place a hand on the small of her back and urge her forward down the hill. He told himself it was only because he felt responsible for her. As sheriff, he had a duty to keep people safe. Besides, he'd promised Heather Finley he'd keep an eye on Amy.

And neither of those reasons explained why it was so tough to pull his hand away again. He forced himself to focus on why he'd come here. Why he needed to talk to her.

"Amy, I wanted you to know what happened with Gabriella. I'm sorry I couldn't give you the whole story at the time." He kept an eye on the woods on either side of the path, unwilling to be caught off guard again. "It wasn't my secret to tell. But Gabby's ready to testify now, so I can finally explain everything to you."

"I understand." She kept her attention straight ahead as they made their way back to the cabin. "And I appreciate you telling me now. I always wondered."

He had plenty of things that he'd wondered about, too. Like why she'd left Heartache right after he did. Like what had happened to chase the warmth he remembered out of her eyes.

But he couldn't afford to think about what

he wanted. He had to focus on the case and Aiden's safety.

"I hoped that, in return, you would spend some time talking to me about what happened to you that summer." He nearly ran into her when she slowed her step suddenly.

He caught himself just in time.

"I told you I don't know anything that will help your case." Her voice sounded strangled.

Because she was hiding something?

Or because there were emotions at work between them that she didn't want to acknowledge any more than he did?

That wasn't going to be easy to untwine.

"But you can't be certain of that," he pointed out reasonably, following her lead in slowing the pace down as they headed back toward the cabin. "I'm not going to ask you anything personal or try to invade your privacy." Nine times out of ten, that was what people were worried about when they resisted police questioning. Unless, of course, they had something to hide. "I just want to try and create a timeline of that summer. Walk through it and try to account for our whereabouts each day. Just see what small memories might crop up."

She seemed to consider it.

Or at least, she didn't protest right away.

"It could jog my memory, too, you know."

He hadn't really thought about that until this moment. "You might remember things that I've forgotten, so when we put our stories together, between the two of us, something new could spring to light."

"So you think us walking down memory lane is going to give you the evidence you need to convict Jeremy Covington?" The look she slanted him told him exactly what she thought of the strategy.

"I have no idea what a walk down memory lane will do, but if there's a chance it will give me a more complete picture of that summer, why not? I've been encouraging more recent victims to come forward. I even went into Crestwood High to talk to the teens about it, but I'm getting a whole lot of blank looks and silence in return. I can't face this guy in a courtroom and not bring all possible evidence to send his ass to prison."

A scuttling sound underfoot startled her, and she moved closer to Sam. He regretted that their walk had made her jumpy, but he liked having her in arm's reach. Liked that her first instinct was to be next to him. He let himself brace her elbow for a solid three seconds.

He slowed his steps as the old cabin came into view through the trees, not ready to let her go until she agreed to see him again. To replay that summer and help him find some clue he'd missed.

Amy turned to face him, leaning against the trunk of a maple as she peered up at him. "One of the reasons I chose to come back to Heartache now is to support my sister when Heather testifies against this guy." She drew a deep breath. "So I promise you, I am committed to putting him behind bars, too. I may have been absent from this family for ten years, but I'm still a Finley, and hearing how that creep threw her in the back of a van with another girl that he'd tied up…" She shook her head, unable to finish the thought. "I am here to see justice done, Sam. But I am not here to testify."

An interesting distinction. Especially considering no one had asked her to testify when she claimed not to know anything. But he didn't want to pick apart that point right now. All he wanted was the chance to talk to her at length about that summer. About any interaction she might have had with Gabriella. He needed to find out if she remembered anything that could help tie the crime against Zach's sister to Jeremy Covington.

"So walk me through those last weeks we spent together and help me spur my own memory," he urged, risking a step closer to press his point. "Give me an afternoon."

"Does it have to be a formal questioning at the police station?" Her worry was obvious. Because she had normal anxiety about speaking to law enforcement? "Or can we do it here?"

The more she resisted, the more he wanted to record her statement. As a cop, he had a naturally suspicious nature, but his instincts told him she knew more than she was letting on. But those same instincts warned him if he pushed Amy too hard, she would shut down altogether.

"All right, your place it is?" He would ask her permission to record the session, of course, and at least then he would be able to review it at length.

She nodded. "Fine. Not tomorrow, though. I have a permit inspector lined up to come and help me apply for some of the renovation paperwork."

"The day after, then." He wasn't budging from this spot without a commitment.

"I'll be there." Her green eyes narrowed as she looked him over. "Are you sure you're ready to relive that summer? Fourth of July? That night we took the late shift to close up the pizza shop together so we could be alone? Because like it or not, those are the times I remember best, and I don't think they're going to shed much light on the case."

She'd deliberately chosen some of the most heated moments they'd shared. And hell no, he wasn't sure he was ready to hear them chronicled from her point of view. He couldn't afford that kind of distraction while he was building his case and trying to figure out how to raise a son on his own.

"Maybe not." He'd put Amy Finley out of his mind a long time ago, knowing that was best for both of them. Yet with the feel of her hip still imprinted on his skin, he wasn't sure he could keep her as part of his past. "But I'm glad to know you have some good memories in spite of how it all ended."

He'd never meant to hurt her, but a whisper of something in her eyes said clearly he had.

Shoving away from the tree, she straightened.

"No sense denying what happened. Especially since it will be a matter of public record soon enough." She headed toward the cabin, her fine hair gently swaying with her movements. "Thanks for standing between me and the wild boar, Sam," she called over one shoulder. "It's been a long time since anyone put himself in harm's way for me."

A damn shame, as far as he was concerned.

He watched her walk away, his eyes drawn to her hips as he remembered what she'd felt like in his arms all those years ago. The attraction hadn't died. It was still plenty hot. Only now that awareness was tempered with suspicion. Something wasn't right.

Once she reached the cabin door and retreated inside, he pointed his feet home, wondering why she had tried so hard to avoid this conversation. And why she had goaded him about their past to distract him and throw him off guard. He'd like to think it wasn't going to work.

But the truth of it was he'd be reliving those nights with her in his dreams anyway. And he already remembered them very, very well.

A WILD BOAR was chasing her.

Amy ran and ran through dark woods. Branches scraped at her face and tore at her clothes as she scrambled down the hill toward the hunting cabin. She was close. So close to safety.

She could almost reach out and touch the familiar rough-hewn logs...

But the grunting pig was faster.

Steaming breath scorched her ear as she struggled. Hairy hooves pawed at her. She wanted to scream. But fear robbed her of sound. Every time she opened her mouth, noth-

ing came out. Tears burned her eyes. Fury fired her insides.

Silently, she lay there as the beast nuzzled under her clothes...

Knifing upright, Amy blinked out of the dream. Drenched in sweat, tangled in her sleeping bag, she felt around to discover she was safely inside her father's hunting cabin. Tools lay all around her from the remodeling project; the cabin floor was still covered in dust from where she'd removed the wall. She must have been more rattled by the wild boar than she'd guessed since the thing had given her nightmares for two nights straight.

Then again, she had struggled for years to forget about other predators that lurked in the woods around Heartache. The boar was just another way for her brain to relive that long-ago horror—the night when she'd been too shell-shocked to scream or defend herself.

Bad enough a faceless man pawed at her in that memory. Now she contended with a two-hundred-pound pig.

Same difference, she thought ruefully.

The urge to get in her car and drive that rattling heap the hell out of Heartache was strong. Yesterday, after she'd dreamed about the man-pig the first time, she'd tucked her car keys in the attic crawl space, just far enough out of reach that she'd have to really think hard about leaving town before she did it. It had taken ten years to get back here. She wasn't going to turn tail and run without good cause.

And bottom line, no matter how scary things got, Jeremy Covington was still in jail. Based on what Sam had said, Amy had good cause to think Covington was the same man who'd hurt her. If that was true, she was safe from faceless molestation in the woods as long as the man stayed behind bars.

A surge of anger prompted her to sift through her purse and pull out a cell phone. She'd come home to support her sister when Heather gave testimony against the bastard. It was high time she actually delivered on that support and stopped hiding in the woods.

Opening her contacts, she scrolled down to the Hs and pressed her sister's name. Two rings later, a groggy voice answered.

"Amy?" Heather sounded like their mom on the phone, although at least she spoke her name with more kindness than their mother usually had.

"Hi." She gripped the device tighter. "Sorry it's taken me so long to call." Had it been almost a week? "But I've been working on the cabin. If you want to stop by—"

"I can come in the morning," her sister offered quickly, sounding more awake.

In the background, Amy could hear a man's voice. Zach, no doubt. Probably asking who was calling in the middle of the night.

"Okay." Better to follow through before she lost her nerve. "I have to meet Sam later in the day, so morning is good."

"I'm glad you called, Ames." The warmth in her voice chased away the last remnants of the dream that had gripped Amy.

For a moment, she was transported back to the old bedroom the three of them had shared—Erin, Amy and Heather. Heather would tell stories until they fell asleep. Or they would act out fairy tales like "The Three Bears" and fall asleep giggling. Quietly, though. Always quietly.

The game was over if they disturbed their mother.

"Good. I'm up early. Come anytime." She disconnected the call, forgetting to say goodbye. Regretting it.

She didn't mean to be rude. She was just out of practice being a sister. A friend.

But she was here, damn it. Back in Heartache, trying to do better.

Unable to get back to sleep, Amy slid out of her sleeping bag to walk around the cabin.

Finding her purse, she searched for her retractable baton, a weapon she'd carried with her since the early days in Atlanta. She'd found it in a pawnshop, where the old couple who ran the place had given her a good deal that she still hadn't really been able to afford. Holding it in her hand now, feeling its familiar weight, helped settle her nerves. Seeing the boar and having the disturbing dream had stirred old anxieties. Hell, just being in Heartache was an anxiety.

Baton in hand, she forced herself to unlock the front door—the original lock as well as the new dead bolt she'd installed her second day in residence. She wasn't crippled by her old fears. She'd learned tangible ways to own them, manage them and keep them at bay. The locks helped, as did the assortment of self-defense devices. Plus she was more physically equipped to handle herself now than she had been as a teen.

Her first year in Atlanta, she'd taken a free class at the YMCA to learn how to get away from an attacker. Each year, around the anniversary of The Incident, she rewarded herself with a new class. Karate. Kickboxing. Krav Maga. She still wasn't strong, but she was a whole lot smarter than that paralyzed, silent teen in the woods had been.

Breathing in the cold night breeze, she leaned

against the porch rail and hoped the fresh air would help her sleep. In the distance, when the wind blew the trees a certain way, she could just catch a glimpse of a light farther down the hill. It had to be Sam's house, the only other residence within half a mile from hers.

Would he be awake right now, too? Did worries about his son have him pacing the floors? She hated that someone had threatened that tiny baby simply because Sam was good at his job. It also unsettled her to think that whoever had made that threat was not behind bars. Sam didn't believe he had the wrong man in jail, but who else besides the man who had assaulted Gabriella Chance and the others would want to stifle new evidence in the case?

The attacker—whoever he was—might still be free.

Her gaze slid from the light in the woods to her car parked out front. She could leave whenever she wanted. Whenever she needed to. She wouldn't allow this trip to Heartache to undo all her hard work to put the past behind her.

But for now, she would stay. She still wanted to reconnect to the family she had since she'd never have one of her own. Life was too short to live with regrets.

Slipping quietly back into the cabin, she locked and bolted the door before settling back in her sleeping bag. Tomorrow, she'd see one of her siblings face-to-face for the first time in a decade. She'd offer whatever help she could to Heather since her big sister had proved braver than her to testify against a local menace. If Covington went to jail, maybe her nightmares would end. But as she laid her head on the pillow, Amy didn't think about vindication or revenge, or even her family. Instead, the image that settled into her tired brain was the moment in the woods when Sam Reyes had stood between her and everything scary. The moment when he'd touched her with shocking intimacy that had stirred long-forgotten pleasure.

After the fear and dread of the nightmare, she didn't bother to fight thoughts of Sam. Reality would set in soon enough that he was off-limits to her now.

But not in her dreams.

CHAPTER FIVE

"Doesn't it make you even a little bit nervous to watch the baby in a house full of foster kids?" Bailey chewed a fingernail as she stared up at the white clapboard Colonial where she and Megan had been hired to watch Aiden Reyes for a few hours after school.

A bank of wire cages sat in the shade of a side porch that had been added on to the original house. A colorful patchwork quilt shaded the cages, preventing her from seeing what was inside. A heap of bicycles in a rainbow of colors lay under a hickory tree in the front yard.

The sheriff had told them to wait for him out front and he would introduce them to his foster mother, Lorelei Hasting.

"Are you listening to yourself right now?" Megan snapped across the roof of the Volvo. She bent down and pulled a stack of textbooks from the car so they could study in their downtime. "You remember I'm adopted, right? You say 'foster kids' like it's a synonym for delinquents."

The knot in Bailey's stomach tightened. The last thing she wanted was to alienate her last friend in the world. A girl she really admired.

"I'm sorry." And she was. "I just remember that some troubled kids lived here at different times, right? That Damon dude, who robbed the pizza shop?"

The story had been in the news. The boy had been kicked out of their high school afterward, and Bailey hadn't seen him since.

Megan slammed the car door and came around the vehicle to stare up at the house with her.

"In all fairness, my dad brought him up this morning over breakfast, too." Meg shook her head, a strand of newly purple hair brushing her cheek. "And I'm going to tell you what I told him. That was an isolated incident. And perfectly traditional homes raise kids who are just as likely to be bad apples. Witness J. D. Covington."

"Right. Agreed." She understood to a far better degree how much of a bad seed J.D. was since he'd been the one to leave bruises on her throughout their relationship. But Megan knew only that J.D. had helped his father try to kidnap Meg and her music teacher, Heather Finley, a few weeks ago. Which was plenty bad enough. With any luck, J.D.'s role in the kidnapping attempt would send him to jail, where she wouldn't have to worry about him.

"Speaking of J.D., did you hear his lawyer asked for another bail hearing?" Megan passed half the stack of textbooks to her while they waited for Sheriff Reyes.

"He won't get it, will he?" Bailey feared for Megan as much as for herself.

"I don't know. The cops have been trying to dig up more evidence against both J.D. and his dad, but my father said they're having a hard time. That's why Sheriff Reyes came to the school last week, remember?" Meg pointed to the car slowing down a few hundred yards away. "I think he's here now. We can ask him."

She followed her friend's gaze to the black pickup pulling into the driveway.

"How can he find more evidence when there haven't been any other kidnappings?" Bailey muttered, her nerves eating her from the inside out. She hadn't eaten lunch today because she didn't want her stomach to launch a full-out panicked protest when she talked with the sheriff. Even so, the stress of seeing him mixed with her guilt over not coming forward about J.D. combined to send a shooting pain through her gut.

"J.D. helped his father find girls online, hacking into their accounts. The police call it... I forget the charge. Something like accessory to cyberstalking?" Megan shrugged and pulled Bailey forward toward the sheriff. "We should ask around to see if anyone else has been harassed online."

"I can do that." Latching on to the idea, Bailey promised herself then and there that if anyone in their school had been hassled online, she would find out about it. "We'll ask everyone we know. And we'll keep J.D. in jail."

"He's not in a real jail, though," Megan answered under her breath as they neared the sheriff. "He's underage, so he went to juvie."

"Don't ask him about J.D.," Bailey asked softly, hoping Meg heard her. She didn't want to draw attention to her interest in the case and what happened to her ex-boyfriend. "Not our first day on the job, okay?"

"Hello, Sheriff," Megan said brightly as their new employer stepped down from his truck.

Bailey had seen her give a quick nod, though, so she knew Meg had heard her. Agreed not to say anything.

Thank you, God.

Her stomach stopped roiling a little, especially as she looked into the truck where a bright blue blanket squirmed. She was only too glad to focus on an adorable baby for a few hours and not worry about secrets and abuse.

Nearby, a screen door slammed. Bailey glanced up to see an older woman in worn jeans and a bright sweater wave to them from the porch. She'd met Mrs. Hasting at the pizza shop she owned with her husband, a guy who sat on the town council with Meg's father and—before she was jailed—Bailey's mom.

Her mother had called Mrs. Hasting "unkempt," a snide assessment delivered with her mother's trademark Botox frown—a stiff glare that only made her look ridiculous. But the sheriff's foster mom was kind of like that rainbow pile of bikes—untidy in the way that made you want to smile. Even now, the woman was grinning, her face full of lively wrinkles that suggested she was no stranger to happiness.

"Hello!" She hurried up the path toward the driveway, dark curls bouncing out of a headband. "Samuel Reyes, you're taking far too long unloading my grandson." She edged the sheriff aside and clambered into his truck to work the belts and buckles of the baby's car seat. "I hope you warned these nice girls they might have to fight me to hold him." Pausing from her work, she leaned back out of the truck cab to wink at Meg and Bailey. "Not really, girls. I will share."

"Mom, this is Bailey McCord and Megan Bryer. Girls, my mother, Mrs. Hasting."

"Nice to meet you, ma'am." Bailey tried not to cringe at the introduction. Lately, people in town tended to do a double take when they heard the McCord name.

"Of course." Mrs. Hasting carefully handed Aiden out to the sheriff while she climbed back out of the truck. "The McCords are two double cheeses and the Bryers are a single pepperoni family. Running the pizza shop, I can tell you almost everyone's usual order. Come on in, girls, and I'll get you settled."

Doing as they were told, Bailey noticed the imposing sheriff fell in line, too, making him seem a little less scary. He tucked his aviator shades in his shirt pocket as he followed them toward the door.

"She'll slow down for a breath soon—don't worry," he told them quietly, brushing a knuckle over his son's cheek with a tenderness that melted her heart.

Seeing that made her regret her words about foster kids all the more. The sheriff had grown up here, and he'd obviously turned out to be a good guy.

They bypassed the front door to walk up the steps to the railed side porch she'd noticed earlier. As they approached the wall of stacked cages, Bailey saw a few rabbits inside. Three of the cages had elaborate houses that looked like craft projects for elementary kids. Made out of empty Kleenex boxes and covered in watercolor paint, the houses had bunny-size doors and carpets made of old pot holders. One fat gray rabbit sat inside his cardboard castle under a painted sign that said Clover's Crib.

Distracted by the cuteness, she hadn't noticed a teenage boy emerge from the house. She just turned and suddenly there was a tall, lanky kid on the porch flanked by two younger boys playing tug-of-war with a plastic car. Bailey stilled, feeling awkward to be caught ogling the rabbits, her skirt riding up her calf as she leaned over the cages. Straightening, she tried not to stare at the older boy, whose brown hair fell over one hazel eye.

"Girls, I'd like you to meet my sons." Mrs. Hasting put a hand on the teen's arm. "This is Dawson. He'll be starting at Crestwood after the holidays. And that's Tucker." She pointed to the dark-headed boy who'd won the car he'd been wrestling over. "And Nate." She ruffled the ginger hair of the smaller child. "They know to keep out of your way, but if you need anything and I'm not around, Dawson can help you."

"Cool shirt," Megan said to the guy. He

wore a T with the silhouette of a dinosaur on a spaceship that must be a video-game reference.

Megan Bryer was not only an A student; she was also a gamer girl extraordinaire. She held the record high scores for just about everything. This gave her a lot more to work with when it came to talking to most guys. She could dazzle anyone who'd ever picked up an Xbox controller in the first five seconds of conversation. Bailey had no such superpower.

"Hi," she finally said, and probably only managed that because Mrs. Hasting and the sheriff were both standing right there.

Her cheeks heated.

"Good to meet you." Dawson nodded, making eye contact briefly before stepping aside. "I'll round up the rug rats."

He jogged across the lawn after Tucker while Mrs. Hasting invited them into the house. Bailey followed her, eager to move past the awkwardness of meeting new people so she could start her job.

Between what had happened with her mother and her new mission to find anyone who might have been harassed by J.D., she wouldn't have thought it possible that some random stranger could make her feel even remotely interested in boys again.

She definitely was not.

So about an hour later when she found herself looking out the nursery window to watch Dawson throw a football with the other kids, she couldn't account for the fluttery feeling in her stomach. It was different from the burn of acidic fear that had been her constant companion for weeks.

It was almost pleasant.

"He's cute, isn't he?" Megan's voice startled her. The sheriff and Mrs. Hasting had left them alone with Aiden.

Embarrassed to be caught staring, Bailey spun from the window.

"I don't know. I guess," she blurted. "He's okay."

"I thought you loved kids." Megan tipped her head to one side to study her, frowning. Too late, Bailey realized that her friend held Aiden in her arms.

She'd been talking about *the baby*.

Realization hit Meg the same moment it hit Bailey. Her friend stood, crossing the large wool braid rug to stand next to her at the window.

A slow smile spread across her face.

"He's okay is right." Meg passed Bailey the baby, and she gladly took comfort in holding the warm, sleepy infant. "Something tells me you're going to become a convert on the topic of foster kids."

"I should have never said that," she admitted. "But just because a boy is cute doesn't mean…whatever you think it means."

"Relax. I won't tease you again about that—I promise." Meg slung her arm over Bailey's shoulders. "But after having dated J.D. myself, I can tell you how awesome it is to be with a real guy. A kind, decent, amazing guy."

"I'm so not interested in being with anyone right now." She couldn't imagine trusting someone not to yell at her. Hurt her.

And even if she could? Who would want to date the town jailbird's daughter?

"Don't give J.D. that kind of power over you, Bailey. If you stop having fun because of him, he wins."

Easy for Meg to say. She had been born kickass strong. But Bailey was just a normal, regular girl. She couldn't just stop being scared because Megan said so.

And yet being scared didn't have to mean she was powerless.

"He's not going to win." The fierceness of her words surprised even her. "Because we're going to canvass the entire school starting tomorrow and find out if J.D. harassed anyone else."

"We are?"

"Damn straight." She whispered it, though, because she didn't believe in swearing in front of children.

Not even sleeping newborns.

"Then you'd better put that baby in his crib so we can get a jump on that homework."

Bailey did just that, tucking Aiden's blanket around him before she moved to the stack of texts she'd carried inside. Only when she was sure Meg wasn't looking did she risk one last glance out the window.

Dawson wasn't out there anymore, which was just as well since she didn't need any distractions. She'd probably only imagined that moment of connection when their eyes had met.

And even if she hadn't? Once he found out who she was, he wasn't going to like her anymore.

BABY CARRIERS WERE a godsend.

Sam vowed to write a personal thank-you to the creator of the invention. It kept Aiden safe and sleeping against his chest while leaving his hands free to hammer away on his laptop at the kitchen table. Finally—finally—he could get some work done at home.

Staying up most of the night, he'd inputted

all the incidents of assault in a five-mile radius of the quarry into a spreadsheet. He had already used it to confirm no incidents had ever been reported while Jeremy Covington was out of town—a narrow window at best since he only had access to a small portion of the guy's vacation dates from the town council. But, more interesting, he'd discovered a higher number of incidents during the annual social-studies teachers' conference that Covington's wife attended every year.

All circumstantial, of course, but given how little he had to work with, he considered every nugget a victory. Especially with almost fifteen years' worth of data to look at.

He would begin cross-checking the cases against the list of victims they'd already interviewed, then identify anyone else he needed to speak to. He would review the MO of all the assaults and then double-check physical descriptions to see how many of them matched Jeremy Covington.

Sam emailed the file to himself to examine further at work just as his doorbell rang. Clamping a protective hand against the carrier, he practically sprinted to answer it, hoping Aiden would stay asleep a little longer.

Flinging open the door, he found…the mayor? Sure enough, Zach stood on his front step looking as disheveled as if he'd stayed up all night. In other words, he probably looked as bad as Sam.

"What the hell are you wearing?" Zach's eyes narrowed as he took in the baby carrier.

"I believe it's called a pouch sling." He glanced down at the carrier, where Aiden was starting to stir, his face scrunching up in that pre-cry, wrinkle-puss expression that meant food would be required soon. Sam rocked from foot to foot, trying to soothe his son while lowering his voice to a low hiss. "And it works like nobody's business to keep the baby asleep unless you have clueless friends who ring the doorbell."

"It's purple, dude." Zach squinted at the strap over one of Sam's shoulders. "And plaid."

"Right. And when you have kids you'll be begging me to let you borrow it." He stalked toward the kitchen to get a bottle started. "But I'll just come over and ring your doorbell while your firstborn is sleeping instead."

"Sorry." Zach kept pace behind him, his leather shoes echoing on the hardwood. The guy still dressed more like a corporate raider than a small-town mayor. "I'm just not used to seeing you sporting anything from the lavender family."

"Keep it up and I'll pass you the bottle and the boy to see how *you* do."

He shook the formula-and-water combination, glad he'd taken the time to do dishes earlier so everything was clean and ready.

It made for the fifth night in a row he hadn't slept more than a handful of hours, but on the upside, at least he'd caught up on work.

"You're going to wish we could go back to talking about purple baby carriers when you find out why I'm here." Zach flung himself on a bar stool at the counter and turned his attention to Sam's coffeemaker.

"Bad news?" Lifting Aiden out of the carrier, Sam cradled him in one arm and offered the boy the bottle. The kid latched on to it like he hadn't eaten in days instead of hours. Would he ever sleep through the night at this rate?

"J. D. Covington walked out of juvie three days ago." Zach concentrated on making the coffee as he turned on the water and filled the pot.

Sam managed to stop himself from uttering most of the curses that passed through his brain, not wanting to upset Aiden's digestion.

"Why? And how come we're only just finding out about it?" A message should have come to his department ASAP, damn it.

Did no one follow protocol anymore?

"You know the juvenile system. They write their own rules. Apparently, they had a detention hearing and decided he could be supervised at home until the pretrial screening, but someone must have forgotten to inform the arresting officer." Zach dumped in some grounds and hit the start button. "I only found out when I went to the quarry to see what kind of Wi-Fi connection I could pick up—long story." He waved away that thread of the conversation. "Anyway, I ran into the kid and his mother, and she told me the good news."

"Meaning J.D. could have sent me that message on my phone."

"Or his mother." Zach shrugged, reaching for a mug. "She reminds me of the way my mom was when Dad went to jail—faithful to the end."

Sam remembered all too well. Mrs. Chance had fallen apart when her husband had gone to prison for white-collar crime. But somehow he could understand her reaction. He had no idea how Jeremy Covington's wife could forgive him for assault and sex offenses against teens.

"No luck pinpointing where that message came from?" He took a seat on a bar stool two down the counter from Zach, leaning an elbow on the granite to make it easier to feed Aiden.

"None." Zach slid the phone across the breakfast bar. "If you get any more, don't touch anything after it happens and bring it to me as fast as you can."

"Right." He ground his teeth together, anger building. "And how do you suggest I document threats that disappear seconds after they're delivered?"

"You're the cop," Zach reminded him. "But I'd write down times and dates."

"You say that like I'm going to have more than one."

He stared down at the innocent face in the crook of his arm, hardly believing the boy was his. His ex-girlfriend might have found the baby overwhelming, but for Sam, the boy was already a part of him. The best part. "But I'm telling you now, there'd better not be another threat against my son."

"We'll find out where it came from." Zach said it with a certainty that eased some of the defensive fury building in Sam's chest.

Sam knew he meant it. And he trusted him. If there was any way to prove a digital crime or find a cybertrail, Zach's company would do it.

"Good. I'll assign someone to watch J.D. now that I know he's circulating again." He set aside Aiden's bottle and patted the baby's back even though the boy was already falling asleep. In the middle of the morning of course.

Rarely at night. "You didn't need to come all the way out here to bring me my phone. I've got to stop by the office later to set up some interviews with victims who reported trouble out in the quarry in the last few years."

He hadn't forgotten about the spike in incident reports during the week of the teaching conference.

"I drove Heather to her sister's house before I came in here." Zach craned his neck to look out the kitchen window, maybe trying to glimpse the cabin from here. "I figured I'd talk to you until she was done over there."

"If I know Amy, that'll be any minute," he said drily, grateful to see Aiden was now fully asleep again. "She's not one for idle conversation."

Zach chuckled softly, leaning in to center the coffeepot perfectly under the drip of the steaming-hot java.

"What's so amusing?" Sam moved toward the infant swing in the center of the dining room, where he'd never bothered to set up a table. Gently, he lowered Aiden in it. To his surprise, the boy stayed asleep, settling his heavy head against one side of the cushioned seat, his baby Buddha belly stretching the snaps of his onesie.

"Just trying to picture the two of you talking if *she's* the quiet one."

In spite of himself, Sam grinned back at him.

"Compared to her, dude, I'm chatty."

"Is that right?" Zach pulled two stoneware mugs off the wrought iron stand near the coffeemaker. "Heather did say that her sister's invitation to come over consisted of about five words. And those were delivered via a call at two in the morning."

He split the brew between the two mugs before searching Sam's fridge for creamer.

Sam sipped his black, wondering why Amy had been awake at that hour. Was that unusual? Or had she been thinking about their conversation this afternoon?

He sure as hell had thought about it a lot last night.

But Amy hadn't called him at 2:00 a.m. She'd called her sister—the one who was testifying against Jeremy and J. D. Covington at the end of the month. Had she been thinking about that?

"When is your sister flying in for the trial?" Sam hadn't spoken to Gabriella in weeks.

It occurred to him now that if Amy had secrets about that last summer, maybe Gabby could shake something loose. Spark a memory.

"I don't know how much time she can take

off from work, but I imagine she'll be here at least a week before the trial begins in order to prepare." His coffee fixed, Zach returned to the counter stool. "Why?"

"Maybe we ought to get together everyone we can from that summer." The idea took shape, feeling right as he said it. "The friends you hung around with. The other foster kids living in the Hastings' house. Anyone who worked at the pizza shop."

"Haven't we already talked to a lot of them?" Zach opened his phone and flipped through the digital files that Sam had been sending him.

"The local ones. But how many people left town, the same way we did?" He wondered how he could hunt down those people. "Lorelei probably has contact information for everyone who's gone through her house."

Zach nodded. "It could be a great time for a Hasting fosters' reunion."

Why not?

"I'll get on it." He'd ask his foster mother to help him. But first he needed to speak with Amy.

"Good." Zach's phone chimed before he'd sucked down half his drink. "I'll see if I can get Gabriella out here sooner rather than later." Standing, he shoved his phone in his pocket.

"Looks like Heather's ready to go. It was a fast visit after all."

No surprise there.

Sam walked his friend to the door. "I know you don't want J.D. anywhere near your fiancée," Sam observed just as Zach reached the door.

"I'll kill the kid personally if he breaks that restraining order."

Sam believed him. Zach wasn't a fighter, but he'd held his own that day they'd found the Covingtons trying to kidnap Heather Finley and Megan Bryer.

"You'll have my help, of course. But maybe so it doesn't come to that, you could dip into that impressive Chance financial reserve and put a PI on the kid."

Zach frowned, scratching the back of his neck. "I don't want to do anything that could harm the case. Aren't there conflict-of-interest laws at work there? Me being the mayor and all?"

"Heather will be your wife soon. How could any court deny you the right to protect her however you see fit?" That area of the law was far too gray for his liking. But sometimes, common sense counted in the legal system.

"But any information a PI gathers is going

to be tough to use as evidence when I'm footing the bill."

Sam shrugged, rubbing the kink out of his neck. "Not necessarily. All I know is that Heartache doesn't have a dedicated police force, per se. I don't have enough manpower to keep constant watch on everyone in town. We can't even try the case in Heartache." Criminal matters were heard in a court at the county seat. "You have a right to use your resources to make sure your family is safe."

"I like the way you think." He clapped Sam on the shoulder. "I'll look into it this afternoon. But I know you've got another angle here that you're not sharing with me."

Oh yeah. The angle where Amy Finley was keeping something from him. But he couldn't connect the dots enough to share with Zach yet. And he had a lot of angles to work before the pretrial screening in less than two weeks.

"Don't look at me." Sam held the door open, letting the cold fall breeze clear his head. "I've got a foster family reunion to plan."

"Not in a million years would I have guessed you'd beat me to the land of family reunions and baby carriers." Zach didn't bother to hide a grin.

"Bite me." Sam closed the door and padded

back into the house in his socks, ignoring his friend's laughter.

He was more interested in how soon he would see the woman who had never been far from his thoughts this week.

CHAPTER SIX

"I DON'T KNOW how you and Erin got all this construction talent while I struggle to tell my wrenches apart." Heather stared up at the new support beam Amy had added to the cabin after demolishing a wall. "Seriously. I don't even remember setting foot in the family lumberyard until I was at least a teenager."

Their first meeting in ten years hadn't been as awkward as Amy had feared, but that had everything to do with her bighearted sister and very little to do with Amy herself. Heather had breezed in with a quick hug that had ended just before Amy could start to feel smothered, then proceeded to fill the dead air with chatter about Heartache and questions about the remodeling of the hunting cabin.

So far, they'd avoided anything too personal, including talk of the trial and the family.

Or at least, they'd only talked of the Finleys as it related to their construction business.

"That's because we were forever sticking you with Mom." Amy unplugged the cord for the reciprocating saw, not wanting her sister to trip since Heather wore heeled boots with her pink paisley shirt dress, a bold choice with her long red curls. "Erin and I were always the first to raise our hands when Dad gave any of us a chance to tag along on a job or help in the warehouse."

She hadn't thought about that in a long time. She and Erin would race shopping carts down the wide aisles, sometimes using them like go-carts and vaulting into the baskets at the last second.

Their oldest brother, Scott, had hated it when they did things like that, always trying hard to make the family more upstanding and respectable. Less…wild. But their father didn't seem to mind. Or maybe he hadn't really noticed.

"That's funny." The long fringe on Heather's sleeveless maroon sweater swept through the sawdust on a pile of planks as she peered into the open floor joists. "I remember being relieved when the house was quieter. I think Mom was easier to manage one-on-one."

The fact that Heather seemed to be examining the remodeling project more than quizzing her about their mother made it easier to talk about Diana Finley. A topic Amy normally shut down faster than any other.

"Five kids would probably make anyone a

little twitchy." She'd gained that much perspective at least. "Don't ask me why Mom, of all people, would have that many children to care for when she'd barely been able to care for herself more often than not."

After miscarrying her only pregnancy, Amy would have traded anything for just one healthy baby. The ache of that loss still hit her at unexpected times.

"In the early days of their marriage, I doubt she had any idea how bad the bipolar disorder would get." Backing away from the gaping hole in the cabin floor, Heather turned her attention to the small kitchen. "I can't believe this place doesn't even have a cooktop. I think Mack has a propane camp stove that you could set up on the counter. Want me to bring that next time?"

"That would be great." A wave of gratitude rolled over her at the realization that her sister was trying to make this visit easy on her. Because, hell yes, she'd rather talk about cook stoves than Mom. And yet it was nice to hear Heather acknowledge that their mother's condition had worsened over the years. Sometimes, as a teen, Amy felt like she was the only one who could see that. "Can I ask you a question?"

"I've waited a long time to have a conversa

tion with you, Amy. Ask me anything." Heather leaned up against the kitchen counter and waited.

"When the Covingtons tried to kidnap you, they didn't try...to touch you?" Amy couldn't reconcile the man who grabbed Heather with the one who had made her life a living hell ten years ago. She was trying to connect the dots and would feel better if she could say for sure that Covington had been the one who'd grabbed her, too. But she just hadn't seen him well enough. "I mean, how can Zach and Sam think that Jeremy is the same guy who tried to sexually assault Gabriella when the MO with you and Megan Bryer was so different? Gabby was an underage girl lured out by an internet predator to a remote location, and she would have been raped if not for Sam. Why do Zach and Sam believe that perpetrator is the same man who grabbed an adult woman in a public place and threw you in a van?"

Heather paused and seemed to consider the question. She tucked her hair behind one ear before answering.

"I haven't heard all the evidence myself, so I can't say for sure. But there have been other victims. And it sounds like Jeremy operated by himself ten years ago, whereas now they believe his son is working with him, so that could change how he preys on women. Plus, Megan is underage, and she was targeted online through a video-game chat message, so there are similarities there."

"Are you nervous about testifying?" Amy folded her arms across her chest, feeling the chill in the morning air. She should have gotten a fire going before her sister arrived.

"No." Heather's answer came immediately. "I'm so furious about what he did—to Megan especially—that I can't wait for my day in court to reveal him as a bastard to the world."

"Good for you." Admiring her attitude, Amy traced a pattern in the sawdust along a plywood plank. "Has Mom said much about the trial?"

Heather frowned, no doubt thinking it a strange question.

Amy had her reasons for asking. She wondered how much her mother remembered about their last argument. The one where Amy had told her about The Incident, looking for guidance or maybe just a little empathy. Instead finding only irrational anger directed at Amy and not at the guilty party. Her mother had not been well that summer; Amy understood that. But had she been medicated enough to have forgotten what Amy had confided?

"Not really. Mom insists that she saw Jeremy Covington giving me sidelong glances during Erin's wedding reception, and somehow that was enough to mark him as a villain in her mind." Heather shrugged. "Some days she seems really solid on her new medicine, but other days..." She shook her head, not finishing the thought. "She's always been eccentric, though, right?"

Understatement of the year.

"She did set my daily chore list to the tune of 'Twinkle, Twinkle, Little Star' when I was in preschool." It was a memory of mixed emotions. Sad because their mother couldn't find any energy to do any household chores herself. But happy because she really had tried to make it fun.

"Exactly." Heather came closer, tilting her head to see what Amy had drawn in the dust on the plywood.

Only then did it occur to her she'd sketched a tree at the edge of the forest, with a window in the distance.

Fighting the urge to erase it, she told herself that it wasn't all that legible anyhow. Sawdust wasn't exactly her medium. Besides, that image didn't hold meaning for anyone but her...

"Sam's coming over today," she blurted, moving away from the site of her impromptu artwork. "He thinks talking about that summer before he left town with the Chances will somehow uncover new evidence."

"Really?" Her sister leaned over the sawdust drawing and added a few flourishes that Amy couldn't quite see. "Do you mind being around him? I always got the impression that your breakup was part of the reason you left."

Was that what everyone thought? That they'd broken up, and Amy had left town because of it? Or that Sam had dumped her for another girl?

It didn't matter now. None of it was true anyhow, a fact that had altered a lot of her view of the past.

"Sam was easy to be around ten years ago, and, in a lot of ways, he still is."

She'd had a hard time admitting it to herself, but the truth revealed itself now. She liked Sam. Still.

"It's funny you say that because a lot of people think he's the most intimidating man in town." Heather kept her head down, using one thick strand of the fringe from her sweater like a paintbrush to feather through the soft particles.

"He's just quiet." But she liked that, too. His silences gave her room to think.

"Well, all that quietness mixed with so much

muscle makes it seem as if Heartache has its very own Secret Service agent."

"That's not a bad thing for a cop. And he seems good with his son." She tossed that out there, curious if Heather knew any more than what Sam had already told her.

"I have no doubt that he'll keep any child of his safe." Heather arched back from her work. "Zach said Sam's already looking to legalize his full custody to keep Aiden here."

"He wants full custody?" That surprised her given his experience with the foster system. She remembered him saying two parents were optimal. It was a conversation that had come up once when she'd been so upset with her own mother she'd suggested she would be better off without her.

A cruel comment, she now realized. So many regrets. So much distance. And so damn hard to figure out how to work through it all.

"I guess he doesn't want his son to ever feel unwanted, and he's afraid that the mother could walk away at any time if she's already floundering at parenting when the baby is so young." She waved Amy over. "Come see it now." She pointed to the plywood plank. "Doesn't it look like the Chances' house?"

Amy stilled.

Her sister had added a horseshoe-shaped

driveway to the dwelling Amy had only half started. Heather had also finished the tree out front. Added dimension to the house with a door and a deep front porch.

"Does it?" She kept her face carefully blank. "It's been so long since I've seen it—I don't remember."

Memories swelled, clamoring to be acknowledged. Freed.

A cold sweat started to bead on her forehead, and she hoped it wasn't visible.

"Amy?" Stepping away from the plywood table near the saw, Heather moved closer. "Are you okay?"

Panicked that her emotions were showing, she nodded fast.

"Fine. Great. Just thinking about that interview with Sam and wondering if I should make some notes before he comes. Or a timeline." Words tumbled out fast in her haste to put distance between them and the previous conversation. "I don't want to overlook anything that might help Sam solidify this case."

She hated that she couldn't share the most important piece of information. But she was being completely honest about wanting to help with any other aspect of the trial preparation.

"Sure." Reaching for her phone, Heather hit the screen a few times. "I told Zach we wouldn't be long, anyhow. He's down at Sam's right now, waiting for me so we can drive into work together."

"Is he?" Amy looked out the window. Her nervousness with Heather wasn't anywhere close to what she'd feel with Sam once he arrived to take her through that last shared summer.

"Yes." Her sister beamed as she toyed with her engagement ring. "I'm lucky to have him. He's been nothing short of amazing to me."

"I'm happy for you, Heather. I really am. Just because I haven't been here doesn't mean I haven't been rooting for you. All of you."

"I hope you'll come to the wedding." Heather headed toward the door, peering out a front window of the cabin as she retrieved her purse. "I'm praying the trial is done before then."

Amy was, too. Although it would move faster if they couldn't make all the charges stick where Gabriella was concerned.

"I'll see what I can do." Thinking too far in the future made her nervous. It seemed to take everything she had just to remain in Tennessee for a week, let alone a month. "A lot depends on how quickly I can finish the renovations."

"Oh." Heather dug in her purse. "Speaking of which, Scott gave me a check for you if you need to buy supplies from any store besides Finleys."

Their oldest brother had given Amy an open account for the work on the hunting cabin, keeping track of her expenses so the family could divide them equally. The check, apparently, was for anything Finleys Building Supply didn't carry.

She read the amount. "I'll never need that much." She'd gotten used to living on a small budget and didn't see herself changing anytime soon.

"But we did decide to go higher end on the appliances and cabinets, right?" Heather bit her lip as her gaze darted around the small lodging.

"Yes. But I don't pay full price for anything." She couldn't help the pride in her voice.

"Then we gave the project to the right woman." Heather leaned in for a quick hug. "It's so good to see you."

Amy savored the words as much as the closeness, even if she didn't squeeze back.

She wasn't ready to rely on her family yet, not even a sister who'd been so kind to her. Waiting until Heather left the cabin, Amy moved back to the plywood table to stare at the familiar lines of the scene she'd seen in her nightmares for ten years. Her rudimentary rendering had been enough to make Heather recognize it and flesh out the details.

Which ought to serve as a reminder that she couldn't afford to even think about that horrible night while she was here, surrounded by people who could be tipped off by the slightest detail. She needed to lock down that memory fast and not let it out anytime soon. No easy feat with the sheriff on his way to sniff out the truth about that summer.

Picking up the wastebasket, she held it under the edge of the wood and swiped all the sawdust into the basket's depths. If only the memory could be discarded as easily.

But she'd do whatever she needed to in order to keep her secrets private. And if that meant distracting Sam from his questions? She was just the woman for the job. Lucky for her, he was the only man on the planet she'd never had trouble flirting with.

HE WASN'T SURE she'd really show up.

Sam had phoned Amy shortly after Zach left, asking her to come to his place instead since he had the alarm system and extra security in place for Aiden here. She'd agreed easily enough, and an hour later, he pulled open the front door to find her there, wind sweeping fall leaves in a swirl behind her.

She wore a gray sweater that was as long as her matching dress, and a pair of black leggings underneath that. Layers of gray and black, the colors of a woman who didn't care to be noticed. Even her auburn hair was hidden under a dark gray knit beanie. He wondered what life had brought her way in the years since they'd dated to turn her into a more reserved woman than the one he remembered.

"Thanks for coming." He led her through the front room and past the kitchen, toward the back of the house. "I'm doing everything I can to protect my son. And while I know he'd be safe with me at your place, I also know I wouldn't be able to concentrate fully on our conversation if I always had one eye out for a threat."

Stopping in the family room closest to Aiden's nursery, Sam pointed to a tan microsuede couch that he'd cleared of all baby gear. He did most of his work in here, and a computer station had been built into a back wall. A couch and love seat sat adjacent to one another in front of the river-stone hearth, where he'd taken the time to lay a fire. The dried hickory wood smelled nice as it burned and, he hoped, detracted from the general disaster of his housekeeping.

Amy slid off her cap and pulled off her boots, leaving both of them close to the fire before she took a seat. The sweater she kept on. She draped it over her knees like a built-in blanket as she drew them up onto the cushion. He liked the way she made herself comfortable. It pleased him to think that she wouldn't do that move with just anyone.

"I don't mind coming down here. The cabin is freezing even when I have a fire going. I've got a big hole in the ceiling since I took down that wall, and the heat seems to go straight through the roof." Even now she tugged the sleeves of her sweater over her hands, tucking slender fingers into the wool. "But I tried to save you some effort on this interview by making you a timeline of that summer."

She withdrew a crumpled sheet of paper from her sleeve and set it on the coffee table.

"You did?" He reached for it, smoothing the notebook sheet's ragged edges against his knee. She had a list of dates and events, some of them with a few extra details.

"The dates I underlined are ones I'm certain about." She fidgeted with the hem of her skirt. "The other ones are approximate."

"This is great." He couldn't believe the details she'd captured, from a notation about the date her father bought a used truck to logging her shifts at the pizza parlor, where they'd both worked. "Did you have a diary for this time period?"

"No. Why? Do you need supporting documentation?" Frowning, she straightened on the couch as if she was prepared to run off and obtain just that.

"Hell no. I'm just surprised you could put all of this together so quickly." He couldn't wait to feed it into his computer against some of the other events in town that summer, including the movements of Covington and Gabriella.

"I have a degree in accounting. I tend to think in data and details." She shot up off the couch to wander around the family room while he read her notes. "Besides, I remember that summer particularly well since it was my last year here. I've had a lot of time to relive my mistakes."

That caught his attention. He raised his gaze to where she was studying a photograph he'd taken of the Harpeth River at sunrise, back when he'd had time to do things like drive out to the lake and fish.

"What do you mean? What mistakes?" He watched her carefully, studying her body language, which always told a story all its own.

Amy Finley had walked into this house well

prepared with her list and her willingness to provide primary sources for her memory.

If she'd been on the witness stand, he'd think she had been coached. In fact, she didn't seem surprised by his question. Almost as if she'd steered him into it.

"I argued with my mother. She heard about the skinny-dipping—I guess Harlan Brady saw me streaking through the cornfield toward the water that day. And you can imagine how well that went."

"That's why you left town?" He'd never known. And while there was a ring of truth to it, he'd bet money she was leaving something out.

Because she walked the perimeter of the room instead of looking him in the eye.

"You remember what she was like back then." She wrapped the sweater tighter around her waist, pausing to test the spring action of a baby bouncy seat.

"Only from what you told me. You never brought me home with you." He was used to that, being a foster kid who lived with the Hastings.

The townspeople had been reasonably nice considering the family had taken in a few bad seeds over the years who had earned the rest of the foster kids an unfair reputation. But Sam had never had many friends, which was why Zach's friendship had meant a hell of a lot.

And which was why dating Amy had been a sweet surprise in a life full of hardship.

"I stayed at home as infrequently as possible myself. I never subjected someone I liked to Mom." She toyed with the fuzzy animals hanging from a mini-mobile that dangled over the baby seat, turning each creature toward her so she could see its face.

"Where did you stay when you weren't at home?" He set aside her list, more interested in what she had to say.

"The hunting cabin. The swimming hole out behind the Spencer farm. My dad's office, which was a converted shed."

"You never spent time anywhere near the quarry?" He braced himself for the answer, even though they were talking about things that had happened long ago.

Things he couldn't change.

"No." She met his gaze, perhaps sensing the answer was important to him.

Thank God. He couldn't imagine how easy of a target she would have made as a teen— out by herself, with little parental supervision and a damaged relationship with her mother.

Of course, Gabriella had been in the same situation.

"Did you have a laptop? Or a family computer you used?"

"No. My parents said we should be outside doing things, not indoors and plugged in. And given how much my home life sucked by then, I wouldn't have wanted to be glued to a laptop." She rose from where she'd knelt by the baby seat and returned to the couch.

Did that mean she felt like the most stressful part of the conversation was over? He hated to think in terms of catching her off guard when he liked Amy. A lot.

But this case was too important to overlook key pieces of evidence just because he was attracted to her—then and now.

"When was the last time you remember seeing Gabriella?"

Her expression shifted. Shuttered. She went back to flipping the hem of her dress over her knees, tugging and tucking it under her.

He hadn't been imagining it. She knew something.

"I listed a couple of occasions when I thought I might have seen her. I can't remember for sure."

Vague information from the woman who liked data and details.

He debated how tough to play it. How much to push.

But before he knew what was happening, she was on the love seat next to him.

"What about the last time I saw you, Sam?" Her voice had a soft, intimate quality to it that changed the air in the room.

Her knee brushed his. Her cool fingers landed on his arm.

Everything in him stilled for a moment. Right before his heart rate jacked up.

"What about it?" He had thought about that night a lot—especially lately. But he hadn't planned to make it part of this conversation.

"I can remember a lot of details about that." Her soft words weren't flirtatious. She wasn't a flirt.

So if she was bringing it up now, it meant…

She was totally serious about what she was saying.

His pulse moved into overdrive and stayed there.

"I don't think a ten-year-old discussion of us going all the way affects the outcome of this case." Because that had been the topic of their last conversation. He remembered that day just fine, and that was not the direction he wanted to take this visit.

So when his gaze slid down to the soft fullness of her mouth, he cursed himself for being ten kinds of idiot.

"I took a lot of grief from my mom about us having a physical relationship that we never *actually* had."

"That seems like a technicality. Witness the skinny-dipping day." Things had been physical, to say the least. Teenagers excelled at pushing those boundaries. They'd both known where the relationship had been headed.

"Still." She tipped her head sideways against the love seat, contemplating him from just inches away. "It always struck me as damned unfair that I bore the punishment without any of the fun."

He closed his eyes to try to dilute the appeal of this woman who'd gotten under his skin from the first time they'd met. Like she'd been born knowing how to turn him inside out when other women called him unapproachable. Intimidating.

And, occasionally, an unfeeling bastard.

Why the hell had she never seen what everyone else did when they looked at him?

"I can't afford relationships that are just for fun anymore." That time in his life had ended when Cynthia showed up on his doorstep with Aiden in her arms.

"Or maybe you need fun in your life now more than ever." Her fingers walked along his shirt cuff.

The smallest, least sexual touch he could imagine. Yet his temperature spiked like someone had thrown gasoline on the fire in the hearth.

Clearly, the woman he remembered with the sparkle in her eyes and the urge to live on the edge was still buried under all those gray clothes.

"Some people would point out that kind of thinking is the reason I have to buckle down now." He nodded in the direction of the room where Aiden slept. "I'm still trying to get my feet under me after finding out I'm a father."

Her fingers stopped their tantalizing walk. Her eyes flipped up to his.

"Lucky for us, 'some people' don't ever have to know. Only you and me."

She was propositioning him on his family room couch.

Something was wrong with this picture. But his brain had a hard time figuring out what when his heart slugged an insistent, pounding rhythm inside his chest. His hands itched to be on her, to pull her across his body and pick up where they'd left off ten years ago. He wanted to see if she still kissed the same way. If she'd still tunnel her fingers through his hair and press into him like she couldn't get close enough.

Would she make those tiny noises in the back of her throat? Encouraging sighs when he touched her where she liked best? Remembering every detail of that last night together—when things had gotten way too hot and out of hand in his truck behind the closed pizza shop—Sam could almost convince himself it was okay to touch her again. To kiss her again.

To make her cry out his name while he helped her find release.

Except they weren't together anymore, his brain chimed in at the last second. And she had changed gears during this sorry excuse for an interview when he'd mentioned Gabriella.

"Are you purposely trying to distract me?" His voice was so dry and hoarse he hardly recognized it.

She withdrew her touch. He felt the loss all the way to his toes, damn it.

"No, Sam." She shook her head. "I was trying to distract myself. I have a lot of unhappy memories from that time in my life." She crossed her legs and shifted away from him, all her body language communicating that she wouldn't be coming on to him again. "Excuse me for thinking I could indulge in one of the pleasant ones."

He wanted to ask her about that. Had so many follow-up questions he didn't know where to begin. But before he could even form words, his son's cry blistered his ears.

"Aiden's awake." He closed his eyes for a moment, mentally shifting gears before he headed to the nursery.

But Amy shot right off the couch. "I'll get him."

CHAPTER SEVEN

"WE'RE GOING TO be late for school."

Bailey ignored Megan's warning, her hand hovering between the hazelnut and pumpkin spice coffee carafes at the convenience store across the street from Crestwood High School. The fluorescent lights hummed overhead while a few other customers picked out doughnuts or ordered hot breakfast sandwiches to go.

They were running behind schedule this morning because Bailey had been fighting with her father. Over breakfast, she'd mentioned that she wanted to speak to her mother—to visit or arrange a call from the jail. Her father had lost his mind that she would even suggest it.

And while Bailey understood he was devastated that his wife had had an affair—and with an alleged sexual predator, of all people—the woman didn't stop being Bailey's mother. They had things to discuss. Or argue about. Or maybe she just wanted to yell at her mom for being so selfish. So stupid.

So hurtful.

"I'm a senior. I've earned the right to be tardy for a day." Bailey put her cup under the pour spout of the hazelnut and filled it with steaming-hot java. "Besides, we have a test in calculus. I will literally fall asleep over the first problem without this."

"You're right." Megan grabbed a cup for herself and tucked it under the carafe marked "Hot Water," then dug through a basket to choose a flavored tea. "I'd better get something, too."

While they were bringing the cups to the checkout, Bailey noticed two girls by the candy display staring and whispering behind their hands. Nothing unusual about that. She'd been the subject of everyone's gossip since her mother went to jail. Or since her mother had been caught having an affair with the social-studies teacher's husband.

"Get a life," Megan snapped at them as they walked past the girls and out of the store.

But then, Megan had dealt with that kind of crap for months after J.D. broke up with her and spread rumors about her. As a star athlete at Crestwood and the son of the richest guy in town—except for the mayor—J.D. had a lot of clout around school.

Now it was Bailey's turn to be on the outs with everyone. She slumped into the driver's seat of the car so hard a few drops of coffee splashed on the dark floral skirt she'd paired with a grunge-inspired flannel shirt.

"You okay?" Megan asked her as she smoothed a hand over her own neat denim skirt and tights that she wore with some kind of video-gamer T.

Bailey edged the Volvo out onto the street for the quick trip into the student parking lot.

"Fine. It wasn't that hot."

"I don't mean the coffee."

"I know." She sipped her drink and welcomed the jolt of caffeine into her exhausted body. "I don't care what they say." *Much.* Although it did suck to be the topic of gossip all the time.

"Some girls get off on drama. It's their oxygen. They'll die a painful, suffocating death if they're not constantly immersed in a soap opera." Megan sipped her tea through the plastic top of her cup and pointed to a vacant parking space.

"I know. And seriously, they don't bug me as much as that fight with my dad." She'd already told Megan the basics since she'd picked her up that morning. "Can he really cut me off from Mom if I want to talk to her?"

"I'm not sure." Megan didn't say much as they crossed the parking lot, and it occurred to Bailey she probably shouldn't have brought it up since Bailey's mom had to be high on Meg's list of despised people.

And, of course, who could blame her?

She sipped her coffee, berating herself for being a crappy friend, and hurried toward the side gates leading into the campus. There was still a chance they could beat the first bell.

But why were so many kids still outside? The lawn and outdoor hallways were crowded with kids in Crestwood's B-wing.

"What's going on?" she heard Megan ask a girl from the school band on the fringes of the mob.

"Look who's back in school." The blonde hefted her violin case higher in her arms, simultaneously raising her phone to take a photo of the drama. Then, before Bailey could figure out what she was doing, the girl gave a shrill whistle and raised her voice. "Hey, guys! Bailey McCord is here."

The crowd quieted. Other students lifted their phones in unison, as if the whole world wanted a photo.

What the hell?

But then the group parted suddenly, opening up to make a path for her and Megan.

"Oh God," Megan whispered, sliding an arm around Bailey's shoulders.

Because in the center of the students stood J. D. Covington.

Her ex-boyfriend.

Her abuser.

Out of jail and walking around her high school like he belonged here.

Bailey's coffee fell out of her hand as Megan pulled her away. Numb and scared, she followed her friend blindly. It didn't matter where they went as long as it was far away from here. She didn't care about the drama or the fact that her reaction had just been captured on cell-phone video by at least a hundred kids and would go viral before lunch. She felt a passing hysterical moment of gratitude that she hadn't at least peed her pants, and she giggled.

"Whatever is so funny, you'd better share it now because I want to throw up." Megan sounded terrified.

Only now did Bailey realize her friend's hand was shaking where she held hers. She squeezed it tight.

"I'm thanking God I didn't piss myself when a thousand camera phones were trained on me."

"I guess that's about as much of a bright side as we could expect, isn't it?" Megan opened a door as the bell rang.

Only they weren't in class. Her friend had brought them to the guidance office.

"What are we going to do?" She looked around the waiting room, where a handful of other kids signed in to see their counselors, class schedules in hand. If only her problem was as simple as changing math teachers.

"Call home. Call the cops. Find out how to get a restraining order against that piece of crap if the police aren't going to keep him in jail."

"Language, ladies." One of the younger counselors walked in the door carrying a leather binder and a yoga mat.

"Seriously?" Megan rounded on Mrs. Trestle. "I just ran into the guy who tried to kidnap me three weeks ago. He's out of jail and walking around school. That is *not okay*, and I will not watch my language if you can't protect me from him."

"He's here?" The counselor peered past Megan to the office secretary behind the front desk like she needed confirmation of the fact.

Apparently "he" did not require a name.

"I just got in." The secretary shrugged while she cradled a phone on her shoulder and typed something at the same time. "I haven't heard anything yet."

"Okay." Mrs. Trestle nodded toward her office at the end of the hall. "Come with me, and we'll get this sorted out. I don't want you walking around this school if he's here." The woman put a protective arm around Megan's shoulders and led her away, yoga mat still tucked securely under her other arm.

Because, of course, everyone knew that J.D. and his father had tried to kidnap Megan and her music teacher. Whereas Bailey was simply J.D.'s ex-girlfriend.

No one had any idea that she had every reason to be terrified of J.D., too.

"Bailey, are you coming?" Megan turned before entering the smaller office.

"I'm going to call my dad first." She needed a minute to catch her breath. To stop shaking.

To figure out her next move.

"Honey, you can use your phone in the testing center right around the corner. You know where I mean?" The office secretary looked up from her desktop screen and pointed the way until Bailey nodded.

Rounding the corner, she pushed open the door to the small testing area. The lights were on in the back of the room but not the front, as if no one had come in yet today.

Not that it mattered to her.

Still, maybe that was why she didn't notice

the boy seated at the first testing corral until he stood suddenly.

"Dawson." She recognized him from the Hastings' house right away, even though his face remained in shadow.

She'd spent half her babysitting shift mooning at him out the window of Aiden's nursery.

"Bailey." He moved to pick up a pile of papers on the desk of the corral where he'd been sitting. "I can work on this out front if you need to be in here."

"No. You don't have to go." She rushed the words out, realizing that she was simultaneously sidestepping to block his path. Could she be any more obvious? "That is… I'm only texting my dad." She held up her phone for proof.

Adding to her dork quotient exponentially. Nice.

"And I'm only filling out paperwork to start school here." He waved the papers before sliding them back on the desk. "Not in any special hurry."

She stared at him dumbly for a long moment, taking in his T with cutoff sleeves that would never pass the dress-code rules but that showed off better muscles than J.D. would ever dream of having. The girls of Crestwood were going to go nuts for him.

"Can't blame you for that." She fidgeted with

her phone case, picking around the edge of the purple cover, hardly believing she'd ended up in a room alone with him on a morning that had started out about as badly as any day possibly could. "I wouldn't go to school here either if I had a choice."

Outside in the waiting area of the guidance office, she could hear some teachers laughing and joking.

Did anyone care that a boy who had harassed and threatened Megan was back in class today?

"That bad?" He leaned over to slide a second chair out and flipped it to face her, the metal feet scraping the cracked terrazzo. Wordlessly, he offered it to her before lowering himself into his former seat.

"Worse." She eyed the chair, knowing it had to be meant for her but scarcely remembering how to react to a boy being nice. "Unless you like high drama and lots of cliques."

Dropping her backpack on the floor, she sank into the cold metal that put her just a few inches away from him. Well, their knees were that close since the chairs were angled. But the rest of her still sat two feet away from him.

Had he done that on purpose? Her heart skipped a few beats.

"That's every school." He slouched lower,

his long legs sprawled so that one knee loomed even closer to her.

He smelled good, like shampoo or soap, maybe. This close, she could see a fresh cut just under his chin, a tiny red slash that might have been a shaving mishap.

Overhead, an old institutional clock hummed away the minutes.

"Where did you go before this?" Was it okay to ask that? She didn't know how long he'd been in the foster system, so maybe he'd just left his real home. Or maybe he'd gotten transferred from one foster family to another.

Either way, it couldn't have been easy. But it was too late to take the question back without another awkward moment.

"Memphis. Three schools in two years. And they're all alike." He shifted toward her to tick off items on his fingers, the angle making the thin gold chain around his neck glimmer dully. "Same athlete pricks. Same entitled rich kids. Virtually identical cliques."

"Really?" She couldn't imagine any student body being as mean-spirited as this one. She tried not to envy him the opportunity to try out other places, knowing his life couldn't have been easy.

Then again, she wondered if his mother was

in jail the way hers was. That had to even the score a little.

"Definitely." Straightening in his chair, he peered over at her. "Who's your clique, Bailey?"

Something about the way he said it sounded like a challenge. As if he already assumed she would be in one of his predictable groups? She saw no point in denying where she stood in the social pecking order. He'd find out soon enough once he enrolled.

"Currently, I've been abandoned by all my former friends except for Megan—the girl you met who babysits with me. So I guess I don't have a clique these days." She avoided his eyes, wishing they could have gone on talking for a while before this subject came up.

"Been there." He nodded, his expression remaining neutral. If he thought she was a giant loser, he didn't show it. "But you know what? Better to have one real friend than ten bogus ones."

Out in the hallway, a woman's shrill voice rose to a shout.

"I know my son's rights! You can't deny J.D. access to his education. He is as entitled to be here as those girls—"

"Oh God." Bailey stood, her reprieve from her real life effectively over. She did not want to face J.D.'s mother. And what if J.D. himself were out there in the front office? "I need to get out of here."

"Why?" Dawson stood, instantly alert. "What's wrong?"

He looked ready to bolt, too. Together? The notion calmed her a little.

"Nothing." She shook her head, still feeling jittery and scared. Why had she let herself get separated from Megan? "I mean, there's a lady out front who will be really—and I mean really—unhappy with me. You can stay. I just… I have to go."

Hurrying over to the door of the testing center, she gripped her backpack under one arm and peered toward the front office. It was around a corner, though, so her view was blocked.

She strained to hear the lowered voices speaking nearby.

"…there is no restraining order in effect," J.D.'s mother, the social-studies teacher, was telling someone.

"But perhaps the young ladies didn't expect him to be out of jail…" That sounded like the vice principal, Mr. Cornish.

"He was never in jail!" Mrs. Covington insisted. "He's just a boy who got caught up in his father's mistakes—"

She was shushed again, and the rest of the

conversation became more garbled, as if they'd stepped deeper into one of the offices off the reception area.

Bailey's stomach knotted.

"You want a ride home?" Dawson's soft voice in her ear was an oddly pleasant sensation in the midst of a firestorm of scary shit.

Bailey wanted to cling to it with both hands.

She really didn't want to be here. She needed to speak to her father about what to do now that J.D. was back in school. And even though her car was out in the student parking lot, she was already shaking in her shoes at the idea of walking through the front office to leave. Her old Volvo would be wrapped around a tree if she tried driving herself anywhere.

So no matter that she knew it was selfish to rope this boy into her problems, she nodded.

"Ready when you are."

BRIGHT BLUE EYES stared up at her from the most angelic little face.

Amy had sprinted into the darkened nursery, grateful to escape an awkward conversation and her failed flirting attempts with Sam. But she'd gone from the frying pan into the fire because now she held a warm, wiggling bundle that was every bit as precious as she'd once imagined a newborn would be.

Only in her imaginings, it had been her child she'd held in her arms. She'd spent months dreaming about her baby, envisioning herself as a mother, and knowing somehow that the journey to being a parent would heal the broken pieces inside her.

"He likes you," Sam observed over her shoulder as she held him.

She hadn't even heard him enter the warm yellow nursery decorated with brightly colored dinosaurs. It smelled like baby powder and infant laundry detergent, with a basket of half-folded tiny clothes near the crib. She had to close her eyes to shut out the vision of Aiden's sweet expression, the moment so beautiful and painful at the same time after what she'd been through.

"It's probably my rocking technique that he likes," she said finally, her voice husky from the mix of emotions tugging on her heart. She'd spent too many hours staring into the hospital nursery after her miscarriage, watching the nurses care for the newborns. Hastily she swiped at a tear that welled in her eye.

She told herself to hand the baby over. To walk out of the nursery and away from Aiden before the boy stole another bit of her heart. Instead, she kept rocking and patting the infant's warm back where she'd wrapped him in a thin cotton blanket.

"Maybe he misses his mother." Sam's voice took on a hard note, and she turned to find him scowling. "She called me this morning to ask for more time—"

He stopped himself as if he'd changed his mind and didn't want to talk about it. Amy, for her part, was all too glad to talk about something besides all the dark feelings inside her. Loss. Regret. Longing for the kind of life she wouldn't have now.

"For what? She wants you to watch him longer?" Curious, she pivoted to face him, her socks sliding on the hardwood.

"According to her, she's in treatment for postpartum depression."

"You say it like you don't believe her." She remembered what her sister had said about everyone in town thinking Sam was intimidating.

Just now, with the dark scowl on his brow, she understood why.

"I'm not sure I do. She hasn't given me many reasons to trust her, though I'd hate to think she would use such a serious condition as a cop-out. It's damn unfair to the new mothers who truly suffer from postpartum depression." He retrieved a black gym bag that had been stored under the changing table and started filling it with diapers, wipes and baby clothes.

"I have to drop Aiden off at my mother's before I make a few stops around town. Any chance you could take a ride with me? I figure the more we reminisce, the more likely it is that we'll stir some memories that could help the case."

She watched him collect supplies from around the nursery, his broad shoulders stretching the cotton of his blue button-down in the most appealing way.

She had been crazy to try coming on to him. But then again, he'd grown only more appealing in the years since she'd seen him last. She liked that he was a serious guy. He never made her feel that she needed to pretend happiness or lightness. Even better, he made her feel safe just with his presence.

"I thought you weren't interested in my kind of reminiscing." She shifted Aiden when he stretched like he might cry again, holding him upright against one shoulder and rubbing his back.

It took all her willpower not to tip her temple to his and sing him a lullaby. What was it about a baby that inspired such an immediate need to cuddle and care for them? It wasn't just her own loss. Even before the miscarriage, she remembered how fun it had been to care for her brother Scott's daughter when Ally had been a baby.

Across the nursery, Sam straightened. He set the bag on the top of the changing table and stuffed in a blanket before turning to face her.

"I am very interested." He stalked toward her, his cool gray gaze unflinching as he watched her. "If I didn't have a job to think about—or my son to consider—I can promise you this afternoon would have proceeded very differently." He let the words simmer between them for a minute while she took in the import of the suggestion. "But I'm going to view this extra time to think as a good thing."

He smoothed a strand of her hair away from where it was caught on Aiden's blanket. He hadn't even touched her and her heartbeat tripped over itself.

"You've had ten years, Sam Reyes." She narrowed her gaze. "How much more time could you possibly need?" She could almost hear the argument brewing in his head. But she didn't want to hear it. So she tucked Aiden closer to her chest and brushed her cheek along his downy head. "Don't answer that. I'll go with you, and we can argue all you like on the road."

Heading toward the door, she wound her way back through the white utilitarian kitchen toward the entrance, picking up her boots along the way. Sam followed her, shouldering a duffel on one arm and stuffing a few items in a leather messenger bag.

Fifteen minutes later, he parked his pickup truck outside the Hastings' home, waiting for a sheriff's car to meet them. He'd arranged extra protection for Aiden after the threat he'd received.

"It must be hard letting him out of your sight." She leaned over in the black leather passenger seat to stare at the infant. He was nestled in his car seat between them in the full-size truck cab. "Not because of the threat. Just for the sake of being with him. I'm sure you're enjoying getting to know him more every day." She stroked a finger over the fuzzy terry-cloth sleeper that covered one bowlegged knee. "If he was mine, I'd—"

Her voice caught awkwardly while Aiden blew bubbles. She was grateful the police car showed up just then, saving her from having to explain why she was an emotional basket case around Sam's baby.

She unfastened the car seat while Sam stepped out of the truck to speak to the uniformed patrolmen tasked to watch the house—and Aiden— for the rest of the day. Five minutes later, Sam took the baby, the car seat and the gear and disappeared into the house before reemerging with a small brown basket covered with a white-and-blue cloth.

When he got back in the truck, she caught the scent of apples and held her hands out for the mystery basket.

"Was your mom baking?" She'd been alone with Sam for two seconds and already it felt like a date from the past. How many times had his mother sent him out with something homemade?

"Apple muffins." Sam's arm snaked along the back of the seat, ostensibly to turn around and see where he was going as he put the truck in Reverse.

But Amy didn't mind the warm brush of his fingers on her shoulder and hoped that part wasn't accidental.

"We got apple muffins for your afternoon of running errands?"

"She might have seen you sitting out here in the truck and drawn her own conclusions about the errands I had in mind." He kept his expression neutral, but she heard the teasing note in his voice.

"Clearly she knows you much better than I do since I don't have a clue what you could be planning."

"I figured I'd use the muffins to bribe information from you." He slid the basket from her hands and set it in the console as he headed in a familiar direction—out toward the Spencer farm, where they used to sneak away to be alone.

"Did they teach you that in police school? Bribing with Baked Goods 101?"

"No. I improvise my technique based on the situation. And since you're proving to be a tough customer, I'm upping my game." He turned down a quiet road that ran in the same direction as Main Street.

She smiled to see it was still deserted. She used to drag race bicycles with her siblings here. As the youngest, she never won contests like that, but the best days were the ones when they left the house in the morning and didn't return until dinnertime.

"Well, now that I can smell those muffins, I'm starving. So what is it you need to know, Sheriff?" She tucked her boots under the truck's floor heater to take the chill off her toes. It wasn't cold out—the truck's thermometer read sixty-four degrees—but she liked her feet to be warm.

"Why did you have tears in your eyes when I first walked into the nursery earlier?" He kept his eye on the road, slowing down for a wide pothole in a place where live oak branches from trees on either side created a tunnel of Spanish moss.

She wanted to lie and say it was because he'd turned down her flirting efforts. But not even ten years apart would make him believe she'd changed that much.

And, truth be told, it was better than having to talk about that last summer. She'd made some peace with her miscarriage at least.

"I had a second-trimester miscarriage last year and it…wrecked me." There was no other way to describe the devastation that day had caused on her life.

"Oh, Ames." His use of her old nickname slid right past her defenses and melted her heart, his hand coming to rest on her shoulder with a gentle squeeze. "I'm so sorry. I never would have asked if I'd had any inkling it was something like that."

"I know." She did, too. He wasn't the kind of man who would pick at a wound to see it bleed. "It's not as raw now. But seeing Aiden reminds me of those hopes and dreams I had."

He turned the truck onto a dirt road around the back of the Spencer farm, close to where the creek ran. The old orchards weren't as full as they used to be since the farm hadn't been working for years, but small peaches littered the ground from trees that still produced fruit.

"What about the father?" he asked quietly, shutting off the engine near a wooden bridge. Old Mr. Spencer had built the bridge over the creek decades ago, but it had held up all these years.

"He lasted about five minutes into my pregnancy and decided fatherhood wasn't for him." She'd been too in love with the news that she was expecting to spare much thought for her ex. A sure sign she'd been with the wrong guy anyhow. "I was more than prepared to be a single parent."

"You want to go sit on the bridge?" He pointed toward their old spot.

He'd kissed her for the first time there.

Had he thought about that when he'd brought her to this place?

Dappled sunlight danced on the water, and the sound of the gurgling rush was apparent now that he'd turned off the engine.

"If you bring the muffins." She reached for the door handle but waited to lift it until he nodded.

In the short walk to the creek's edge, she moved to skirt around a muddy ditch, not wanting to ruin her boots. But Sam lifted her up easily, his arm circling her waist and plunking her down on the other side of the ditch before she had nearly enough time to savor his touch.

Still, her skin tingled beneath her dress for long moments afterward as they stepped up onto the gently rounded arch. The bridge supports were a naturally bowing tree branch that the old man must have sawn down the middle since the curved log halves perfectly matched. Sam rinsed his own boots in the water before he climbed up beside her and then lowered himself to sit on the planks, their legs dangling over one side.

With the sound of birds and rushing water in her ear, and the warm splash of sunshine on her shoulders, Amy felt more at home than she had at any other time since arriving in Heartache. Sitting beside Sam, with his strong arms and easy way with her, was a tantalizing memory she knew she shouldn't get too caught up in.

She wasn't staying in Heartache. And Sam had plenty of problems of his own to work through with a new baby at home.

But for now? He was not in a relationship. And their past had ended on a giant question mark that had lingered in her mind and in her heart for years.

"So you brought me here to reminisce?" she clarified, wanting him on board with whatever happened next.

"That's correct." He looked around the forest and then shifted to see her better. "This was one of a few places that came to mind as being an important part of that last summer."

Tension curled through her at the reminder of the information he wanted.

"Are we back to the interrogation?" She crossed one leg over the other and gazed down into the water below.

The rush of shallow water could have mesmerized her if she hadn't been in the middle of a very intriguing conversation.

"I think you know damn well no one has interrogated you yet." He had moved closer while she'd been looking away.

His shoulder brushed hers, the warmth of his body heating her straight through his shirtsleeve and hers.

"So I'm free to reminisce about whatever I like?" She played with the hem of her dress until his hand covered hers and stilled the movement.

Could he feel her heartbeat pound where one of his fingers lay on the inside of her wrist? The sunlight found lighter hints of brown in his hair and illuminated the rough shadow along his jaw.

"Now that we're alone, I'm very interested to see what kind of memory you'll bring up next."

She smiled then, confident now that it wasn't

an accident he'd brought her here. To this bridge. Where they'd first kissed.

"I don't know." She shook her head, feigning confusion. "It's been a long time. Maybe you ought to tell me what *you* remember. That might help me."

"I remember getting hypnotized by a wild girl who loved to run through forests." He tunneled his fingers into her hair, igniting shivers down her spine.

She wanted to curl into that touch and seek more of it.

"A wild girl?" She wondered how much he was teasing and how much he had seen her that way.

"Oh yeah. She was hell on wheels." His thumb stroked a path over the middle of her cheek, back and forth, a warm brush of calluses. "I could never keep up."

Her heart turned over on itself. After all the years she'd spent hiding from the world since then, it was nice to remember a time when she'd felt strong. Desirable. When life was more exciting than scary.

"I don't know that I remember her. Tell me more." Looking into his eyes, she recognized the boy she'd been crazy about so long ago.

She still wanted him to kiss her every bit as much as she had that first day.

"I always had fun chasing you, Amy." His lips neared her ear where he spoke the words softly against her skin.

More shivers. More want.

"I'm not running now." She lifted her hand to his chest, where she could feel powerful muscle and the steady thrum of his heartbeat.

"Looks like I'm going to catch you for sure, then." His words were a soft breath of minty air over her lips in the moment before his mouth slanted over hers.

Everything else stilled. His hand in her hair. Her fingers splayed against the placket of his shirt. He moved only his lips as he kissed her. A slow, tantalizing pressure until she opened for him, her tongue darting out to see if he still tasted the same.

He shifted then, circling her waist with one arm to draw her closer. His hand cupped her hip so their thighs pressed flush together, her right leg tight to his left. She ended up crossing her other knee over his too, half in his lap as she looped her arms around his neck.

He tasted like toothpaste and kissed like he had all the time in the world for her. She couldn't get enough of him. She pressed nearer still, her breasts grazing the wall of his chest while she lost herself in the feel of him.

She hadn't been touched like this since she'd

been with him. He traced a path down her spine with slow deliberation, as if he could somehow press her closer, vertebrae by vertebrae. When he reached the waistband of her leggings, a ridge he must be able to feel through her thin cotton dress, he followed the line to one side and then backtracked to the other, as if he was contemplating sliding away a barrier.

Or maybe that was just her wishful imagination. Nerve endings flared to life all over her body. Her skin was tingling from his touch, and he hadn't peeled away even so much as her sweater.

He broke the kiss to lean back, his gray gaze raking over her like a fiery touch.

"Bring back any memories yet?" He arched a heavy eyebrow, his focus returning to her mouth.

"I remember how hot and bothered your kisses make me." She couldn't imagine how she could sleep tonight after the fever he'd stirred inside her.

"That's the most encouraging news I've had all day." He rested a palm on her knee, his fingers teasing along the hem of her dress.

"But since I'm not sixteen anymore, I can't just go home and be content with daydreaming about you." She disentangled her arms from his neck before she started peeling off her own clothes. Or his. "And since you told me you weren't in the market for anything fun and simple…"

What were they really doing here?

His cell phone buzzed in the silence hanging between them.

She knew he'd have to check it. So, sliding her legs off his, she reached back to satisfy her physical cravings with apple muffins instead of a sexy cop.

"Damn." He scrolled through the screen and shoved the device back in his pocket. "I've got to get down to the high school before all hell breaks loose."

CHAPTER EIGHT

"You can't drop me off at home?"

Back in his truck, Amy sounded worried as he peeled out of the gravel road that led away from the creek. Away from the site of a kiss that had him seriously questioning his sanity.

He had wanted to coax secrets from her, not just breathy sighs and hungry touches. *Ah hell.* He wanted all that and more. But he needed the truth about whatever it was she was hiding, damn it.

"Not enough time." He cursed himself for not having J. D. Covington followed sooner. But the police department was stretched thin to the point of breaking. And who would have thought the kid would go right back to school his first day out of juvie? Shouldn't a family-court advocate have been making sure he stayed out of trouble? "Zach's place is on the way to the school. If you think your sister is there, I could drop you off at the Chance house."

"No." The adamant refusal was followed by

Amy tucking herself against the passenger-side door.

Retreating.

Had she argued with her sister to inspire that strong of a reaction? Amy was prickly as they came.

Except when he kissed her.

Damn, but he wished they hadn't been interrupted. That there had been more time to explore the attraction. Things had been intense with her during their teenage years. But nothing like this.

Shit. He needed to get his head back to the task at hand. The safety of the town came first.

"I'll try to wrap things up quickly at the school, but I should at least check in." Turning out onto the main road again, he pressed hard on the accelerator but didn't bother to slap a flashing light on the roof. Heartache was quiet this time of day—the calm before the storm when classes let out at Crestwood and student drivers took to the roads with more speed than sense.

"Something's going on in the parking lot." She pointed to the teachers' parking area near the football field.

"Fender bender, maybe?" He noticed one car was pulled up tight to another. Even from a distance he could read the body language of angry people leaning in toward one another. They were adults out there, not kids.

He really didn't want to get involved in a faculty dispute when he'd heard J.D. was causing trouble. Apparently the principal had tried to handle the uproar the kid's return to school had caused, but by noontime, the superintendent had gotten involved and phoned the local police.

"Shit. That's Kate Covington. She teaches social studies at the school." He could see her now as he pulled off the road and into the lot. "And the woman she's arguing with was behind bars up until a few hours ago. Tiffany McCord had an affair with her husband."

Who damn well still better be in jail tonight. The court system was hemorrhaging Sam's arrests, it seemed. But there was enough evidence against Jeremy Covington that the guy couldn't have possibly been given bail.

But Tiffany McCord... Sam had been surprised she'd remained locked up for as long as she had.

Belatedly wishing he'd put the flashing light on the hood, he navigated the truck through rubbernecking teachers and students who'd somehow filtered out of the school to witness the drama fast bordering on a reality-show shit storm gone rogue. When he'd pulled up as close as he could without running anyone over, he slammed the gearshift into Park.

"Wait here. Keep the doors locked," he told Amy before jumping down to the pavement.

"You cheating slut!" Kate Covington screamed, her face a mottled red headed toward purple. Tall and thin, the woman was normally soft-spoken and a well-liked member of the teaching staff. "How dare you show your face here?"

Tiffany McCord, a former pillar of the community with her position on the town board and a prominent area business owner, appeared to be unfazed by the other woman's fury. Virtually every other time Sam had seen her, she'd been slathered in makeup and sporting coordinated, expensive-looking clothes as if her life depended on her appearance. She wasn't so made up today, though, with a clean face and blond hair in a ponytail. She looked more like her daughter, Bailey.

Tiffany's eyes narrowed. "I'm not the only one who cheated. And if you would stop protecting him, you could put his ass in jail—"

"Ladies." Sam stepped between the women before Kate could wring Tiffany's neck. "Everyone should take a step back right now before this escalates any further. I think we can all agree the school parking lot is not the place for this discussion."

Even though he'd been more than a little curious what Tiffany McCord had been about to say next. Did she really think Covington's wife had actionable evidence? A wife couldn't be compelled to testify against a husband. But it would do Sam's case a hell of a lot of good if the woman felt so inclined.

Kate Covington bared her teeth like a rabid dog. "Good. Keep talking, bitch," she shouted at the other woman. "You'll be right back in jail, where you belong."

Sam had no choice but to tighten his hold on her waist while she struggled forward.

A few of the other teachers in the crowd tried to help him by urging her to settle down. Others ushered kids back toward the school—a losing proposition—and a couple of brave souls circled the wronged social-studies teacher and tried to catch her flailing fists.

"You want me in jail?" Tiffany asked, an amused smile on her face. "Where Jeremy is? It's almost like you're trying to matchmake."

Kate Covington lost her mind then. Windmilling her arms, she shrieked and swore until spittle flew from her mouth. Tiffany McCord could have gotten into her car and out of harm's way at any time since she was the one blocking the other woman's exit. But instead, the newly freed McCord remained just an inch or two out of reach, like a cat taunting a chained dog. What the hell was her goal here?

So much for his quick stop at the school.

"Mrs. Covington." He kept his voice low and attempted to be as calming as possible. "Please regain control of yourself. You don't want to put your job at risk—"

She slashed at his face and tried to make a grab for the gun at his waist.

Which was how she ended up on the ground in cuffs.

Damn. It.

He read the woman her rights while the school principal belatedly put in an appearance. Reaching for his phone to call for backup—something Sam had hesitated to do earlier since he didn't want to pull the patrolman away from guarding his son—Sam realized he'd left his cell in the truck in his haste to reach the scene. He glanced toward the pickup and met Amy's gaze through the windshield. She had a phone to her ear.

Hopefully she'd decided to call the station.

Either way, he didn't think he'd be giving her a lift home anytime soon.

AMY QUICKLY REALIZED she should not have answered Sam's phone.

She had debated what to do when it rang the first time, but she'd ignored it. When it rang again shortly afterward—the caller ID showing a local number but no contact name—she started second-guessing herself.

Sam didn't appear to have any kind of police radio in the truck. What if the only way his department could contact him was by the phone? For all she knew, there could be a holdup taking place nearby or a kidnapped child.

He'd want to know.

But as soon as a young woman's voice had burst through the phone, pleading with Amy to reassure Sam that the caller was working hard to get her life in order so she could see Aiden again... Amy was in way over her head. As in drowning.

"Ma'am." She cut the woman off midsentence while watching Sam try to reason with the feuding pair in the parking lot. Her grip tightened on the portable baton in her purse, the stress of the conversation making her tense. "I just happened to have been holding the sheriff's phone. He's on police business. I don't know him well at all. Could you call him back?"

She didn't want to get involved in his personal affairs. Even if she hadn't kissed him, she'd want to keep the mother of his child at arm's length. Now? She didn't want to end up in a hissing match like the two ladies ready to draw blood on school grounds.

Thank God Sam could handle himself. Her heart had been in her throat when the teacher tried to reach for his weapon. But Sam had moved with ease for such a large man, quickly incapacitating the woman while not harming her, which she knew from her self-defense classes wasn't as easy as he made it appear. Thankfully, a police car had pulled into the parking lot a few moments after the scuffle.

"No. Please. He hasn't been picking up when I call." The woman sounded urgent. "I just want to hear how Aiden is doing." Her voice hitched. "I miss my baby so much even if I'm not in a good place right now to take care of him."

Amy closed her eyes and wondered what to do. As much as she wished she hadn't fielded this call, she couldn't just hang up on the woman if those emotions were real. Still gripping the baton in her lap, she watched out the windshield as Sam turned over the social-studies teacher to a young uniformed officer.

"Aiden is fine," she admitted, aching for whatever this woman was going through. "I saw him this morning, and I can assure you he's being well taken care of."

"Oh, thank you. So much." Her tearful relief

was so obvious Amy had no doubt the other woman's condition must be serious. Otherwise she'd be taking care of the baby she clearly cared about. "I just—" She sniffed on the other end of the call, the connection a bit unsteady as if she spoke from somewhere rural. "Can you tell Sam that I'm working hard to get better? That I will come back soon to see Aiden?"

She was uncomfortable getting involved in Sam's personal life, but she couldn't find it in her heart to refuse. Her gaze locked on the too-damn-sexy sheriff as he strode toward the truck even now.

"I'll tell him." She disconnected.

The driver's-side door opened, and he took a seat beside her. "That mess is done, and apparently J.D., Megan and Bailey have all left school anyway. Sorry."

She passed him the phone. "Sam, I hope you're not upset, but I have a message for you. I really debated answering your phone when it rang, but I was worried it could be your work. The number was local but unidentified." She realized she still had the baton in her other hand and tried to slide it back into her purse discreetly, but she noticed his gray gaze followed her movements.

"Everything okay?" He shoved the phone

back into an open slot on the dashboard and pulled the door shut behind him.

Outside in the parking lot, the principal had corralled the bystanders away from the drama. The bell rang, signaling the end of the school day. Sam must have been trying to beat the rush since he threw the truck in Reverse and wasted no time backing out of the teachers' parking area.

"The call was from Aiden's mother." *So awkward.* She hadn't even gotten the woman's name. "I told her you were unavailable and asked her to call back, but she was upset, really upset. She seemed very anxious and wanted reassurance that Aiden is doing well."

She watched Sam's jaw flex while she spoke. He seemed to be focusing on the thinning crowd outside the window, but when he turned to meet her gaze, his gray eyes flashed with anger.

"Kind of Cynthia to check in on the child she abandoned." He did not seem to have the same empathy for her that Amy had felt.

But perhaps he had reason not to trust the sincerity of the woman's pleas? The woman had walked away from her baby, something Amy found difficult to fathom. But then, she also understood postpregnancy hormones could be very tricky. She readjusted the restraint on her seat belt as Sam headed in the direction of town.

Away from where they lived on Partridge Hill.

"She asked me to let you know that she is working hard to get better, and that she'll come back soon to check in with you." Her obligation complete, she told herself not to ask anything more about it.

Cynthia wasn't her business.

But Sam appeared so unmoved by the message that Amy couldn't help but wonder why he'd been screening calls from the mother of his child, especially when he'd always said that two-parent families were better than one.

"Then it's a good thing Aiden isn't old enough to ask where his mother went." His grip was tight on the steering wheel as they passed the pizza joint on Main Street that his foster family owned. "Like I was."

Amy remembered the little bit he'd told her about his life before foster care. His birth certificate lacked a father's name, and his mother had abandoned him one day while Sam was in first grade. He'd taken the bus to school and come home to an empty house.

"Have you looked for her?" she asked.

"My mother?" He shrugged. "I needed her as a kid. Now?" He shook his head. "I can't see the point."

"You told me once that even a bad mother is better than no mother." She wondered if he still believed that. Would he try to work things out with Aiden's mother?

And if so, she needed to be very careful about what she let herself feel for him.

"It's human nature to want to know your birth parents. I suppose I can't deny Aiden that."

Her stomach clenched at the thought of Sam with another woman. Not just any other woman, but Aiden's mother. They could be a real family one day after Amy went back to her life in Atlanta.

"Is Aiden's mother ill?" She found herself asking the question as they drove past Last Chance Vintage, the consignment shop her sister Erin owned.

Forcing herself to focus on the scenery and not the idea of Sam with his old girlfriend, she squinted into the sun's glare to see the display in the consignment-shop window. Her sisters had told her about the store in their letters over the years, and the storefront was every bit as quirky and charming as she'd imagined it. The faceless mannequins in the window wore Ts featuring 1970s-era rock bands paired with full, feminine skirts that had a 1950s vibe. The hand-painted sign out front used purple lettering on driftwood. Very eclectic and reflective of Erin's aesthetic.

But not even the sight of the store could lessen her interest in Sam's answer. Like it or not, he was bound for life to the woman through the child they shared.

"The last time I checked one of her messages, she claimed she's suffering from postpartum depression." He made another turn that took them away from Main Street and toward the town hall and the sheriff's office.

"You don't believe her?" Amy tensed, feeling defensive on the woman's behalf.

Did Sam have any idea how strong the hormones associated with pregnancy could be? How deeply emotional they could make a woman? During and after?

"I have a difficult time trusting someone who disappeared from my life after a one-night stand, never revealed that she was carrying my child and only reappeared because she couldn't care for our son." His voice remained level, but the cold judgment in it was evident. "And before you jump down my throat, let me remind you that if the situations were reversed, and your partner had deprived you of getting to know your own child, you might feel every bit as resentful as I do."

He parked the truck in the town-hall lot with a hard jolt of the gearshift and switched off the ignition. They stared at each other across the cab, the engine ticking in the quiet.

Guilt pinched as she considered that she had judged him unfairly. He had a right to be upset. And to worry about the well-being of his son.

"You're right." She would. "She should have told you about the baby." Sam would never have bolted like Amy's ex. "But if she's truly trying to get better for Aiden's sake—"

"She has to." He said it fiercely, his gray eyes flashing a cold, fiery determination. "It wrecked me when my mom checked out on being a parent. I won't see my son go through that kind of pain."

"He won't." She knew that for certain. "No matter what happens with Aiden's mom, your son will always have you in his life."

Unlike Sam, who'd grown without his father.

"Yes." His jaw flexed, and he seemed to weigh his words. "But no one takes a mother's place."

The words hinted at a wealth of unspoken hurt, making Amy ache for the child he'd been.

Not sure what to say, she reached to squeeze his wrist. Just a brief touch to indicate that she understood. Sam wasn't the kind of man who revealed his emotions lightly, and she wanted him to know she appreciated him letting her in—if only for a moment. Too bad the glimpse he'd given her made her more wary than ever about getting involved with him.

"True." She cleared her throat, allowing her thoughts to stray to her own mother and their lack of relationship for the last ten years. That had been a unique hurt that never went away. "And for what it's worth, I do realize that this is none of my business. It wasn't my place to ask about any of it."

Because no matter that she and Sam had just re-created their first kiss out on that old bridge today, they weren't going to pursue a relationship, and she wouldn't be staying in town any longer than it took to heal the family rift and renovate the cabin.

"I don't mind you asking me tough questions." His forthrightness had been something she'd admired about him long ago. He might be quiet, but he'd never been secretive—aside from his disappearance, which he'd now explained.

"No?" She found it difficult to meet his level gaze, more confused than ever about where they stood with one another.

"Not at all. I'm going to keep asking you tough questions until I find out what you're hiding. So it's only fair you put me on the spot sometimes, too. Keeps us even."

With a few concise words, he'd made it crystal clear to her. He wouldn't stop looking for witnesses to testify against Jeremy Covington.

But for better or worse, she hadn't seen the face of the man behind The Incident. So as far as she was concerned, she didn't have anything else to tell him.

"Is that why you brought me to the cop shop with you?" She pointed to the town hall and sheriff's office. "To interrogate me about whatever it is you think I'm hiding?"

"Hardly." He retrieved his phone and pocketed it. "I need to file paperwork about what just happened at the school and how we dropped the ball with J.D. I spoke to the principal in the parking lot, and she assured me J.D.'s mother took him home before lunchtime after the uproar he caused."

"Seems weird how Tiffany McCord was in jail this morning and now Covington's wife will take her place tonight." The argument on school grounds had rattled Amy, bringing back ugly memories of her own disputes with her mother.

One quarrel in particular had made her mother

so angry she'd turned the same shade of red that the social-studies teacher had today.

"Kate Covington is not going to jail. She'll get an appearance ticket and be back home in no time. But it will be a good chance to ask her some questions. I'll let Linda Marquette talk to her until Kate cools down—she's got a lighter touch than I do." He pointed to the uniformed officer pulling up to the building now. The same one who'd arrived at the school just before they left. "I should go give her a heads-up on details of what shook down. But I can arrange someone to give you a ride home if you wait a minute."

"That's okay." She'd been avoiding downtown Heartache long enough. "I'll walk over to Erin's store. I haven't seen her or the shop yet, and it's time."

A furrow in his brow deepened. "Are you sure?"

"I'll be fine." She could use a walk to clear her head, a little time away from the attraction growing between them all over again.

"Let me get your door."

As he exited the driver's side, she gathered her purse and checked her face in the flip-down visor. She felt an odd flutter of nerves at the idea of walking down Main Street, where anyone could see her. At least her mother stuck close to home, so she didn't have to worry about running into Diana Finley unexpectedly.

But there was always that uncertainty that the man who'd haunted her nightmares could still be free. That was, if Sam had locked up the wrong man and the real bastard who'd tried to hurt Gabriella still lurked out there. A man Sam was working hard to keep behind bars.

Still, Amy felt for her pepper spray in her bag as Sam opened the passenger door. Stepping onto the truck's running board, she moved the spray to an exterior pocket where she could reach it easily.

Sam shook his head as he shut the door behind her.

"What?" She smoothed her dress straight, wondering about his expression.

"Just trying to guess why you need a personal armory in that bag of yours." He nodded at the purse, where only the cap of the spray was visible.

How had he guessed?

Then again, it shouldn't surprise her that he'd be an observant man. He'd been on the police force in San Jose for years before moving back to Tennessee. No doubt he'd had to stay on his toes in a bigger city like that.

"Doesn't hurt to be safe." How many other

things had he seen or guessed about her that she thought she'd kept hidden?

"Can't argue with that." He held up his phone as he backed up a step. "Call me if you want a lift afterward. I should be done in an hour or two."

What was he suggesting? That they spend more time together? Something monumental had shifted between them this afternoon with that kiss, but they hadn't really addressed what it meant.

"And who will show up if I call? The man who kissed me? Or the sheriff who wants to interrogate me?"

She probably couldn't afford to see either of them again. Because even though she liked kissing Sam—a lot—his personal life didn't leave much room for a passionate affair.

More's the pity. Because that kiss with Sam had been one helluva toe curler.

"Maybe it'll just be your friend. Seems like we're both in need of one." Jamming the phone in his back pocket, he waved goodbye and stalked toward the town hall.

The fact that Sam Reyes wanted to be her friend more than he wanted to interrogate her made her feel special. Just knowing he was looking out for her gave her a stronger sense of security than any baton or pepper spray.

Call her crazy. But it was the most romantic proposal she'd heard in a long time.

CHAPTER NINE

"I NOTICED KATE Covington is in the interrogation room." Heartache's mayor pointed to the door at the end of the corridor on the opposite end of the town administrative building.

Sam had come down the hall to give his friend an update on the case, but Zach must have heard all about the argument in the teachers' parking lot. Zach stuffed an expensive-looking fishing pole under one arm as he glanced over the arrest report Sam handed him.

"It's hardly an interrogation. Just a relaxed interview." Or so he hoped. He hadn't done many true interrogations since he'd left San Jose. Besides, Kate Covington was hardly the kind of lifetime criminal that Sam had questioned on the San Jose drug-crime unit. "My gut says she was as shocked by her husband's activities as the rest of the town. But if she knows anything, I sure hope she's ready to give something up."

Because while there was no doubt in his

mind that Jeremy Covington would do jail time for the attempted abduction of Megan Bryer and Heather Finley, Sam wanted to pin more on him than that. In his bones, he knew that Covington was a longtime sexual predator. Clearly the guy had been very careful over the years, covering his tracks and keeping his identity hidden from his victims. But Sam and his staff were reinterviewing assault victims from the last ten years, hoping to connect their cases to Jeremy Covington.

He'd also requested a special investigator out of Franklin who dealt with teenage victims to see if she had any more luck than he had with the local high school population.

Yet even if he got more current witnesses to come forward, he still wanted better evidence to connect Covington to the crimes against Gabriella. Soliciting a minor for sexual contact online came with tough penalties—tougher even than the attempted sexual assault that Sam had witnessed with his own eyes.

"I heard Kate was riled up when you took her in. Maybe today she'll be ready to give us something." Zach peered down the hall again. "Where's Amy? I heard she was with you at the school."

"You damn well have the most up-to-date information about my day, don't you?" Although at least he'd managed to keep their trip to the old bridge a secret. Those hours—and the kiss that had left him reeling—were strictly between Amy and him. He needed to keep his personal life and his work separate. Not so easy to do when Amy seemed to have one foot in both.

Zach slid the fishing pole out from under his arm and took a step toward his office. "The Tastee Freez is still open for the season, you know. That place has all the best informants."

"You mean the eighty-year-old patrons that have nothing better to do than share the latest gossip?"

"They're rarely wrong." Zach grinned unrepentantly. "Besides, the coffee is good there."

"Right." He didn't buy it for a second, but Zach was the mayor because he was Mr. Personable and everyone liked him. "So did you take the day off to fish and hang out at the Tastee Freez?"

"Since I worked all night, I figured I could afford a lunch break out by the river."

"To fish." Sam happened to know Zach couldn't cast a rod to save his life.

Zack turned the rod over in his hands, studying it like a piece of rare technology. "It shouldn't be so damn complicated."

"Ever heard the saying 'don't bring a gun to

a knife fight'?" Folding his arms, Sam couldn't help but enjoy his friend's puzzlement since Zach was one of the guys who seemed to sail through life—from acing school and college, to launching a hugely successful business.

"Too much firepower for the Harpeth River?"

"Just try something simpler until you get the hang of it. Is Heather outfishing you again?" He'd heard she had reeled in a prizewinner at a recent fishing derby and apparently Zach had been struggling to keep up ever since.

He gave a self-deprecating laugh. "A ten-year-old kid could outfish me. But Heather is like…a fish whisperer. They swim for miles to hang themselves on her hook." Backing into his office, he leaned the rod against a wall. "I took her to the river to make peace with her because she was not too happy about the body-guard idea."

Sam frowned. "Did you tell her it was either a private bodyguard or someone from my of-fice protecting her?"

"I did." Zach ran a hand through his hair, a furrow of concern scrawled on his brow. "And she eventually saw reason. I called your old foster brother—the guy whose name you gave me."

"Excellent." Sam hadn't found much time to work on the Hasting family reunion today between his morning meeting with Zach and his afternoon with Amy. But he had pulled up a few contacts and remembered one of the guys who'd passed through the house at the same time as him now worked as a private investigator in Memphis. "I hope he'll be in town for the reunion anyway. Lorelei's birthday is in two weeks. I'm going to have it then."

"Makes sense. Good luck with Kate Covington."

"Thanks."

Stalking toward the interview room, he prepared himself to face Jeremy Covington's wife, hoping she'd had enough time to cool down. And as much as he wanted any information he could get from the woman, Sam found himself wanting to get the interview over with in a hurry.

Partly so he could pick up his son and reassure himself Aiden was fine despite the threat someone had made against the boy.

Also because he wanted a chance to give Amy Finley a ride home.

He had no idea how she'd crawled into his consciousness so fast and made herself important to him all over again. But there was no denying it. He'd brought her out to that bridge today because he couldn't stop thinking about kissing her. And now that he'd done it, he only wanted more.

Cursing the direction of his thoughts, he shoved open the door at the end of the hall and found Kate Covington dry-eyed and pale, her shoulders slumped over a cheap cafeteria-style table that had been repurposed for interviews.

Sam slapped a file down on the table and slid into a seat across from her. It wouldn't be the first time he'd pulled the good cop–bad cop routine with Linda Marquette, a technique that usually yielded more information than if either one of them spoke to the subjects alone.

"I already gave my statement to Officer Marquette." Kate looked like she hadn't eaten a good meal in weeks. Besides the pallor of her skin, her eyes were sunken and her mouth was pinched in a frown. Lank, dark hair hung in her face.

"I have it here for you to sign." He laid a palm on the file folder in front of him. "But I have a couple of additional questions."

She said nothing. Didn't even bother straightening from her slump.

"First, I'm going to ask your assistance in making sure J.D. understands the importance of staying away from Megan Bryer."

The girl's father was a mild-mannered guy on the town council, but he was fierce when it came to Megan. Dan Bryer had already contacted Sam's office a half-dozen times today.

"I'll tell him." J.D.'s mother pursed her lips.

"When I arrived on the scene, Tiffany McCord was in the middle of suggesting you had the power to put your husband behind bars."

She tensed slightly at the mention of the other woman's name. Her chewed fingernail scratched idly at the laminate tabletop. "I won't be compelled to testify against him."

"Of course. But it begs the question why you'd want to protect a man who betrayed his vows. With a woman who would come to your workplace to publicly harass you."

"If you thought she was harassing me, why am I the one who's been brought in for questioning?" She arched an eyebrow at him, making eye contact for the first time.

"Because she proved more skillful in getting under your skin."

Sam had been playing Tiffany's words over in his mind ever since he'd stepped between the arguing women.

Tiffany McCord wanted Kate to testify against Jeremy. Which meant there was trouble between Jeremy and his married lover. Could that be leveraged to turn her against him?

"I'm not the only one in Heartache who

thinks she's a mouthy know-it-all. She would get under most people's skin."

"Except for Jeremy's." Sometimes he didn't like that he got paid to pick at open wounds. But it wasn't hard with this woman, knowing she was protecting such a bastard.

"The rumor I hear is that he grew tired of her, Sheriff." Kate finally sat up straight, drawing herself upright as if with effort. "Is there anything else?"

"You think he's going to come back to you?" He couldn't imagine what the incentive would be to stay with a man like that. He opened the file folder and pulled out the typed statement for her to sign.

"I know so." She scribbled her name on the lines where he indicated. "And since he wasn't the man who tried to kidnap Megan and Heather, it's only a matter of time before he's back home and you'll have to admit this was all a mistake."

She set the pen aside and turned her head to one side as if she'd said all she planned on saying to him.

Sam realized he wasn't going to wrangle any more from her, but he was pleased to have learned one new piece of information.

Tiffany McCord would be a valuable woman

to have on his side. Tomorrow, she'd be the first person he spoke to.

Tonight, however, he planned to find Amy and finish the conversation they'd been having earlier about the secrets she was keeping.

And if he happened to make her dinner while he was at it? After the turns his life had taken in the last month, he damn well deserved a night that wasn't all about the job.

FALL SUNSHINE WARMED her face as Amy turned the corner past Lucky's Grocer onto Main Street. Her worn gray tennis shoes slowed their speed when she saw the handful of shops, brightly painted and welcoming. At the far end of the road sat the pizza parlor, awash in deep reds. Closer to Amy, the hair salon—The Strand— had the door open to let in the late-day warmth. The sandwich place across from Last Chance Vintage must be new.

Her sister had placed late-blooming mums in bright silver buckets outside her consignment shop. As Amy's feet hit a welcome mat, she realized she'd made the whole trip without once reaching for her baton—not even just to feel the weight of it in her hand.

Being back in Heartache—at least this part of town—made her smile. She'd passed a lot of fun summer nights on the town green behind Lucky's. Live bands played there sometimes, and she remembered dancing under the stars while her family ate barbecue on Friday nights. The kids would hurry up their meals to run to the playground.

A bell chimed a happy tune as she entered Last Chance Vintage, but it wasn't her sister Erin behind the counter. Amy recognized the blond ponytail, though, and the wide smile of her sister-in-law, Bethany.

"Amy!" Bethany squealed it more than spoke it, dancing out from behind the counter, already lifting her arms for a hug.

Amy had no chance of refusing. And maybe it was the bright sun of the day—or the fact that she'd been on the receiving end of an incredible kiss today—but she squeezed Bethany back.

Her oldest brother, Scott, and Bethany had already been married for eight years when Amy left town. In her early teens, Amy had gone over to their house for sleepovers sometimes, and Bethany had never made her feel like she'd been an obligation. They'd make popcorn and watch bad horror movies after they tucked in Amy's niece, Ally.

"It's so good to see you," her sister-in-law exclaimed, her rolled-up jeans and work boots paired with a khaki anorak and bright pink sweater underneath. She used to be a teacher until she'd found her niche managing Finley's Building Supply, proving herself invaluable and increasing the amount of money the store made every year since she'd taken it over.

Amy knew because her father used to send her the company statements. All the Finley siblings owned a portion of the building supply company. So even when she refused to take anything from the family, she'd been aware when they were thriving and when the economy hadn't been as kind to them. Even though she'd maintained her distance from the family, she'd kept track of their lives. Missing them and yet unable to make herself return.

"It's really great seeing you, too." Maybe it was easier to be with Bethany because they shared a different kind of history. Amy had never held her sister-in-law responsible for not stepping in to intervene when Mom had her worst days because Bethany had never lived in the same house. Bethany had never knowingly abandoned her.

Stepping back from the hug, Amy took in a quick glimpse of the store's interior. There were stacks of vintage linens arranged in an antique pie chest, to more whimsical touches like a fallen picnic basket spilling shiny, mismatched silverware onto a gingham blanket.

White leather go-go boots and a patch of purple shag carpet decorated a display of Ts for old rock bands. But despite the artsy vibe of the antique displays, the store actually had an expansive amount of floor space devoted to new and gently used clothes. A handful of shoppers picked through the racks even now when it must be almost closing time.

"How's Ally?" she asked Bethany.

"Having fun at college. I miss her while she's away, but it's okay because I know she's happy and thriving." She tucked her hands in the pockets of the anorak and rocked back on her heels.

"I'm so happy for her. And you." Amy had new appreciation for the way a child's life dominated a mother's heart. There'd been her intense grief for the baby she'd lost. But even today, listening to Cynthia's desperate voice on the phone when she had asked about her son, Amy had empathized. Perhaps more than she should have, in light of how Sam had reacted afterward.

"Thank you. Scott and I are very lucky that we repaired our marriage when we were close to calling it quits. But what about you? How's the house project going?" She bit her lip and peered around the store. "Actually, don't answer that yet. We should find Erin so she can hear. And Nina, too."

Waving Amy forward, she headed toward the back of the store, leading her past two dressing room stalls covered with long swaths of blue toile. The planked hardwood floor squeaked in a few places as Amy walked over it, but she liked the way Erin had maintained some of the building's original architectural features. The additions added to the feel of a turn-of-the-century general store with lots of rich wood to anchor all the colorful offerings. The scent of rose potpourri seemed to emanate from a few electric oil burners.

"Nina is here, too?" She hadn't expected to see so much of her family at once. Nina wasn't formally her sister-in-law yet, but she would be soon enough.

While her oldest brother, Scott, had been married to Bethany for ages, her brother Mack had only just gotten engaged to Nina Spencer. But Mack and Nina had been dating at the same time as Amy and Sam. There'd been a big blowup between them a few months before Amy had left town, though. Mack's best friend had been in an accident in Mack's car on the night of their high school graduation. For a devastating few hours, the Finleys had thought Mack had been the one who'd died.

Nina left town shortly afterward, and Amy had often wondered why. But she was back now, and she and Mack were planning a future together. They had opened a restaurant together in Heartache.

"We all came over to help Erin get the mobile unit ready for a Dress for Success event this weekend. That's her initiative to help underprivileged women source clothing to wear to work. Plus, a local woman asked Erin to help her find an outfit to give a deposition against Jeremy Covington." Bethany peeked into a back office and then, when the room proved vacant, she pushed open a heavy rear door labeled as a fire exit. "I think they might be outside helping her find a dress."

Sunlight poured over Amy through the open door. She tried not to linger on thoughts of a down-on-her-luck woman trying on outfits to give a statement against Covington while Amy...

Couldn't.

She shut down the guilt and looked around the parking area behind the shop. It was mostly vacant except for a large custom RV with the store name stenciled on the side. A door to the motor home was open, and the lights were on in the back. Rock music and laughter filtered into the parking area.

"Erin?" Bethany called, leaving the fire exit open so she could see inside the store. "Someone's here for you."

She grinned at Amy.

How strange to be here, waiting for a glimpse of the sister she hadn't seen in ten years. Her stomach jolted with nerves as she wondered if Erin would hold a grudge—no matter how nice of a face she put on her feelings. Erin and Amy were actually more alike in temperament than her other siblings. Heather alone had a sunny disposition.

"Well, hello, stranger. We're just finishing up in here."

Amy halted in the doorway to stare at her. With reverse highlights in her hair and a pink headband to hold it off her face, Erin didn't seem to have aged a minute since Amy had seen her last.

Despite the stern-looking black lace-up boots she wore and the tough-girl jean overalls, her smile was friendly. Genuine.

Amy felt herself return the smile as Nina Spencer leaned out the rear window of the RV.

"Look how gorgeous you are! Amy Finley, you may be the only woman on the planet who does not have a single picture of herself posted on the internet," she chided, retreating through the window to follow Erin out the door and into the parking lot. "You know how often we've cyberstalked you through the years?"

"Atlanta didn't make me any more sociable, I'm afraid." She wasn't used to so much scrutiny at once. But standing in the middle between Bethany, Nina and Erin, she searched her emotions and realized she didn't feel awkward. Or resentful.

Erin hugged her fast, the scent of rose potpourri permeating her clothes. Nina squeezed her like a favorite rag doll.

Behind them, Amy noticed a younger woman step down from the RV, a bright blue suit over one arm, her short brown hair covered by a yellow cap with a fast-food restaurant logo.

"Feel her hair, Erin!" Nina exclaimed, her fingers smoothing over the strands on Amy's shoulders before she pulled away. "You must have never colored it in your life."

Amy had forgotten how effusive Nina could be, but it was no surprise, as her grandmother, Daisy, was just the same way. Erin winked at Amy behind Nina's back before noticing the quiet brunette in the uniform.

"Faith." Erin moved toward the other woman, tugging a plastic bag that had been trailing from her back pocket. "Let me put this around the suit to keep it clean for you. And if you need another suit for an interview down the road, you should come to us again, okay?"

The woman—Faith—nodded, saying nothing. Amy noticed how pale her skin was, how dark the circles beneath her eyes, like she'd been up for too many hours and was too tired to put one foot in front of the other. She'd been that woman once, when she'd first moved to Atlanta and didn't even have a high school diploma to land a good job. Waitressing had carried her through a lot of lean years. She'd only recently started to build a client base for her private accounting business, and her best two clients were the restaurants where she'd waitressed.

"You're giving a statement against Jeremy Covington?" Amy asked Faith, shamed to think this tired lady was giving a court deposition while Amy kept her own knowledge on lockdown.

Scared. Guilt-ridden.

"Yes." She passed the outfit to Erin to bag, her pale blue eyes meeting Amy's. "I don't know how helpful my testimony will be since I can't identify the man who…assaulted me." She swallowed with an effort. "But the sheriff said it might lead to more people to testify."

"Thank you." The words came out fiercer than she'd intended, enough to make Erin turn from what she was doing to study Amy's face. "Our sister is testifying, so the case has been on my mind. You're brave to come forward."

The barest hint of a smile showed in the quick flash of a dimple.

"I'm not brave. It happened a long time ago, and I'm only just giving the police a statement." She smoothed the polyester work shirt that was part of her uniform. "It's long overdue, but I have a younger sister and I'm trying to… I don't know. Model better behavior for Patience's sake, I guess."

"It takes a lot of courage to call up unhappy things from the past." Amy knew that for a fact. "I'm sure other people will follow your example when they see what you're doing."

"Yeah?" Faith took the bag from Erin and pulled her keys from a worn leather satchel slung over one shoulder. "I hope so. And at least I have this suit to wear. It makes me feel more confident. I really appreciate it."

"It looks great on you," Nina supplied.

"I'm so glad we got to help you choose it." Erin fussed over the suit bag, smoothing it so the plastic lay flat over Faith's arm. "Good luck."

Giving an awkward wave, Faith hurried away toward a tan sedan parked on the far side of the back lot. Amy watched her hang the suit in the rear seat before she climbed in the car to leave. The muffler was loud and needed replacing. Amy found herself wanting to run after the other woman and offer to fix it. She'd replaced most of the exhaust system on her old car using YouTube videos and junkyard parts since for years she'd had no extra money to pay a mechanic.

Besides, Faith was her new hero.

"I can't believe you're really here, Amy." Erin's words called her out of the past, forcing her to focus on her family.

That was why she was in town, right? To smooth over old relationships? Time to start trying.

An hour later, the store had been closed, the security system switched on, and the four of them sat in the back room where Erin had a private office and consultation area for clients. The round table had been cleared of fabric swatches and reference books so they could make themselves comfortable to visit over bottles of sparkling water Erin had pulled from an under-counter refrigerator.

After touring the Dress for Success mobile unit, Amy had updated them on her renovations at the cabin. She was more interested in learning about how Erin had done most of the remodeling work on the store herself, but her family seemed determined to keep Amy in the hot seat. They questioned her about life in Atlanta, her plan to go into business as a private accountant and how she was spending the upcoming weeks in Heartache.

"So tell us about Sheriff Reyes." Nina leaned forward, elbows on the table. She wore a gold necklace, and the long chain pooled around the heart-shaped pendant as she leaned forward over the table. "Rumor has it you were in his truck today when he broke up a fight."

With her shoulder-length dark blond hair and gray eyes, Nina was a lovely woman. She had a ready smile and a warmth that drew people in. Amy could see why Mack loved her. Even if she did enjoy putting people on the spot.

"Sam is determined that I remember more about the summer when Gabriella was attacked. He drove me around Heartache today in the hope of shaking loose old memories." She wasn't going to reveal that the best memory they'd relived was a kiss, and that kissing him had been on her mind ever since.

"That's not his usual method of police questioning." Erin tapped her phone screen a few times, and the action seemed to lower the volume of the speakers behind them on a small coffee bar.

"No? I guess he hasn't forgotten we were once good friends."

"How about you?" Bethany sat closest to her. She reached over to lay a hand on Amy's arm for a second, her wedding diamond reflecting the light from a pendant lamp above the table. "Any hope of continuing that friendship?"

"I think Sam has too much on his plate right now to think about that." She gave an honest answer, even as it occurred to her this was the most girl talk she'd had since high school. Or, more accurately, it was the most girl talk she'd had about *her own* life. Because while she'd made a few casual friendships in Atlanta, she hadn't let anyone too close to know much about her private life.

She hadn't actively missed that kind of thing; she'd craved independence when she'd first moved to Atlanta. But she couldn't deny this felt…nice. These women might not have seen her in a decade, but they quickly zeroed in on things that were important to her. Things that weighed on her mind.

"Men don't ever have too much on their plate to think about 'that.'" Erin sipped her water coolly while both Bethany and Nina swung around to look her way. "What? It's true. Remy was still grieving for his wife when he showed up in Heartache. Neither of us was searching for a relationship, but we can't choose when the right person comes along." She stirred up bubbles in her water with a striped straw. "It just happens."

"I'm a long way from having the right person come along," Amy said. She had thought she'd found something special with her last boyfriend, and he'd bailed on her almost as soon as she'd shared her pregnancy news. "Sam is just very committed to this case. And he knows I'm in town to support Heather while she testifies. That's half the reason I came back."

The table went quiet for an awkwardly long moment.

Making Amy realize that the women here might feel shunned that she hadn't come home for other milestones in their lives. Bethany had almost gotten divorced, and her daughter had graduated. Nina had returned to town and became engaged to Mack, starting a restaurant along the way. Erin and Heather had opened this store. Erin had gotten married. And, of course, all of them had been here to help their mother after the death of Amy's father. That had to have been a traumatic time.

But as she cringed inwardly, her sister-in-law leaned closer.

"We're glad you're home." Bethany's hand returned to her arm. This time, her hand stayed for a long moment. "And Heather is, too."

"I know someone else who is glad she's in town." Erin stared down at her phone screen for a moment before flipping it around for the rest of the table to see.

An image of Sam—taken from a security camera—showed him standing just outside the front door of Last Chance Vintage. He pushed a buzzer or maybe an intercom button, his square jaw flexing as he glared at the closed entrance.

Had he come out of a sense of duty? she wondered. Or was he anxious to see her? His eyes gave away nothing.

"He's here for you, Amy Finley." Nina gloated as if she'd predicted it. "And he's the talk of all the single women in Heartache."

"I'm letting him in," Erin announced, stabbing at a button on her phone. "Because I can hardly lock out a lawman."

"That's some high-tech security system," Amy observed, hoping to steer the conversation away from Sam.

Erin's expression shifted, softening somehow. "Remy installed it all to keep me safe."

After another silent exchange of gazes around

the table that didn't include her, Amy wondered what she'd said this time.

"His first wife died during a home invasion," Bethany said softly as Erin jumped up to flip on a light in the store. "It made him very protective."

How awful. Amy hadn't heard that, but then, she and Heather had exchanged a limited amount of information over the years, a dialogue that she'd deliberately kept to a minimum. As much as she wanted to embrace her family now, she didn't know if they would ever understand.

"I should go." Rising from her spot at the table, she tossed her empty water bottle into the recycling bin under the coffee bar. "Sam will want to finish up our discussion."

It was as good an excuse as any to retreat. And besides, he was her ride.

"Of course he will." Nina draped her arm over Amy's shoulder as she walked her toward the office door. "How good of you to do your civic duty."

She didn't bother arguing. She smiled instead and let it go.

"I was the mayor's daughter, you know," Amy reminded her.

Nina tossed her head and laughed as they paused in the back hallway near the fitting room. "You were at that." She squeezed her once before she let her go, her attention shifting to where Erin was greeting Sam near the cash register. "Good luck."

"You ready?" Sam seemed to notice her as soon as she stepped onto the sales floor. He turned at once, jamming his hands in the pockets of dark pants.

Tall and broad shouldered, he was a fine-looking man. No wonder all the single women in town were talking about him.

Too bad for them, he'd kissed *her* today.

As their gazes connected over the racks of rock-band Ts and floral skirts, she felt a ping of electricity. A shock of awareness that bolted straight through her. Maybe he'd been thinking about that kiss, too.

"I'm ready." She was ready to follow where he led. Ready for a replay of this afternoon and maybe more.

Was he?

He gave brief nods and greetings to Nina and Bethany, but he moved closer to Amy. Put a hand at the back of her waist. The warmth of that touch seeped through her sweater. Her dress. It branded her skin and heightened her awareness of him.

Her nerve endings twitched to life.

And as he steered her toward the exit, she realized she'd developed one hell of an attraction for him. All over again.

And as he drove a few yards beyond the exit, she realized he'd stopped the full car-rier once more, pulled ahead again.

CHAPTER TEN

"TELL ME EVERYTHING," Megan demanded over the phone that night while Bailey searched the refrigerator for the ingredients to make a salad.

Since her mother left, there hadn't been much in the way of fresh food in the house unless Bailey remembered to stop at the grocery store herself. Her father could say what he would about her mom, but she'd run the house with precision. And made baked goods that were the first to sell out at school fund-raisers. Pre-pared healthy food with separate menus for newly vegan Bailey and her meat-eating fa-ther. There were always clean clothes and clean sheets. She'd always been available to proof-read homework.

But lately the McCord household had taken a decided downturn. After rejecting an old car-ton of wilting spinach, she closed the fridge with her hip and took the phone out onto the back screened-in porch, dragging a heavy wool blanket from the couch to take with her. She slept out here in the summer sometimes, listening to the crickets and the wind in the leaves. Now, even when it hovered around sixty, she liked the rush of fresh air. With her father out for his poker night and her mother banned from the house even though she'd apparently been sprung from jail today, Bailey had free run of the house to take Meg's call. Well, except for Hazel, her father's Irish setter, who thumped her tail on her dog bed for three swishes before she got to her feet to greet Bailey.

"There's nothing to tell." Scratching behind Hazel's silky right ear, Bailey thought back to the quiet car ride home with Dawson that morning. "He brought me home from school since I was so rattled about seeing J.D."

Thank goodness she'd left before the drama with her mother had unfolded in the school parking lot. She'd received a whole slew of texts reporting the news.

She climbed into the porch swing that was actually a twin-size mattress on a flat frame to keep it level. The sheets that were normally on it in the summer had been traded for flannel— something her mom had done before her arrest. The rest of the cold-weather blankets were folded on the end of the mattress, including a down comforter with a denim duvet. She kicked her shoes onto the planked floor and then tucked herself between the piled blankets. Hazel leaped up beside Bailey despite the arthritis in her hips and the stepping stool that was there to help her onto the swing. *Stubborn dog.*

"But how did he know to bring you home? Where did you see him?" On Megan's end of the call, Bailey could hear electronic gunfire and explosions from whatever video game she was playing.

"He was in a back room in the guidance office, filling out paperwork to go to school at Crestwood." At first, it seemed like incredible luck to run into the boy she'd been crushing on. But after the quiet and awkward drive home, she wished she hadn't accepted the ride. Had he regretted offering? "And he knew I was freaked out because we could hear Mrs. Covington yelling at everyone that J.D. had every right to be in school." She'd started shaking as the woman got all riled up—remembering what it felt like to be around someone who could get angry so fast. "I told Dawson I needed to leave, and he offered to drive me."

It had been really nice of him. So why had he been so quiet after that? She doubled up a pillow behind her head, staring out at the purple streaks of twilight while Hazel circled her feet and tried to find the best possible spot to lie down.

"Well, he's not a taxi service. He must have

wanted to hang out with you. Or help you. Or get your attention. Right?"

"Wrong. He just happened to be stuck in the same room as me when he overheard me having a personal crisis." She felt the dog freeze. "What guy wants to get involved with a girl whose ex-boyfriend will only stay away if she has a restraining order on him?"

Headlights shone along the side of the house, and Hazel leaped off the bed to stand at the back door, her tail wagging. Was her father home early? It didn't sound like his truck in the driveway. Bailey hugged the throw blanket around her shoulders and slipped off the swing to see who it could be, sliding her shoes back on her feet.

"With all respect to guys, do you really believe they consider things that carefully? He's eighteen, Bailey. He thinks you're cute. End of story." A happy electronic tune chimed on Megan's end of the call, signaling a victory in her game.

But by now, Bailey could see the outline of a figure coming around the side of the house. Toward the rear door.

"Someone's here." Panic made her throat close. It couldn't be J.D. Could. Not. Be. She backed up a step, closer to the door to the house.

But Hazel had never liked Bailey's former

boyfriend. And the dog's tail was still in motion. Her arthritic legs high-stepping in excitement.

"Bailey?" Her mother stepped out of the shadows. She wore a man's-style trench coat over pale jeans and a white T—clothes Bailey didn't remember her wearing before.

"Mom?" Her father had changed the locks after her mother was arrested. "I heard you were out and that you went to the school first."

She hadn't been surprised to learn her mother had been released on bail. Her father had been saying Mom's expensive lawyer would win his appeal for bail sooner or later. But it bugged Bailey to think her mother's first stop was to make trouble with Mrs. Covington instead of trying to see her own daughter.

At her feet, Hazel whimpered and scratched to get out.

"My worthless lawyer finally made good on his promise to free me before the trial." Her mother shrugged.

Seriously? Her mother deserved to be behind bars for what she'd done to Megan. How could a grown woman harass a teenager like that, pretending to be a peer? It was totally sick. And her mother had never apologized, never tried to send her a letter from jail explaining why she'd done any of the horrible things she'd done.

Bailey said nothing.

"I hoped I could see you," her mother said finally, perhaps guessing Bailey wasn't going to let her off easily. "I knew tonight was your dad's poker night, so I took a chance." She smiled at Hazel through the screen door. "Could you let the dog out at least?"

"I might as well since she's the only one who is happy to see you." Bailey cracked open the door so Hazel could greet her mother. "Meg, I'd better call you back," she said into the phone, feeling her friend's disapproval even if Megan didn't discourage her.

"Be careful, okay?" Megan warned her. "Want me to call someone? Let your dad know she's there?"

"It's okay." No matter how angry she was with her mother, she felt like she deserved an explanation for some of the things that had happened. "I'll be fine."

"Call me back when she leaves, okay?" Megan asked. "I have something to tell you."

"For sure," she said absently.

Ending the call, she stepped out into the dark evening, still holding her blanket around her shoulders like a shawl.

"I picked up some groceries." Her mother pointed toward the driveway, where her car was still running, the headlights on. "I'll get them for you before I go."

"Yeah?" She watched Hazel rub her doggy face against her mom's right knee and then her left one, happy as a dog could be. It was easier for Hazel, who didn't know Mom's villainous side. "I was just trying to make a salad a second ago. There's nothing."

Her mother pursed her lips and frowned. She looked strangely good, though. Like she'd been to the spa for three weeks instead of prison, which seemed weird. The little worry lines that used to be around her forehead all the time had eased. She wasn't moving around at a mile a minute trying to get things done.

"Bailey, I'm so sorry for everything. I don't expect you to forgive me. I don't deserve anyone's forgiveness." She rubbed the dog's head, and Bailey noticed her wedding ring was gone. "I'm going to try to patch up whatever I can fix, but… I don't know. I just wanted you to hear it from me directly that I understand what I did was so wrong, and I'm going to try hard to be a better person."

"Dad is crazy angry." She'd listened to his tirades—ugly stuff about her parents' marriage that she wished she'd never heard. She knew her father would never take her mother back in a million years.

"Rightly so." Her mother's expression was unreadable, but she didn't look away.

"But setting aside all the ways you hurt Dad? I'm so angry about what you did to my best friend." Her mom had made the anonymous texts sound like they'd come from one of the girls at school. "You told Megan she might as well die."

Her eyes burned to think that level of hate had come from her *mother*. The person who was supposed to love her the most in the world.

"I have regretted that every day since I sent it." She straightened from petting the dog, folding her arms tight. "Every hour. I knew it was stupid at the time. I knew *I* was stupid for letting Jeremy talk me into it." She frowned as if she still didn't understand it herself.

This conversation sucked for about a million reasons. But it was really strange to stand there and be disappointed with her mother for acting like the most idiotic teenager on the planet. Since when was Bailey the adult in this relationship?

"Did you ever stop to consider what could have happened if Megan had taken the message to heart? Like, what if she was having a bad day and she got a note that said 'You might as well die.'" Her mother had—as she was fond of reminding people—run a major electronics company at one time. How could someone so smart do something so dumb just because her boyfriend told her to? "What if she decided her life was shit and she should end it all?"

Her mother shook her head, blond hair slipping out of the elastic in front to hang in her face. "I'm truly sorry. What I did was unforgivable."

Bailey had a whole lot more to say about that, but what was the point? *Sorry. Sorry. Sorry. Blah. Blah. Blah.* The word didn't mean much to her. It didn't change what her mother had done.

Hugging the blanket tighter around her, she nodded toward the car. "Let's bring in the groceries before Dad gets home."

She damn well wanted the food.

"Okay." Her mother followed her along the landscaped pathway they'd put in when they first moved here.

The cobblestone pavers had taken her mother weeks to choose. Was it strange for her to be here, walking on those stones she had picked and knowing she'd never be part of life in this house again? Bailey did not want to care how she felt. But she wondered.

Once they retrieved the bags and carried them to the porch, Bailey stepped back outside with her mom, ready for her to leave. Her mother hadn't offered any great insights or reasons for what she'd done. And the last thing she wanted was a confrontation between her parents when her father came home.

"Are you still with him?" she asked, even knowing her dad could pull into the driveway any minute. "I mean, if Mr. Covington gets out of jail—"

"No." Her mother's eyes narrowed. "I am going to do everything I can to make sure he goes to prison for a long time after—" She shook her head like she wasn't going to say any more.

"Um." Bailey tapped her foot and tried to decide how to express herself. "If you think you're protecting me or something, please spare me after what you've already put me through. I'd like to know where you truly stand with him, Mom."

"Jeremy Covington is a cheating liar who had another girlfriend half the time we were together. And if I can do anything to make sure he goes to jail, I will."

Bailey's head spun from her mother's lack of sense. If she'd been talking to a girlfriend, she would have pointed out that her mom should have *known* he was a cheater by the fact that he was *married* and carrying on an affair. But her mother had lost her marbles. It was like one of those teen movies where the mom and daughter switch places for the day. Except Bailey would never pull the childish crap her mom had.

"How about Mr. Covington's kid?" she asked instead, tracing a path between the pavers with the toe of her shoe. "Can you send J.D. to jail, too?"

"Why?" Her mom stepped closer, all tense like she was poised for action. "Did that boy do something to you?" She put her hands on Bailey's shoulders. "Did he hurt you?"

"No." As much as the episodes with J.D. freaked her out to remember, she didn't want to unload them on her mother now. Not when she already seemed hell-bent on revenge. "I just...hate him for hurting Megan."

J.D. had helped his father shove both Meg and Mrs. Finley into a van. They'd duct-taped Meg's wrists and ankles. Gagged her. That was plenty of reason to want J.D. behind bars.

"Are you sure that's all?" Her mother's voice lowered to a whisper. She sounded scared. And scary.

Making Bailey feel really, really alone. Sure, she had a porch full of groceries. But now more than ever, she felt like her mom had checked out on her and left a flighty substitute behind. Maybe her mother had always been immature.

Or maybe her affair had brought out the worst in her. But either way, she didn't want to confide in this woman. Hazel might still love her, but Bailey wasn't so sure.

"I'd just be happy to see justice done. There should be consequences for what he did to Megan. So if you know anything about him, or if you can help Sheriff Reyes in any way—"

"I will." Her mother straightened, and for a moment, with her expression certain and her voice calm, she seemed like Mom again. "I promise you, Bailey, I will speak to the sheriff about what I know, and I will find a time to speak to Kate Covington when she's not in a mood to rip my head off. Because I guarantee she's got the goods that can send Jeremy to jail."

"Really?" That sounded okay. But Bailey knew darn well that Mrs. Covington wouldn't do anything that would get J.D. in trouble.

Bailey might be the only one who could testify to what a brute J.D. could be, and that made her stomach hurt. She'd left school today before she could look for other girls he might have pushed around. Or worse.

But she'd start asking questions tomorrow. There had to be someone else.

"Really. Jeremy Covington crossed the wrong woman." Her mother pressed a kiss to Bailey's forehead. "You'll see. I can't fix everything, but I can do that much."

She nodded, feeling chilled all of a sudden. "You'd better go before Dad gets home."

"I know." Her mom leaned down to hug Hazel. "Will you hold on to Hazel so she's not as sad when I go?"

"Sure." Bailey nodded even as the dog whimpered and stamped her paws anxiously.

"Things will get better." Mom bit her lip. Hesitated. Then walked quickly toward the front of the house and her waiting car.

Bailey watched her leave, arms around Hazel's neck, her face half-buried in the dog's soft fur. Her eyes burned a little, and she reminded herself that her mother had lied to everyone, cheated on her father and hurt Bailey's best friend—betraying Bailey deeply in the process. But in spite of everything, she couldn't escape the unsettling fact that the dog wasn't the only one sad to see her mom go.

"Come on, Hazel." She tucked a hand under the setter's collar, pulling her toward the porch.

Her tail wag slowed. Stopped. Started again as she turned hopeful dark eyes up to Bailey.

It was hard to watch.

"Come on." She tried again to move Hazel. "I bet there are treats for you in those bags, too."

A sudden creak of twigs and a rustle in the nearby woods startled her. Hazel pivoted, on high alert. The dog sniffed the wind and barked, her fur standing up on end along her back.

Panic jolted Bailey. Letting go of the dog, she hustled up the steps and into the screened porch.

"Who's there?" The words came out even though she wasn't sure she wanted to know. Her voice sounded like someone else's.

What if J.D. had come here to hurt her?

"Bailey?" a male voice called.

It didn't sound like J.D.

She turned toward the voice even as she locked the screen door behind her, leaving Hazel to deal with the intruder.

"Bailey, it's me." The guy sounded nervous. He didn't come any closer with an animal growling at him. "Is your dog going to bite?"

Dawson.

Relief rained over her.

"Hazel, stay," she commanded, reaching into a nearby grocery bag for dog biscuits. "I've got a treat for you, but you have to sit."

She hoped her pet would hear that she was relaxed. Not threatened. She shook the box of biscuits. Hazel sat down immediately, tail thumping.

Thank goodness. Bailey ditched the blanket that she'd had draped around her, tossing it on a padded wicker chair near the door.

"Sorry about that. I didn't know who it was." She edged out the door again, waving Dawson closer as she gave Hazel a treat. "What are you doing out there?"

Now that the fear had faded, her heart beat faster for other reasons all together.

He wore a gray hoodie and cargo shorts and he pushed a bright green bicycle through the damp grass as he came toward her.

"I didn't get your number, and I wanted to talk to you." He rested the bike against the back of the outdoor fireplace. "Is it okay if I leave this here?"

"Sure." She stuffed her hands in the pockets of her pink sweats, wishing she didn't look like she'd just rolled out of bed. Her long-sleeved T actually was a thermal pajama top, now that she thought about it. "My dad will be home any second, though. Is it okay if I introduce you when he gets here?"

"Of course." He held his hand out for Hazel to inspect. "Why wouldn't it be okay?"

"I don't know. You rode through the woods. I thought maybe you were trying not to be noticed or something."

"No." After Hazel showed her approval,

Dawson scratched her neck. "The woods are the shortest path between our houses."

"Right." Puzzled about his trip, she waited for him to offer some explanation for what he wanted to talk to her about. "You were so quiet when you dropped me off before, I'm surprised you still want to talk to me."

"Sorry for that. I wasn't sure what to say to you then." Straightening from petting the dog, he gave her his full attention.

Her mouth went dry. "Am I that hard to speak to?"

Her voice sounded high and strange. But then, she was nervous.

"I wasn't sure you'd want to talk about what was bothering you, and I wasn't sure how to bring it up." He seemed serious. Not flirting with her. But like he had something on his mind.

She tried not to be disappointed about that.

"No?" She didn't know what to say. Because, obviously, the last thing she wanted to talk about was the crap storm of problems she'd run from this morning at school.

"But I thought about it more after I got home." He scraped a hand through his dark hair, and she noticed a scar on his forehead that shone white in the moonlight. "Thought about you. And I just had to come back and talk to you."

"I don't understand." Her heart slugged hard in her chest. Curiosity mingled with worry as her father's headlights turned into the driveway out front. Hazel barked, and the dog sped off to greet her dad.

Dawson lowered his head along with his voice to speak closer to her ear. "How many people know your last boyfriend hit you?"

HE TRIED NOT to think about her secrets.

Sam didn't want the pending Covington trial to come between him and Amy yet, so he forced the thoughts out of his head with an effort while they finished their impromptu picnic on a blanket spread over the living room floor.

"I was going to cook for you tonight," he told her between rounds of peekaboo with his son.

Today the peek game involved lifting Aiden up over his head, then slowly lowering him into his field of vision. This elicited drooly smiles and cooing from the baby while he gummed at three fingers. The kid was too dang cute.

"Good parenting doesn't always leave time for good cooking." She poured him a glass of wine from a forgotten stash of Chianti he hadn't known was in the pantry. "Nice job making the more important choice."

With her shoes off and her sweater sleeves rolled up, she looked at home and comfortable here in his house. In his life. Her clothes—layers of dark garments that ensured no hint of skin showed from her neck down except for her hands—still seemed at odds with the vibrant woman he remembered. Her auburn hair hadn't changed, though. He'd liked running his fingers through it when he kissed her.

"It is cool to spend some time with the little guy." He'd given Aiden a bath and put him in sleeper pj's while Amy had prepped dinner. He'd thought that would mean opening a pizza box, but she'd gone to a lot more trouble than that.

She'd dragged out some mismatched wineglasses—one of which had been on his mantel since it had been part of a golf tournament trophy from a long time ago—and made them suitable for use. She'd used some kind of magic to find salad ingredients in the fridge, and the resulting spinach, curled carrot strips and walnut salad had been damned good.

"Thanks for doing this." He laid Aiden on a baby blanket near the bright quilt with the remnants of their dinner, tucking him under a play gym of red-and-black toys. "I know you already gave up a lot of the day to be with me."

She topped off her own wine, too, a lock of red hair skimming her cheek as she moved. "I was intrigued to see if this evening could possibly be as much fun as the afternoon."

"Not everyone would call being on the scene of an arrest *fun*."

"That's definitely *not* the part of the day I had in mind." She settled herself on the floor beside him, their backs against the leather couch while they kept Aiden in view.

The reference to their kiss heated his blood to a slow, steady simmer. He was in no position to start something with Amy, not with an eight-week-old at his feet. But maybe it was too late to put the brakes on an attraction that had dug into him a long time ago.

"Glad you could look beyond the showdown in the parking lot." He'd dated women who were put off by his job—the dangers, being put out when he had to respond to emergency calls, the decreasing community respect for the uniform. So it made him glad that Amy wasn't rattled by what she'd witnessed this afternoon. "I had hoped Kate would explain what prompted the argument, but no such luck."

Would it do any good to haul Tiffany Mc-Cord in for another interview?

"I met a woman at my sister's store who is coming into the police station to give you a deposition this week." Amy speared some of the leftover walnuts with her fork, all her attention on chasing down the nuts.

It surprised him that she'd shared the information. She'd so far been reluctant to discuss the trial or his investigation.

"Yes—Faith Wilkerson. I'm glad some people are starting to come forward." He'd sent his appeal out in all directions in the community, and it seemed those pleas were finally paying off.

"Faith didn't see her attacker." Amy stirred her fork around the bowl without eating anything else. "So maybe her testimony won't help."

His cop instincts started humming, and he warned himself to tread carefully. Having Amy talk about this voluntarily was far better than him asking and putting her on the defensive. He wanted to maintain the easy rapport with her. Let her feel comfortable sharing things without him pushing his own agenda and asking follow-up questions.

But that wasn't easy when he had about twelve inquiries in mind.

"It will help. Establishing a common MO links the cases and helps show the jury that one man was behind multiple assaults. If he says similar things to his victims, or lures them to the same spots, it shows a pattern." He lifted his wineglass and took a sip to stop himself from diving into interrogation mode. Since it was impossible to talk around a mouthful of Chianti, he leaned forward to tickle his son's foot while the boy's eyelids grew heavy.

Amy set down her fork, staring out over the living room floor littered with baby gear.

"Anything that helps connect the cases is valuable," he continued, unable to stop himself.

What did she know, damn it?

"Even if it's old information?" Her green eyes slid his way.

"I'm actively seeking both old and new information to prove the same guy has been quietly working this area for years. I'm personally invested in nailing him for what he did to Gabby and the other women. And, frankly, what he did to me." He hadn't dwelled on that, of course, since Gabriella had been the intended target. The one who'd been scared out of her mind and screaming on the forest floor while a masked bastard wrenched off her dress. "Helping Gabby through that was hell for me and Zach—it was far more than a couple of seventeen-year-old boys were equipped to deal with. I turned my back on my foster family, on you, on the military career I wanted…"

For years he'd told himself that it didn't matter. But the truth was, his life had taken a radical turn because of Jeremy Covington's attack in the woods.

"It must have been hard on all of you." She leaned forward to peek at Aiden's face, checking on him.

Sam watched his son fall into peaceful baby slumber, envying the kid his simple needs even as Sam vowed to make sure he would always be there to fulfill them all.

"I moved back here to try and close the case." Carefully, he lifted away the play gym and covered the baby with a corner of the blanket he lay on. "I've wanted revenge for ten years."

Amy was quiet for a long moment. So long that he almost excused himself to put Aiden in his crib. But then she drew a deep breath.

"I know something that might help." She spoke quietly. Holding herself very still, she glanced up at him with wide eyes. "That same night Gabriella was attacked, a man molested me outside her house."

CHAPTER ELEVEN

MEETING FAITH TODAY had shifted something inside Amy. She had identified with the woman, from her battered car to her secondhand suit. She'd traveled that hard-knock road herself. Yet Faith hadn't let life's blows keep her down. She'd been determined to speak the truth no matter how much it hurt.

It shamed Amy to think she couldn't do the same. Not when she was sitting beside a strong man who'd been brought low by the same creep. How could she kiss Sam while withholding information from him that he desperately needed? How could she hold his precious son while harboring information that might help Sam figure out who had threatened the boy?

Would he blame her for keeping quiet this long?

The guilt and indecision had her in knots. Or it had, until it occurred to her that she could confide in Sam without committing to making an official statement. For tonight, she would find the courage to do just that much.

"Amy." Sam's hand settled on her shoulder, his fingers gently rubbing along her upper arm. "I had no idea. I'm so sorry—"

"You couldn't have known." She shook her head, unwilling to let him shoulder any guilt for what had happened to her. "I followed you to Gabriella's that night, but I made very sure you didn't see me."

Memories returned, as fresh as if it had all happened yesterday. How many times had she relived the events in nightmares that woke her in tears?

"Why?" His eyebrows lifted, head tipped to one side. "Why would you follow me?"

"I had a weird vibe that day. You seemed anxious to leave me and do something else, but when I asked you about it, you were kind of cagey." Shrugging, she didn't even remember precisely what had set her feminine jealousy flaring. It had been an instinct. A hunch that something wasn't quite right. "I felt stupid for following you, but I just had this feeling you weren't telling me something."

"We'd been at the swimming hole with our friends that day," Sam said, his hand still warm on her shoulders, anchoring her in the present even as her mind wandered back in time. "Zach was there with some others, and he told me he had a shift to work at the nursing home that night. He was worried about leaving Gabriella alone."

"Maybe I overheard something about Gabby." So much else had happened after that, it was tough to recall how it all started. "So I rode my bike through the woods. It wasn't hard to stay hidden since you had on headphones and it was starting to get dark outside anyway."

Her skin chilled at the memory. Her chest tightened with the need to draw a breath as the picture in her mind's eye narrowed. Sometimes she wondered how much of that night she remembered accurately and how much had shifted over the years, growing even more frightening with time.

Sam's brow furrowed. "I took the car to Gabby's, though." His voice was gentle, like he didn't want to contradict her. "Not the bike."

"First you biked from my house to yours. Once you got in the car at the Hastings' place, it still wasn't that hard to follow you. You were headed toward the Chances', and there aren't many houses out that way." That was where her memories really took on the qualities of a scary movie. In her nightmares, there was fog all around her, but she knew that hadn't been the case in real life.

She'd been staring at the Chance house

when she'd been helpless. Choking on her own fear.

"So you pedaled to the Chances'." Sam's voice was low and even. Calm.

Remotely, she realized he was stroking her hair now, but any warmth that she'd felt from his touch before had faded in the face of sharing this moment with him.

Swallowing, she closed her eyes. "Your car was in the driveway, so I hid the bike in the trees and then moved toward the living room window to look inside."

"Why didn't you just come to the front door? Confront me?"

How different her life might have been if she'd done that. But she could drive herself crazy second-guessing everything she'd done that day. If she changed any one of her choices, The Incident might never have happened.

"I knew you and Zach were friends. What if you were just there to see him?" She hadn't wanted to appear irrational. Overly emotional.

Bottom line? She hadn't ever wanted to behave in the same way her unstable mother might have in the same circumstances. And no doubt about it—her mom would have lost it if she'd suspected the love of her life was cheating on her.

"So you looked through the living room

window…" Sam kept the conversation on track, leading her through the night, all the while smoothing his hand down her hair with slow, even strokes.

Amy opened her eyes, unwilling to get lost in those old visions. She focused on the baby sleeping nearby instead, watching his chest rise and fall, the Cupid's bow of his mouth slightly open, his skinny arms spread wide as he lay on his back. So precious.

"I did. And I saw you talking to Gabby." It had looked like a heated discussion, in fact. "It must have been before she was attacked, but at the time, you both seemed upset. Your voice was raised, and I heard you tell her to wait."

"Right. Because she wanted to go out and meet some scumbag who she'd been talking to online." His voice went hard. Frustration evident even all these years later. "If only I could have convinced her to stay home, she would have never been accosted." No doubt he'd had as many sleepless nights as Amy, wondering what would have happened if he'd done any one thing differently that day.

"I couldn't hear all the details." It had been like listening to voices underwater, the conversation distorted and muffled. "But you stood close to her, and I was worried about what was going on between you two. Right up until a man grabbed me from behind."

Sam swore softly. He slid an arm around her waist and drew her close. Kissed the top of her head.

She appreciated that connection to him. It helped her keep her heart rate in check. Helped her manage the urge to run.

"He wore a hoodie pulled up, and his face stayed in shadow." Shaking her head, she wished she could shake off the feel of those iron arms locking around her. One clamped at her hips.

One over her breasts.

"Was he much taller than you?" The question was a welcome reminder that she was speaking to a cop and not just her old boyfriend. In some ways, that made it easier, disconnecting a lot of the emotional baggage from the episode to focus on facts.

She might not want her experience on record, but it was simpler to tell the tale to an officer.

"A few inches. Medium height. But he seemed strong—like I could have never gotten away if I tried."

Of course, she hadn't tried. She'd been paralyzed with fear. As he'd tightened his hold, her chest cramped and her lungs burned with the need to breathe more air.

"Did he say anything?" Sam's jaw rubbed lightly against her hair as he spoke.

"He asked what I was doing there. If I was your girlfriend." Her voice sounded thin. Young. She cleared her throat. "At first I thought it might be one of your friends—a guy from the senior class who knew me even though I didn't recognize him."

"You didn't hear him approach? No car engine? No sound of him walking through the woods?"

"Neither." In her dreams, he showed up like a wraith, ghosting around her in the fog.

"He was probably there before you," Sam mused. "Covington was probably making sure Gabriella was going to meet him. He could have had a BlackBerry or an early smartphone that he used to contact Gabriella even as he watched her through the window of her own home. He could have watched you watching us."

"Maybe." She swallowed over the raw words in her throat. "All I know is that his grip got tighter and he dragged me backward."

She'd hardly fought. The fear and surprise had caught her off guard.

"What else did he say?"

"I blanked for a little while. I mean, I have a vague memory of him saying other things into my ear while he brought me deeper in the woods, but my brain was screaming at me to do something. To shout. Get free."

"Did he have your mouth covered?"

Her eyes burned at the question. At the memory. She shook her head. "He latched on to my chest and my hips. Pinned the back of me to the front of him. I wanted to scream, but I was scared. And when I opened my mouth, no sound came out."

More than anything else that happened that night, that was what stayed with her most. Not the forcible touching. Not the ugly words or things he'd eventually threatened. It was that— when she'd had the chance—she hadn't been able to make a sound.

"Don't blame yourself. Different people respond to fear in unique ways. No one can predict how they will react in a crisis."

And she'd reacted like a frightened child, waiting for someone else to save her.

"Eventually, he told me he had a knife, and he would use it if I made any noise." Her breathing came fast and shallow. Reliving The Incident had that effect. "He put one hand up my shirt. One hand down my pants."

"Amy." Sam's grip on her waist tightened. "I'm so damn sorry—"

"Let me just get it out," she blurted, having come too far to stop. "It could have been worse, and I was afraid that any minute he'd throw me down and rape me. But he seemed content to stare up at the Chance house—maybe looking at Gabby through the window—and molest me with his hands. He rubbed my body against his, although he never got naked or anything."

She'd burned her clothes in the fireplace when she'd gotten home. Then washed for hours afterward, until she shivered uncontrollably in the bathtub, unable to rinse away the feel of his hands in her underwear. Inside her. Years later, a counselor helped her work through some of her intimacy issues, but she'd remained—technically—a virgin for a long time afterward, unable to feel good about her body since her innocence had been lost that night in a terrible way. A way that made it so difficult to face physical intimacy.

She'd numbed herself to everything and everyone, a coping mechanism that had made it difficult to feel pleasure later. She'd tried to explain to one of her college boyfriends. But he'd only remarked that she was lucky she hadn't been raped, and his dismissal had grated on her endlessly. She'd been assaulted. Violated.

And that was when she realized she needed counseling to heal.

Even now, it took her a moment to realize she was crying silent tears. Sam wiped them away gently with his thumbs.

"What made your attacker leave?" he asked, pressing soft kisses to her eyes.

She'd closed them, forgetting to anchor herself in the world around her as she'd gotten lost in that night. *Damn it.* She forced them open now, peering into Sam's gray gaze, which was full of concern.

That connection felt right. Good.

"Maybe the sound of the garage door lifting at Gabby's house?" She sifted through the ugly memories, searching for concrete details. "He ran toward the car as it backed out and shoved me aside."

"You didn't look at him then?"

"At his back? I guess so. He was wearing a dark hoodie and jeans. I couldn't see much in the woods. And he stayed out of the beam of the headlights when the car rolled out of the garage." By then, she'd been so traumatized she hadn't been thinking about Gabriella or Sam. Her thoughts were solely on her body and the way he'd used it. The way he'd made her feel dirty, and the fact that she hadn't screamed for help.

Scared silent.

"Did you see or hear him get into a vehicle?"

"No." After Gabriella had left the house—or at least, she assumed now it had to have been Gabriella—there had been quiet in the woods for long moments until Sam jumped in his car and followed in the same direction.

He kissed her forehead. "Thank you for trusting me with what happened." He brushed her hair off her face. "I'm so sorry you had to go through that, and I'm even sorrier that you carried the burden alone for so many years."

"I didn't have any useful information anyway." She wanted to make him understand why she'd maintained her silence. "If I thought it would have helped you, I would have spoken up sooner. But I never saw his face. I couldn't identify him—then or now. I don't know if I ever met Covington as a teen, and I didn't put the old pieces together until you told me what happened to Gabby." She shrugged, frustrated with her ignorance. "And, for what it's worth, I didn't carry the burden alone. I told my mother after it happened."

She didn't count the crappy boyfriend who'd written off her experience with a few careless words.

"Your mother knew this whole time?" His

hands fell away from where he'd been smoothing her hair off her cheek. Shock colored his words.

"She may not remember. She was on a lot of medication." But telling her mother had only made things much, much worse.

"And she never reported it to the police, either?"

His eyes went wide. And it took a lot to surprise a cop.

"She was struggling with bipolar disorder and new medications." She sat so close to Sam now, his big body curving protectively around hers. She could so easily tip her head to the side and be cradled against his shoulder. The temptation to do just that was strong, but she forced herself to get through the story. "She screamed at me that I was a slut, that I'd led you on and to get the hell out of her house."

"You'd led me on?" He shook his head. "I don't understand."

"Mom was convinced that it was you who molested me in the woods because I'd encouraged you after the skinny-dipping incident. Remember I mentioned how upset she was about that?" Her stomach knotted. She had loved her mother. Needed her desperately. But when it counted most, her mom had blasted her morals and told Amy she needed to move out by nightfall.

"Holy shit." Beyond that, he was speechless. And who could blame him?

"She had a nervous breakdown later that summer." Amy hadn't heard about it at the time, but apparently her mom had fought with Mack's then girlfriend, Nina, too. Nina had moved away for almost as many years as Amy had.

Thank goodness Nina had returned to Heartache, or Mack might never have reunited with her.

"I didn't know the disorder could make someone so…" He grappled for words.

"My father was giving her experimental medication, too." That was another piece of the puzzle Amy hadn't discovered until recently, thanks to Heather's letters. "At the time, there weren't many good options for her on the market, so he imported some drugs that hadn't been approved by the FDA. But Mom secretly went off everything for a while, and no one knew how bad things had gotten until that breakdown."

Amy still wasn't sure if she could make peace with her mother. Would her mom remember the details of that conversation? How could Amy forgive her for not helping her through that time? For convincing her that she had somehow deserved the attack? For kicking her out? It didn't matter that Diana's accusations had made zero sense—Sam hadn't been the one to hurt her.

She'd been vulnerable to her mother's opinions and each one of them had dug deep, taking root. Amy had run from Heartache, but she hadn't had much luck outrunning her mother's damning words.

"Right." He went to work picking up their dishes, stacking them and setting them aside. The tension in his shoulders was obvious, along with the rigid set to his jaw.

She covered his hand with hers when he reached for the wine bottle. "I'm sorry that she thought the worst of you."

Sam's forehead wrinkled in confusion before he shook his head. "You think I care about that? Hell. Amy, I'm upset because you were molested fifty yards away from me and I never knew about it. I'm upset I didn't just tell you I was going to Gabby's that night to keep an eye on her the way Zach asked me to." He set the bottle on the coffee table and then eased to the floor again to sit across from her. "I'm upset that someone hurt you and I could have stopped it. I was so invested in watching out for Gabriella, this bastard got to you instead."

The anguish in his eyes was obvious. A hurt he didn't deserve, but one that soothed something raw inside her nevertheless. For years, she'd faced the fact that she'd handled The Incident alone. That even her mother hadn't cared what had really happened to her.

But Sam cared. He'd always cared. She'd just been so busy worrying that he was having a relationship with Gabby—running off to California without a word to Amy—that she'd never understood it.

"I was hurt. Wounded inside." She threaded her fingers through his. Kissed the back of his hand. "But I'm not hurt anymore. And as for healing? I've come a long way over the years, even more so tonight, thanks to you."

She gave in to that urge she'd been fighting, the need to tip her head onto one of his broad shoulders and savor his strength and presence. She'd craved it ten years ago and never had the chance to let a loving touch take away the hurts of that night.

Now? They were in a very different place emotionally. But she still craved his touch.

"Amy." He studied her with that steady gaze of his. Drew a deep breath. "I hate that I wasn't there for you."

"You're here now." She rubbed her cheek

against the cotton of his shirt, absorbing the warmth and feel of him.

His muscles clenched beneath her jaw, his body tensing. From resistance? Or because he was holding himself back from something he wanted, too?

"I wouldn't want to—" his jaw flexed as he seemed to search for the right words "—take advantage of a vulnerable moment."

"You wouldn't be." She kissed his shoulder before straightening, needing to look him in the eye. "We could spend tonight putting the past behind us." She didn't know where the idea came from. But her attraction to Sam had been simmering ever since she'd come home. And tonight, when he'd been so tender with her and so ready to shoulder blame that didn't belong to him, she wanted to act on that heat. That connection they'd always had.

Something flared in his eyes. A blaze of raw reaction he couldn't hide.

But he shook his head in that immovable Sam way.

"It's been a long day. An emotional day." He swallowed hard but didn't retreat. "You've only just come home. I don't want you to wake up tomorrow and regret something that happened too fast."

"I've had ten years to process what happened to me. Ten years to understand how much that night robbed from me." The more she thought about it, the more right this felt. "We were on the verge of taking our relationship to the next level before that bastard ruined our chance to see what could have happened between us. Why should we let it keep robbing us now?"

His gray gaze dipped to her mouth. Lingered.

"You're a tough woman to argue with." His voice was scratchy.

"So don't try." She ventured closer, brushing her lips along that strong jaw of his. "Tuck Aiden in for the night, and then come take away all the old, ugly memories. I want some new ones, and I want them with you."

CHAPTER TWELVE

"ONE DAY, YOU'LL UNDERSTAND," Sam whispered to his sleeping son, kissing him gently on the forehead before lowering the boy into his crib. "You'll find out how a woman can turn your life upside down. You think you're going to walk away and do the honorable thing one minute. And the next, you can't form a thought that isn't about kissing her."

Aiden curled a tiny fist, his features relaxed as he snoozed. Sam turned on the nursery monitor and covered his son with a blanket.

"Bet you'll be better with the ladies than your old man." He rubbed the baby's back. "Night, champ."

Even now, as Sam wound through the family room looking for Amy, he wondered if it was wrong of him to want her this much after learning what she'd been through. He had no idea what the right response should be to finding out a woman he cared about had been hurt like that—right under his nose. He'd assumed she was home safe and sound that night. Then he'd inadvertently made things even tougher for her by leaving right afterward without a word. He hadn't been around to comfort her when she'd needed him most.

He would change that now, damn it. He would be everything she needed tonight.

"Sam?" Amy called to him from the darkened kitchen, and he followed the sound of her voice.

Knowing she was here, in his house, waiting for him…that amped him up far more than when he'd chased her through the woods as a teen. Maybe because now there was no second-guessing. No wondering if he understood what she wanted. She'd been very clear. They were going to reclaim what they'd been denied long ago.

She straightened from the dishwasher and pressed the start button. The dull thrum of the machine filled the kitchen as they stared at each other over the butcher-block island.

His chest ached with wanting her. He would have slayed dragons for her ten years ago. He'd damn well send her demons running now. Or at least, he'd do everything in his power to make that happen.

He gestured to the sink. "You didn't have to clean up."

"I know. I figured I'd start the dishes to keep

busy. It was no trouble." She stood still, watching him in the muted blue glow of the light from the ice maker. She twisted a strand of hair, a sweetly nervous gesture that cued him in to what she was feeling more than anything else. "Did Aiden stay asleep?"

"He did." Edging around the island, Sam closed the distance between them. "And it just so happens newborns sleep an average of eighteen hours a day." He threaded their fingers together and squeezed her hand in his.

"Really?" She arched an eyebrow at him, the hint of a smile playing around her lips.

"Yes." He wanted to pull her against him and kiss her again. If he let himself do that now, however, they might never get out of the kitchen. "We'll hear him better if we're in my room, though." He nodded in the direction of the master suite. Where he would be with Amy. Soon. Not soon enough. "The nursery monitor is in there so I can hear if he needs me."

"Good. I was angling to visit your room." She backed up a step. "I used to fantasize about where you slept at night."

The smile she'd been hiding before unfurled now. A rare occurrence for Amy. And so damn welcome after the conversation they'd just had. He wanted to see that smile on her face again and again tonight. When she paused near the closed door of his bedroom, he opened it for her.

"Back in those days, I didn't even have a room to myself. I shared with Clayton Travers." The same guy Zach had hired to guard Heather. Sam had called him from the police station that afternoon to invite Clayton to the Hasting fosters reunion. "So it wasn't much to fantasize about."

"I don't know." She gave a deliberately casual shrug that did enticing things to the collar of her dress. "If I remember Clayton right, he was almost as cute as you."

"You always did enjoy starting trouble with me, didn't you?" He flicked on the wall lamps on either side of the headboard, lowering the dimmer to ensure the corners of the room remained in shadow.

"You are a lot of fun to tease." She turned away from him to take in the room, her eyes roaming over the half-made bed with a gray duvet and pillows strewn sideways. "I think it's because you look like you'll breathe fire on anyone who dares to try it."

"I seem to give a lot of people that impression." His eyes wandered over her as she let go of his hand to step closer to his nightstand.

"Which makes me wonder why you never bought it."

Reaching the bedside table, she picked up a framed photo of him with Zach and Gabriella on her graduation day. She touched a finger to his face in the photo, and he felt the ghost of it on his cheek.

"Guess I know you too well, Samuel Reyes." Setting the heavy silver frame back on the bedside table, she turned toward him again. "You'd never hurt me."

Her fingers reached for the buttons on her dress.

His mouth went chalk-dry.

He couldn't take his eyes off her smooth, efficient movements as she unfastened one after another. With an effort, he ground out the word that needed saying. "Never."

And then he was moving toward her, needing his hands on her. The taste of her on his tongue.

Maybe she was feeling as anxious as him, because she immediately forgot about the dress buttons and wound her arms around his neck, pulling him closer. A slight hint of lavender teased his nose, a subtle fragrance that made him want to inhale deeply to catch more of it. He steadied her with a hand on her waist, just above the flare of her hips, feeling the warmth of her skin right through the thin dress and leggings. Her green eyes studied him through half-lowered lashes; her naturally pink lips parted.

His blood pounded through his veins and in his ears, the sound an echo of his harsh breathing. He didn't want to rush this. Because no matter that she said she'd healed from what had happened ten years ago, he knew talking about it must have picked at the wound.

Gently, he brushed a kiss along her lower lip, just enough to remind himself of the feel of her. Her eyelids fluttered closed. She swayed slightly, giving him a welcome reason to tighten his grip on her. He banded one arm around the small of her back. Slid the other hand up her spine, pressing her against him inch by inch.

Her breath hitched, the smallest, softest sound. That whisper of air stroked over his ears and made a fire roar to life inside him. Burning him up. A slow shudder trembled over her skin, vibrating through him until he wondered if it was his own.

"I've missed the way you touch me." Her confession, so direct and honest, rattled him even as he savored the words.

He'd missed her touch, too. But damned if he could think beyond this moment. This night.

"I'm about to touch you a whole lot more." He

kissed the words down her neck, then paused to retrace a path to her ear. Tunnel a hand in her silky hair.

She arched her head back, giving him more access right where he wanted. He risked a look down at her in the dim light from the sconces, her body bowed up to him like a gift. So different from the guarded way she usually moved through the world in her dark clothes and quiet ways.

"Less looking." Her eyes opened, and she pinned him with her gaze. "More touching."

"Soon," he promised, gliding the tip of his finger from the hollow of her throat straight down the open V of her dress, lingering in the shallow valley between her breasts.

She hummed her approval as he skimmed aside the dress to expose one breast cupped in simple black satin. A silver medallion decorated the spot between the cups, and he played with the metal that had been warmed by her skin. Watched as goose bumps played over her skin. Then kissed along the pale curve of her breast plumped high by the satin.

Soft, tender kisses. But as the scent of lavender grew stronger with the heat between them, he found it damn tough to hold back. He gripped the bra strap on her shoulder and tugged it down, swiping aside the thin fabric of her lightweight dress to see and feel more of her.

His kisses turned greedy as he delved beneath the satin cup to find the tight peak of her nipple. Amy squeezed his arms, his shoulders. Her touches grew more insistent, her fingers tugging at the buttons of his gray work shirt.

He lifted her high against his chest before depositing her in the middle of his bed. He followed her down, hovering over her on his arms. Her full skirt clung to his legs while their limbs tangled. He couldn't get enough of her. He unfastened the rest of the buttons on her dress while she finished off the ones on his shirt.

She spread her palms over his chest when she'd bared it, her fingers cool compared with the inferno just beneath his skin. He wanted her hands everywhere.

"I don't remember all these muscles from the last time I touched you," she said suddenly with a breathy sigh of appreciation, her fingers tracing the ridges on the back of one shoulder. "They feel good."

"I took physical training seriously at the police academy." Plus, he'd never forgotten what hand-to-hand combat felt like after that first ugly encounter with Covington. And he'd done everything possible to be sure he had the edge if he ever found himself in that position again. And, of course, in his line of work, he had.

"All the better to protect and serve?" She smoothed a hand down his side. Down. Down. Splayed her fingers along his hip through the lightweight wool of pants he wanted gone. "I approve this plan."

Wrestling his way out of his shirt, he leaned back to slide away her leggings and the rest of her clothes, leaving only a pair of black bikini underwear in place. He meant to shed his pants, too, but the sight of her rose-tipped breasts called to him. He fell on her fast, hungrily, tugging one pebbled tip into his mouth to draw on her.

She made sweetly satisfying noises, twisting beneath him so that she undulated in a wave that rocked his whole world. His vision narrowed. Fire torched up his spine at the feel of her on his tongue, her leg snaking around his calf, holding him where she wanted him.

Sweat lined his forehead at the effort of holding back when he wanted to be inside her. Soon her hips arched into his, seeking the connection he wanted, too.

"Sam?" Her short fingernails scraped lightly against his lower back, a deliberate, teasing touch.

"Mmm?" He wasn't sure he could form words anymore with her hips cradling his erection like that.

"You aren't naked enough." She curved a hand around his belt, the backs of her fingers smoothing along his abs.

"I had good intentions of going slow." He fumbled with his buckle and managed to unfasten it.

"Go slow next time." She stroked him through his pants, and he throbbed against her.

Sam tried to catch his breath.

"I like how you think." He pointed to the bedside table as he slid away from her. "There are condoms in there, in the top drawer."

She lost no time in opening the drawer, treating him to a spectacular view while she lay on her stomach, chin propped on one of the pillows. His pants and boxers were gone in seconds. He'd just stretched out on top of her when she pulled the whole box from the drawer.

It was a large package.

"How many are in here?" Eyes wide, she met his gaze over her shoulder. "Ambitious much?"

He pulled the box from her hand enough to free just one foil packet.

"I may have overbought right after I found

out about Aiden." He'd been upset. Not about being a father. Never that.

But about being kept in the dark. About being with a woman who would keep that from him.

Amy shifted beneath him, rolling to her back again as he took out a condom. The rest of the box fell forgotten to the bare hardwood floor.

"Sort of like closing the barn door after the horse is out of the gate?" She walked her fingers up his chest and kissed a few places she missed.

"Something like that." He didn't want to think about the past, though. Not now.

"The good news is we'll have lots of opportunities to take it slow another time." She snatched the packet from his hand and set it on the bed nearby. Then she rocked her hips into his again, the satin of her underwear a silky caress that didn't come close to satisfying his craving for her.

"Have I mentioned that I like how you think?" He cupped her through the damp satin, and she went utterly still for a long moment, her lips parted as he stroked between her thighs.

She was so soft. So warm.

He was completely lost in touching her

when she gripped his forearm. For a moment, he thought she wanted him to stop. But when he slowed, her small cry of dismay was unmistakable. When he continued, her whole body tensed, trembled and then bucked hard against him. Cheeks flushed pink, she came fast and hard, clamping her thighs tight around his touch.

He wanted to go right over that edge with her. A primal need to be inside her surged. When the aftershocks of her orgasm slowed, he forced himself to wait. Let her collect herself.

But she reached blindly to her side, patting until she found the condom and putting it in his hand. He raked off her panties with one hand and ripped open the packet with his teeth.

In another second he was sheathed and edging his way inside her body. That, he did take slowly. For his own sake as much as hers. He wasn't missing out on a second of this chance to be with her. She'd starred in all his adolescent fantasies—even after he'd left Heartache behind. And now she was here, in his bed, sexier and sweeter than he'd ever imagined.

"Sam." She pushed at his shoulder, and he let her turn him over so she was on top.

He looked up at her; her copper-colored hair brushed her shoulders as she moved with him. He fought the urge to steer her where he wanted her. To clamp his hands around the gentle curve of her hips and drive them both to completion.

Instead, he let her take charge of what she wanted. She moved with a sense of purpose and wonder, her expression easy to read as she found what pleased her most. He settled for molding his hands to her sides, palming her breasts, squeezing gently.

When she started to move faster, however, he lost any focus he might have had. His own need roared hard and he couldn't stop himself from thrusting deep. Once. Twice.

The third time drove her release even as it ignited his. He gripped her hips, holding her where he had to have her. Sensation slammed through him, knocking him all but senseless until he lay there panting like he'd run a marathon.

Amy sprawled on top of him, her hair tickling his nose and neck, her body damp and scented with sex and lavender. He wanted to tuck her under his arm and into his bed—into his life? Sleep beside her until he woke her in the middle of the night to be with her all over again.

Because, damn. He already knew he'd want that. Once was never going to be enough. She was right about that box of condoms. It would serve them well.

Right up until the time she left Heartache again.

He didn't know where the thought came from since he was still drifting on a wave of sexual euphoria. He should be happy just to keep her close for tonight. Still, he couldn't help but wonder what it might be like to have her stick around. They'd been good together once.

Maybe now that she was done keeping secrets, there was a chance they could be good together again. Once she gave her statement about what happened ten years ago, she wouldn't need to run from Heartache anymore. When he put Covington behind bars for good, she would feel safe here again. His decadelong search for justice would finally be over.

Yet even as he told himself as much, all the while stroking Amy's tangled hair and kissing her temple, he had a sinking feeling it wouldn't be that simple.

He still didn't know who was threatening his son. It couldn't be Jeremy Covington because the guy was behind bars.

Some other danger lurked.

And he needed to be very careful it didn't steal away any more from him than the past already had.

CHAPTER THIRTEEN

How many people know your last boyfriend hit you?

Bailey's heart raced as she stared at Dawson in the shadowed lawn off the porch. How could he have figured out her secret?

Already she could hear her dad getting out of his car in the front yard. Hazel barked like crazy while Dad shushed her.

"My father—" she stammered. "He'll come this way to go inside." She pointed at the door behind her, her movements awkward and wooden. "Please." She swallowed a lump of panic. "Don't say anything."

Dawson's jaw went rigid. With anger? Disappointment? She couldn't tell. But something in his expression indicated he didn't much care to keep her secret. He nodded stiffly.

"How did you know?" she whispered, her ears attuned to the sound of her father's uneven gait. He'd been injured in Afghanistan when she was in grade school, retiring from the military with a lot of honors but—as her mom put it—more ghosts than medals.

"I've seen the signs before when a friend went through it." Dawson didn't bother lowering his voice. "With you, though, it was only a guess."

A guess she'd just confirmed.

Heart sinking, she cursed herself for being so easy to read. Although how could this boy who hardly knew her figure her out so fast? Before she could worry that one to bits, her father called to her.

"Bailey?" His uneven footsteps slowed for a second before picking up pace again. Hazel beat him around the corner, tail wagging, a fluorescent orange ball in her mouth. "You out here?"

He must have heard their voices.

"Yes, Dad. My friend Dawson is here." She kept her eyes on him, hoping he was as good as his word.

Didn't he owe her his silence after tricking her?

"Do I know a Dawson?" Dad asked as he limped around the corner. His prosthetic had never fit him well, but he had gotten tired of having it adjusted.

Mom said that was because he liked to punish himself. But it occurred to Bailey now that most of what she knew about her father had been filtered through Mom. And how reliable was that information?

"No." She took the damp ball from Hazel's mouth and tossed it across the yard, sending a furry torpedo hurtling into the woods after it. "He's new to Mrs. Hasting's house."

Everyone in town knew the pizza-shop owners took in a lot of fosters. Mr. Hasting had been on the town council with Mom.

"Welcome to Heartache, Dawson." Her dad was still built like a marine with his square shoulders and heavy arms, and when he reached to shake hands with Dawson, she hoped he wouldn't flex too much muscle. "Cole McCord."

"Nice to meet you, sir. Thank you for your service."

Bailey watched her father's eyebrows shoot up in surprise. But the "First In, Last Out" ball cap he wore must have been what had given him away. Still, she couldn't remember any of her other friends ever commenting on her father's veteran status, no matter that half his clothes bore some version of the eagle, globe and anchor.

"You're welcome, son. Although all the thanks in the world doesn't take away the fact that Bailey's not allowed to have male company unchaperoned."

Oh God.

"Dad." She spoke on top of Dawson, who'd already blurted something about being there only a minute. "He rode his bike over a minute ago and we didn't go inside."

Her father was already squinting into the screened porch, though, his attention now on something else.

"What the hell are all those bags?"

She tensed. As if she hadn't been tense enough to start with. She stuffed the toe of her gym shoes into the patchy grass.

"Um. Mom was here. She brought groceries."

"You did not let her in that house." Her father glared at her.

Bad enough to bully Dawson, but he wasn't going to bully her, too, damn it.

"I helped her unload the bags from her car, and then I put them on the porch so my favorite granola did not sit outside on the ground where Hazel could sneak it into the bushes to eat." She folded her arms around an ache in her heart that hurt 24/7, missing the mother she remembered all the more.

Mom had been good at standing up to Dad.

But then, she'd also lied and cheated on him.

Her heart softened a little as Hazel returned with the ball, nudging her hand insistently to throw it again. Dawson took it from the dog without a word, throwing it for her and making a new friend.

"Fine." Dad headed up the steps. "You and your friend can visit while I put away the groceries. But it is a school night."

"I saw some beef jerky in there." Bailey wished he'd at least be civil to her mother again. No matter who was wrong, it sucked that she was caught in the middle.

"I'll buy my own damn groceries," he grumbled. "These are all for you."

"There's beer, too," she couldn't resist adding, winking at Dawson behind her father's back until she remembered that Dawson wasn't happy with her, either.

"No doubt trying to butter me up before I hear from her attorney," he groused through the screen as he leaned over to pick up the bags. He jostled them both to one arm, reached inside and pulled out a six-pack. He dropped it in the industrial-size trash, and a few of the cans hissed open.

"Should we help him?" Dawson watched Cole's awkward movements as he edged around furniture. This time, Dawson did lower his voice so only she could hear.

"Not unless you want your head bitten off for suggesting he can't handle it himself." She'd learned that at the tender age of ten when she'd wanted to attach the straps on his prosthetic for him.

He'd yelled at her so hard she'd cried the rest of the afternoon. That was one of many times her mother had tried to explain to her about the "ghosts" that had come home with her father after his last tour of duty. There'd been a lot of years since then, but her father had never sought help for the temper, the bitterness or the nightmares that sometimes woke the whole house.

"Guess I'll pass." Dawson shrugged out of his hoodie and handed it to her. "You should put this on. It's getting cold."

She wanted to refuse. Still miffed about the way he'd tricked her into revealing the truth about her relationship with J.D., she had a retort at the ready. But he simply lowered it to her shoulders like a shawl.

Surrounding her in warmth and boy scent. Not sweat, either. Something good-smelling.

"Can we sit on the swings next door?" he asked, squatting down to greet Hazel's triumphant return.

The dog eyed Dawson sidelong and refused to give him the ball back even though she kept nudging his knee with her head. *The flirt.*

"Sure." She didn't want her father to over-hear this.

Tromping through the wet grass, she held on to the sweatshirt to make sure it didn't fall off her shoulders. Then again, maybe she was trying to burrow deeper in it.

When they reached the old swing set that had belonged to the family that used to live there, Dawson wiped off one of the plastic seats with his palm and indicated she sit before lowering himself into the other.

Thoughtful.

"Why haven't you told anyone?" he asked as he wrestled the ball from Hazel and threw it again.

Nearby another dog barked from someone else's backyard. She could see into her kitchen through the back window. Her father had re-moved his marines cap and was working to unload the groceries.

Alone.

"Because it's over. Done." She kept telling herself that, anyway.

"How is it over when you're still ditching school to avoid him? He still scares you." He leaned forward, one shoulder pressed to the chain.

"He caught me off guard today." Seeing him had triggered a sick feeling in her gut. "I didn't know until I saw him that he'd gotten out of jail. Or juvenile detention. Or wherever he's been."

Digging her toe through the clumpy old sand beneath her seat, she felt stupid for letting herself crush on Dawson even a little bit. Hadn't she known from the start that her past with J.D. made her a loser? A stronger girl— like Megan—would not have put up with being talked down to. Being shoved around.

Worse.

"But now he's free to walk around town." He reached for the chain on her swing, bringing her closer. So close her denim-clad knee brushed his. "You can't afford to hide the truth anymore."

A million thoughts tumbled through her mind. Like how Dawson had guessed the truth in the first place. Why he'd cared enough to come over and talk to her about it. What he thought of her.

But all of it got overridden by that touch of their knees. By his hand so close to hers on the swing chain. A finger's width apart, maybe. Her heart pounded wildly.

"Everyone will think I'm a coward for not standing up to him." Which she supposed was true.

Hazel returned, running around them in circles before lying down nearby to gnaw on the orange ball.

"If you out him for the bastard he is, Bailey, everyone is going to see you've got plenty of spine." Even as the words were kind, his voice was hard.

His eyes took on a steely challenge.

She pulled her swing chain from his grip and let the seat straighten itself out again, her feet whirling in the moonlight for a moment before she righted herself.

"I still don't understand how you could tell."

"The Hastings' house is my fifth foster home. I've been around other kids who've been hurt by people they trusted. I know what that looks like."

"There are no bruises." She slanted a glance his way.

He shook his head. "I've survived the foster system this long by being able to read people. And I can spot fear and betrayal almost as fast as I can spot an abuser."

She hated to imagine how he'd come by that kind of knowledge.

"Someone hurt a friend of yours?"

"Yeah, a girl in my old neighborhood—her boyfriend hit her sometimes. It took me a while to understand why she'd cover for him." He stared up at the stars for a long moment. "But things were complicated for her. No matter how much shit the boyfriend doled out, I guess she thought he was still a step up from her parents. And maybe he was. But all I know is, when things got rough between them and the guy would show up around school searching for her—she got that same panicked look in her eyes that you had today."

Bailey scuffed her toe through the wet grass while the swing twisted, trying to imagine herself as Dawson had seen her today. She wasn't used to anyone paying such careful attention to her. For a long time, her parents had been too embroiled in their own drama to appreciate the nuances of her life.

"Did that girl get away from the boy eventually?" She hoped that Dawson's friend had saved herself.

"I'm not sure. I don't keep up with people from that neighborhood anymore. Too many of them wanted to give me updates on my mother's condition—she's an addict—and I got to the point where I just couldn't hear it." He traced the pattern of the metal chain links on his swing. "That might sound callous, but—"

"No." Bailey turned to face him. "It sounds really smart."

Nodding, he seemed to weigh that idea before continuing. "But I didn't come here to talk about me. I came here because I want you to tell someone. Start with your dad." He pointed to the house, where her father was now wrestling a bag of dog food into an overhead cabinet where it didn't belong. "Having people know what happened—that'll keep you safe."

Her belly turned to ice at the thought of talking to her dad about J.D. She hadn't even been able to tell her mom, and they'd been close once. But her dad? Even before he'd been hurt, they'd had a weird relationship—more for show than anything since he'd never been home much.

But ever since he'd lost half his leg, she and her mom had done whatever they could to make things easier for him without looking like they were. Or, at least, her mom used to do that until she'd cheated on him with J.D.'s father.

Maybe her mom had gotten tired of tiptoeing around Cole when all he did was bark back.

"I've got to go." Dawson sprang to his feet, all athletic grace and impatience. Hazel stood with him, tail wagging hopefully. "I told Lorelei I forgot something at the pizza shop, and I don't like lying to her. Will you be over this week?"

For a second she thought he was asking her out. *Will you be over?* But then she remembered her job babysitting Aiden at the Hastings'.

"I watch Aiden on Tuesday and Wednesday."

She wasn't sure about the rest of the week. Standing, she tugged off Dawson's hoodie and handed it back to him.

"Good. I'll see you then." He made no move to leave. He watched her like he might have more to say.

"Why would you want to?" The thought drifted from her brain right past her lips even though she didn't want to know the answer. He was just being nice. "Actually, don't answer that."

A sad smile lifted one side of his mouth.

"That girl I told you about? The one whose boyfriend hit her? She was older than me, and I got sucked into the foster system before I could figure out how to help her." He leaned down to pet Hazel's head. "It sucks to stand by and watch someone else be hurt, Bailey. And I'm not going to do it again."

"In other words, I'm some kind of pity project for you." She peered up at the sky, unable to look him in the eye. A plane flew high over her head, silent but steadily blinking, its destination far from Heartache, Tennessee.

"But you won't be. As soon as you tell your dad what happened." He tugged his bike out from the spot where he'd left it earlier. Then, leaning the frame on his hip, he pulled on the sweatshirt he'd let her borrow.

"Then you'll be off the hook." She was his personal charity case.

Flattering.

"Then I don't have to worry about you." He straddled the seat and pushed off with his feet. He looked over his shoulder as he pedaled away. "I can just like you."

BRIGHT SUNLIGHT SLANTED through the blinds overhead. Odd snippets of conversation drifted to Amy's ears as she pulled herself out of sleep. Had a television been left on somewhere?

"I drove all this way. Please." A woman's voice—vaguely familiar—was pleading in a nearby room.

Amy's limbs were pleasantly sore, her hair a rough tangle under one cheek where she lay in sheets that weren't her own. Dove-gray sheets that smelled good.

Like Sam.

Her night in his bed had been far more satisfying than her teenage self could have ever imagined.

"When you brought him here, we agreed I could have him for six weeks." The tone of Sam's voice brought her upright. Stern and unyielding.

Nothing like the lover who'd whispered tender encouragement to her when she'd woken him with kisses a few hours ago, wanting him all over again.

"I didn't know that I would miss him so much." The woman's tearful voice prompted Amy's memory then.

She'd heard that same voice on Sam's phone the day before. Aiden's mother, Cynthia, was here. At Sam's house.

Sliding out of bed, Amy searched for clothes even as she told herself not to get involved. It wasn't her place; this was Sam's business. But the tone of the conversation worried her. She remembered how resentful Sam had felt toward Cynthia yesterday. But if Aiden's mother was truly suffering from postpartum depression, how unfair would it be for him to send her away?

All Amy's deprived maternal instincts flared to life as she slid into her leggings. Fastened her bra hooks.

Dropped her dress over her head.

Sam's voice rumbled something low, and Amy hoped it was something reassuring. As Aiden's father, he would have the boy's best interests in mind. She trusted that absolutely.

So when she found herself opening the bedroom door, it wasn't to interfere. It was only to extend...

Forcing herself to stop in the middle of the

hallway, she waited for that thought to finish itself.

She wanted to offer some kind of empathy
toward the woman who—according to Sam—
had abandoned her own baby. Where the hell
was that need coming from? Normally she ran
headlong from getting too involved in other
people's affairs.

Pivoting on her bare feet, she retreated to
the bedroom. A floorboard creaked beneath
her step.

"Amy?" Sam called to her from the front
room.

She cursed herself for leaving his bed.

"Yes?" She didn't move.

"There's someone I'd like you to meet." He
didn't sound happy about it. Because he didn't
want Cynthia in his house?

Or because Amy couldn't mind her own
business?

At least she'd put her clothes on. It would
have been awkward to meet the mother of his
child while wrapped in a sheet.

Make that *more* awkward.

She stepped into the front room, taking in a
pale brunette dressed in sweats and a T-shirt
with an olive-colored army surplus coat over
it all. Cynthia clutched a yellow stuffed bunny
under her arm, the head squished like she'd

forgotten about it. This woman wasn't at all what she'd expected.

But before she could take the thought further, Sam nodded curtly.

"Amy, this is Aiden's mother. Cynthia." Sam offered the woman a seat as he made the introductions. "I'll get Aiden, but he's not leaving the house."

"Of course." The woman shuffled her boots along the welcome mat before she darted into the spot Sam indicated. "I just want to hold him for a few minutes," she explained while Amy took a seat on the couch nearby.

"Do you live in the area?" Amy asked, hoping it sounded like friendly conversation and not like she was gathering intel on a rival woman in Sam's life.

Although perhaps, in all honesty, it was a bit of both.

"I live in Franklin." Cynthia went to tuck her hair behind her ear, and, as she moved, the stuffed bunny fell to the couch. She righted the animal and set it on the wooden coffee table. The sleek, polished surface of the hickory was a nice balance for the rough exterior shape of the wooden plank.

The piece gave her an idea for the rafters in the loft room she wanted to build in the hunting cabin. She tucked it away for later.

But it was easier to think about her renovation project than about what to say to Sam's former girlfriend.

Cynthia shot to her feet at the sound of Sam's footsteps in the hallway. He held Aiden in his strong arms, the boy tucked securely against his father's wide chest.

Amy's breath caught in her throat just seeing him. She wondered vaguely if Cynthia felt the same. She knew they'd only shared a fling but still—they now shared this baby and a whole life she'd never be a part of. That stung more than it should have.

Yet the woman's eyes seemed to be all for her son. Their son. Seeing the three of them together—however briefly—Amy couldn't help but wonder if Sam would be trying to work things out with the mother of his child if not for her presence in his life.

Was she a distraction when he needed to focus on family?

"I'll make his bottle if you'd like to feed him while I get ready for work." Sam handed over the baby as Aiden started to fuss. Amy followed him into the kitchen to leave the new mother with her child.

"Sam." She kept her voice low while he moved around the island to flip on the bottle warmer. "I should go."

"No. You shouldn't." He wore the same basic clothes as he had the day before. Not a uniform, per se, but the black pants and gray shirt had a generic look about them, even if he happened to be fiercely handsome no matter what he wore. "We haven't even gotten to talk this morning."

The long look he gave her heated her skin.

Until she remembered the woman in his front room. A woman suffering from postpartum depression, separated from her child and at a truly vulnerable point in her life.

"We can talk later. Cynthia drove all this way to see you and Aiden—"

"She's here for her son. Not for me." His tone rumbled a hint of anger before he raised his voice to be heard in the next room. "Cynthia, would you explain to my friend why I'm so sure you're not here to rekindle some old flame between us?"

Amy stiffened. "That's unnecessary."

"I think it's very necessary." He heated the bottle in the warmer.

Cynthia stepped into the kitchen, holding Aiden on her shoulder, her cheek tipped to the baby's down-covered head. She'd removed her coat and tossed a cloth over one shoulder to protect her T-shirt.

She looked comfortable with her child in

her arms and younger somehow. Less unsure of herself.

"Sam and I had a one-night stand," she explained quietly, her blue eyes locking on Amy's. "He didn't know I was still married at the time."

"Whoa." Amy dropped into a bar stool. Had she said that out loud?

No wonder Sam was having difficulty sharing parenthood.

Wordlessly, Sam passed the warmed bottle to Cynthia, his jaw flexing before he retreated to the coffeemaker to start a fresh pot.

Cynthia repositioned her baby and settled into the cushioned banquette built around a corner of the table in the breakfast nook.

"The night I met Sam, I thought my marriage was over. My husband had sent me the divorce papers, and I signed them." She focused on the baby while he ate greedily, readjusting the blanket when he kicked a foot free. "I drove into Nashville and went out as a mental farewell to my old life. I found Sam."

Amy wondered what Sam had thought that night. Had he hoped for a relationship with her? Had he known it was only temporary? She'd be willing to bet they'd met at her brother's bar. Finleys' was a popular night spot, and when people from Heartache went into Nashville, they often stopped there since both Mack and the Finley name were well-known.

"The next morning," Cynthia continued, "I freaked out about the divorce. I realized how much my husband and I were throwing away. We'd been having trouble conceiving, and it had put a tremendous strain on our marriage. But was that any reason to toss it all in the trash?" She looked to Amy, telling the story for her benefit and seeming to relive some of the emotions as she did.

And no wonder. It hadn't happened all that long ago.

"So you tried to work it out with your husband?" she guessed as the scent of freshly brewed coffee filled the air. She was beginning to understand why it had taken the woman months to let Sam know he was a father.

"Yes. We agreed to try again." Even as the woman stared down at Aiden, Amy could see a tear on her pale cheek before she swiped it away. "And when I found out I was pregnant, there was a minute where I thought—I hoped—" She clamped her lips together, trying to hold back the rest. When she looked up again, her voice was stronger. "I kept right on hoping. All through the pregnancy I told myself that it was safer for the baby not to get a paternity test anyhow since I wouldn't have wanted anything invasive no matter how minimal the risk."

Amy's heart ached for the emotional turmoil Cynthia must have gone through. True, none of this had been fair to Sam. But she certainly understood Cynthia's dilemma. Especially if she'd already been under the strain of infertility and marriage problems. The struggle with depression might have started well before she'd given birth.

Those were battles that Amy understood after growing up with a bipolar mother. Sometimes the causes for an episode were wound up in things that happened weeks before a breakdown. Strange that it was easier to empathize with this total stranger than it was with her own mother.

"So you waited until after Aiden was born to get a paternity test." Out of the corner of her eye, Amy saw Sam checking his phone.

Because there was news at work? Or to tune out of a conversation that aggravated him? She hoped for Aiden's sake that Sam would make an effort to forgive Cynthia.

"Yes. I'd told my husband about Sam earlier in the pregnancy and he said he could forgive me—if the child proved to be his." She readjusted the baby to her other arm as the feeding slowed down. "But when the results of the test came back…he moved out the next day."

"Cynthia, I appreciate your being honest about what happened." Sam interrupted before Amy could respond. He set his phone aside and filled an insulated travel cup with coffee from the machine. "I don't mean to cut this short, but I have to take Aiden to my mother's house before I go to work. We both agreed that Aiden couldn't stay with you until you're feeling more stable."

"I understand." The woman brushed a kiss along Aiden's forehead. "I'm so happy I got to see him. Thank you, Sam." She seemed to remember Amy was there, too. Looking up, she gave her a small smile. "Nice meeting you, Amy."

"You, too." She moved to take the baby from the other woman as Cynthia slid carefully out of the banquette seat. "Good luck with everything."

"Thank you." Her blue eyes darted over to Sam, but he didn't echo the sentiment. "I appreciate it."

Sam walked her to the door while Amy patted Aiden's back and wiped a milky smile with the bib he wore. The infant stared up at her with blue eyes that probably wouldn't stay blue—there was a gray-brown muddiness around the edges.

No matter the circumstances of his birth, at least his mother and father both seemed to appreciate that he was a beautiful gift. A tiny miracle.

One she'd been denied in that painful miscarriage.

And, oh yes, she could identify with how infertility might rip a woman's heart apart. But she also saw it from the other side of how much it must have hurt Sam to lose those months of pregnancy. To miss ultrasounds and the birth, the precious first days, memories he would never have with his child. God, this was tearing her apart inside from all angles. She needed space. Fast.

"Amy?" Sam's voice startled her. "You okay?"

She hadn't heard him return. Hastily, she handed Aiden over to him, not getting too close.

"I'm sorry." Sniffling, she realized she'd been close to tears just thinking about the baby she'd lost. "I really do have to get going."

"I could drive you home." He reached for her, stroking a hand along her hair as she shuffled back another step.

"That's okay. I've got so much to do. I'm

going to fall behind." She found her purse where she'd dropped it the night before.

She'd been ready to deal with the morning-after feelings she might have for Sam. She hadn't been at all ready to face morning-after feelings about his complicated new role as a father.

Or his adorable son.

"I'll call you later." He gestured to the coffee mug on the counter. "You want a cup to go?"

"No, thank you." Not wanting to end the visit on an awkward note, she stepped closer. Kissed his cheek. "I don't mean to rush out."

"Cynthia's story is a lot to take in." It was the least adversarial comment he'd made about her yet.

Still, Amy wondered if they could work out a future together. Didn't they deserve a chance to at least try? Sam had said in no uncertain terms that no one could take a mother's place. His loss of his own mom had devastated him. He wouldn't let the same thing happen to his son. Maybe, with a little more time to forgive Cynthia for keeping Aiden a secret, Sam would be ready to reconsider a future for the three of them—Cynthia, Aiden and Sam. A family.

Even thinking about it hurt.

"I'm not leaving because of that." She was leaving before she fell in love with his son.

"Good." He moved to set Aiden in the baby swing. "Then we'll talk later to set up a time for you to come into the station. Give a formal statement about what happened to you."

She almost tripped over her feet on the trek to the door.

Turning, she stared back at him while he gathered his keys and his wallet.

"What statement?"

"What you told me last night. Your testimony against Jeremy Covington. We can get it recorded and submitted for evidence today along with Faith Wilkerson's."

Oh crap.

He thought she was going to tell her story publicly.

Because he was one of those people who identified a clear line between right and wrong. And he assumed everyone else saw that line in the same way he did.

At that moment, she understood Cynthia's decision to keep a lid on her pregnancy for as long as possible. Amy wished she could keep a lid on her news, too.

But she wouldn't hurt Sam that way.

Not when her refusal was already going to upset him.

"I'm sorry, Sam." She took a deep breath and hoped he would understand. Knew that he wouldn't. "When I confided in you last night, that was just between us."

His coffee mug hit the counter with a thud. "Excuse me?" His voice was deep.

She wished she had better news for him.

"I'm not ready to give a statement about what happened that night." She watched his face fall for an instant before it hardened in resolute lines.

"Even if it would help your sister? Even if it would increase Covington's jail time and keep a public menace behind bars?" He tilted his head slightly as he studied her, as if her decision would make more sense to him if he viewed it from another angle.

But there was more at stake here than just his case.

Her new sense of self-worth was fragile. A shell she needed to protect until she was stronger. Until she made peace with her family and with her past.

"I can't, Sam." Shaking her head, she wished their night together had ended on a different note. "I'm not ready to do that yet."

She half expected him to stalk after her and demand answers about when she *would* be ready.

But he didn't say a word as she walked out the door. He just let her leave, his disappointment ringing in her ears louder than any parting argument.

CHAPTER FOURTEEN

"OF ALL THE foster kids I met in my years in the system, you are the last guy I would have pegged to go into the party-planning business." Clayton Travers's voice boomed through Sam's truck later that morning, delivered in stereo thanks to Bluetooth.

His former foster brother's call wasn't exactly unexpected since Sam had sent out the first round of electronic invitations for the Hastings' foster family reunion. But he had a world of other things on his mind after being with Amy.

He'd thought they'd really connected last night. Turned a corner in their relationship. He'd awoken twice during the night with her arms around him and her hands roaming...

Hell. It had been damned amazing. But apparently sleeping together had been more about exorcising demons for her than about any deeper bond with Sam. Yet he'd let himself read into it. Made assumptions about it. But no matter what he'd thought, she had no intention of letting him use her story to build his case.

"Catch you at a bad time?" The disembodied voice filled Sam's truck again, forcing him back to the present.

"Definitely not." Sam appreciated the call, in fact. "I'm on my way to work but I've got an eight-week-old son and I've clocked about ten minutes of sleep in the last two weeks. My reaction time has suffered, to say the least."

On the other end, Clayton chuckled. "Well, congratulations are in order, then. Is that why you decided to have a family reunion now? Introduce the little guy to all your sketchy relatives?"

Sam had forgotten how easygoing his old roommate could be. He steered the truck out of Heartache to a motel past the town line. Tiffany McCord had given the place as her address when she got out on bail, so he hoped to find her there.

"Hardly. I would have given my kid a free pass on that for a few more years, but aside from celebrating Mom's birthday, I'm also trying to talk to some of the residents who lived here when Gabriella Chance was in high school." Covington's trial was in three weeks. If there was more evidence out there, he needed to find it fast.

Sticking to the road that ran along the Harpeth River, Sam drove under a canopy of oaks with bright yellow foliage—a sign of the season. Fallen leaves swirled in the breeze as he passed the turn for a popular fishing spot.

"Right." In the background of Clayton's call, Sam heard the sounds of a diner or coffee shop—the clink of plates and glasses, a waitress calling out an order number. "Gabriella's brother called me about a job protecting his wife. I'm coming into town today to start." There was a pause, and Clayton seemed to move to someplace quieter. "The mayor thinks there is someone on the outside helping the guy in jail?"

"Definitely. Someone is sending threatening texts around town, and there's no way Covington could have sent those from jail. He must have an accomplice who is still on the loose. And whoever it is threatened my kid." The need to find out who was helping Jeremy Covington had become every bit as high priority as ensuring Covington got as much jail time as possible.

Clayton blew out a low whistle. "That's some kind of desperation to threaten an infant. And a cop's kid to boot."

Sam hadn't thought about it quite that way before, but it was true. Their perp had to be stupid or desperate to do something that would attract so much attention from the sheriff's office.

"You can see why Zach called you. Heartache is a small town, and we don't have a lot of resources." He had about five irons in the fire with this case and not enough time to follow up on everything he wanted to. Especially not with Aiden to care for and the major—welcome—distraction of Amy Finley in his life again.

"I'll do whatever I can," Clayton offered right away. "I'm taking this job because the mayor said it would only be for a few weeks, and I wanted to be there for the reunion anyhow. But it sounds like you've got a lot more at stake than just a party."

"I'd appreciate anything you can contribute." Sam would put a PI to work in a hurry. Especially one he could trust. "I know it's been a long time but—"

"Family first." Clayton obviously remembered the former mayor's motto. It had been on all the reelection signs around Heartache for years back when Amy's father had run the town.

Hearing the words—applied to him, of all people—meant a whole hell of a lot.

"Thanks, man." He hadn't expected the strong

statement of support. And it resonated all the more for him now that he was a father.

Now that he had a boy of his own to protect.

"I'll call you when I get into town, and you can tell me what you need." In the background, an engine fired to life before Clayton disconnected the call.

Sam was just pulling into the motel when he spotted Tiffany McCord almost immediately, walking from the main building toward one of the small cottages that surrounded it. Still dressed in striped pajama bottoms and a T-shirt, she had her hair piled on her head and a foam cup of coffee in one hand. She held a phone in her other, and that was where her attention was focused as she hurried between the buildings, slippers scuffing the pavement.

A stroke of luck to spot her so soon. And he needed the break after the way Amy had walked out of his house this morning. Did she even have plans to see him again? Or had last night been a one-off for her? Memories of the night before flashed through his head like a steamy movie trailer, replaying on a loop he could repeat endlessly.

Right up until the part where she walked out with no other explanation than "I'm not ready yet." Had that only been about giving her testimony? Or had it applied to their relationship, too?

Cursing himself for getting distracted all over again, he shoved open the driver's-side door of the pickup. He slammed the thing shut and headed in Tiffany's direction.

She stopped outside one of the cabins. But she made no move to enter. She stared down at her phone, her mouth open in surprise or maybe dismay.

Her eyes went wide. She backed up a step. Dropped her coffee on the pavement.

"Oh my God." She didn't seem to notice that the liquid had splashed down her pant legs and was pooling at her feet.

"Tiffany?" He forgot to be formal. He'd known the woman from her town council job well enough.

She turned toward him, her narrow face ash white.

"Sheriff." She shook her head, her brows knitted. If she was surprised to see him, the shock was small compared with whatever news she'd just received. "I got a message on my cell. A threat to Bailey."

Her grip on the phone's protective case turned her knuckles white. Wavering on her feet, she backed up another step.

Gently, he took her elbow, knowing it felt

like a gut punch to have your child threatened. Would she make the connection that this was how Dan Bryer had felt a few weeks ago when Tiffany herself sent those ugly texts to his daughter, Megan? Tamping down the thought, he reached for her phone.

"May I see?" He also didn't want the thing to fall and crack on the pavement, a real risk now as her hands were shaking.

"The message disappeared." She jabbed at the screen. "I was reading it, and it vanished."

Sounded familiar.

"All the more reason not to tamper with evidence." He was tempted to wrestle the damn thing out of her hand so he could get it to Zach, but Sam couldn't afford a confrontation with her. Let alone overstep his rights as a law-enforcement officer.

But damn. Any hope he had of finding out who'd sent the threat diminished with each urgent press of her shaking finger.

"The message said I'd better not talk to the cops or Bailey would be sorry I did." Her voice hit a high, frantic pitch. Her head swiveled as she glanced around the parking lot. "What the hell does that even mean? Is someone watching me?"

Turning desperate eyes toward Sam, she finally thrust the cell into his hand.

"Probably not." He pocketed the evidence and steered her toward the bench outside her cottage. Or what he assumed was hers. "But it's easier to trace the message if you can get your phone straight into the hands of an IT expert. The mayor's company specializes in that kind of thing."

"Right." She dropped onto the bench awkwardly, banging her hip on the way down but not even seeming to notice. "I just saw Bailey last night. I should tell her father—"

"Let me call this in, and I'll make sure an officer notifies Cole, the school and Bailey, too." Jogging back to his truck, he used the police radio to contact the station and make arrangements, texting Zach about another disappearing threat at the same time.

It was a damn good thing Clayton had offered to help. Even so, he would have to call the county for more uniformed reinforcements.

When he returned to Tiffany's side, her color had improved a little. Her movements remained stiff and uneasy, however, as he neared.

"Sheriff, I haven't mentioned how grateful I am to you for hiring my daughter to watch your son. It means a lot to me that Bailey hasn't been alienated...because of me." She folded her arms around herself tightly, bear-

ing little resemblance to the aggressive busi-
nesswoman he remembered from town council
meetings.

Sam couldn't remember her ever thanking
anyone in town for a damn thing, unless it was
at an event documented by the media. She'd
been a press hound for her small business—
a sporting-goods store she'd opened with her
husband the year before.

She reminded him of alcoholics he'd seen
who'd turned their lives around—people who
operated at a whole different pitch once they
rid themselves of a bad influence. For Bailey McCord's sake, he hoped that her mother
had learned a lesson in the hell of the last few
weeks.

"I believe each of us are only accountable for
our own actions and no one else's." He leaned
against a post that was mostly decorative in
front of her cottage. Judging by the vacant
parking lot, Tiffany McCord was probably the
only guest at the Country Cabins Motor Lodge
this week. "And since my son has been threatened, too, I have a uniformed officer keeping
watch over my mother's house whenever Bailey is there."

"You think that makes the kids safer or puts
them more at risk if they are together?" She
crossed her legs, one foot twitching nervously.

"With a cop car out front?" There was no question in his mind. "Safer for sure."

She nodded, seeming to accept this, but her foot kept right on twitching.

"Mrs. McCord, do you have any idea who might have sent you that threat?" He'd come here to question her about her argument with Kate Covington yesterday, not add to his already long list of items that needed investigation. But if this incident helped lead him to whoever had threatened Aiden, he was just as glad to put the rest of his questions on hold.

"Patience Wilkerson." She tipped her head forward, squeezing her temples between her hands. "The bitch."

"Faith Wilkerson's sister?" Faith was coming in later today to give her statement. She'd been groped by a faceless man in the woods near the quarry in an episode similar to what Amy had experienced.

He was so close to proving a pattern of behavior. But he'd need more people to come forward before the trial. At first, Sam had hoped for the usual legal motions and delays to slow things down in the justice system. But Covington's lawyer was pushing things through at full speed, undoubtedly aware the evidence against his client remained thin considering the years Covington had been quietly molesting and stalking girls and young women in the area.

"I guess they are sisters." Tiffany shrugged as a big rig roared by on the highway. A few moments later, the motion blew through the bushes at their feet. "All I know is that Patience thinks she's the true love of Jeremy's life, and she's crazy enough to hate anyone else who has ever held that position before."

Sam was doing the math to figure out the age difference between Faith and Patience—three years, maybe. One sister was giving testimony that could keep the guy in jail, and the other wanted to protect him? Sounded like some serious sibling rivalry he could use for leverage.

"This is what you brought up to Kate in the teacher's parking lot yesterday?"

"I did. Kate is in major denial about her husband." She picked at some green peeling paint on the arm of the bench. Flicked off a dry piece.

"So now you think he's guilty?" She'd defended him in previous interviews, insisting the police had arrested the wrong man.

"I think he's a lying, cheating bastard. And if he could fool me so thoroughly—" She pursed dry lips. Pressed a hand to her forehead. "I have no evidence of anything, okay?

But I'd bet Kate could find enough in his files to fry his ass if I can convince her how big of a cheater he is."

"Kate seemed very angry with you yesterday. Could she be the one who threatened Bailey?"

"Kate? She's won teacher of the year in this state five times in a row or something." She rolled her eyes and shot to her feet, restless all of a sudden. "She likes kids too much to pull that crap. Don't ask me how she wound up with such a loser for a husband. She must have a savior complex or something. But to answer your question—no way."

Interesting. He made some notes on his phone to check out the Wilkerson family, as well as Kate and Tiffany. Tiffany paced in front of the cottage, biting her lip.

"I'm going to talk to Kate again. And don't worry—I'll do a better job not pushing her buttons. I took the wrong approach with her yesterday." She jammed her hands in the pockets of her blue-striped pajama bottoms. "We need to work as a team."

"You slept with her husband." Sam didn't mean it as a jab or even as a judgment. Hell, who was he to look down on her when he'd had a one-night stand with a married woman himself? "What makes you think she's going to talk to you?"

"I realize, Sheriff, that I allowed myself to become the town joke between sleeping with Jeremy and pushing so hard into town politics. But I didn't head up multiple companies over the course of my career without some sense of interpersonal dynamics. I can do this." She dug her room key card out of her pocket and used it to open the door of her cottage. "Besides, I told my daughter I'd make this right, and I've failed Bailey too many times to screw this up too."

He believed her. Understood the fierceness of her commitment to her kid, if nothing else.

"One last thing." He hadn't asked all the questions he'd wanted, but the case had taken a new direction, and he was eager to follow it after all the dead ends of the last week. He didn't want to wait to speak to Faith Wilkerson and—he hoped—her sister, too.

"Shoot. I'm listening." Tiffany leaned her hip into the doorjamb, her tiny cottage dark and lonely behind her with the TV set tuned to an infomercial.

What a sorry state for a woman who once seemed to have the perfect life and family.

"How did you find out about Patience and Jeremy?" Tiffany had been in lockup until two days ago. Had she heard the news while she was still in jail? Or had someone told her as soon as she was freed?

"She sent me photos of them together in the corn maze at Harvest Fest. There was no mistaking the time and date since I recognized the spot." Her mouth twisted in distaste and maybe a hint of pain. "It was the same damn place he'd taken me, right near the banner for the sporting-goods store, in the back west corner."

"And you're sure it couldn't have been more innocent than she made it seem?" He hadn't met Patience, but he didn't think she could be more than twenty-one or twenty-two years old. "There's an odd breed of woman who fixates on a man behind bars."

"The pics were stills pulled off a video she'd made. They had their hands down one another's pants. So…" She shrugged, her lips still pursed. "Definitely not innocent."

"Did you save the photos?" Linking Covington to new women could only help his case.

Even better? If he could shift the focus to what Covington had been doing recently instead of ten years ago, he could ease up on Amy.

"Hell yes, I saved them. Just in case that cheating bastard ever tried to deny it." She gave a smile that was mostly a baring of her teeth. "They're password protected in about ten different locations in my files."

And just like that, he recognized shades of the Tiffany McCord he remembered. Ruthless, tenacious and arrogant.

Right now he was grateful for those qualities. Not just because they were going to help him nail Covington's ass to the wall. More important, they could help him and Amy put the unhappiest parts of their past behind them by bringing a predator to justice.

That was a good thing. Assuming, of course, that Amy hadn't already found other reasons to close the door on their relationship. They hadn't had an opportunity to say much on the subject of Cynthia and what she meant in his life and Aiden's, but the woman's arrival had definitely complicated things.

He'd told Amy he wasn't in a position to have a simple affair, and he meant it. He cared about her, and he wanted more than just one night. But something told him that pushing her on the issue right now would only send her running back to Atlanta, and he didn't think he could handle that, either.

After ten years, he finally had her in his life again. And he would do whatever it took to keep her there long enough to find out if the connection he felt with her was as real as he'd always thought it might be.

"ARE YOU SURE you don't want me to go with you?" Heather asked Amy as they stood on her small porch overlooking a neat lawn dotted with colorful chrysanthemums in garden beds.

Most of the Finleys lived within a mile of one another, their homes visible to each other across the converted land their dad had once farmed. Heather owned a converted bungalow closest to the original house, while Erin and Scott had built custom houses on their plots. Mack and Nina had converted an old barn on the property but also kept a residence in Nashville. Only Amy had ignored the land her father had given her, never building on the corner she'd been deeded as a teenager.

Now, standing with Heather in front of the bungalow that used to be their father's office, Amy stared up at the home where she'd grown up. A home she hadn't seen since the night she'd packed her bags and left following the argument with her mother.

Finally—thank heaven—finally, she was done hiding from her past. After revealing the truth of The Incident to Sam, Amy was ready to see her mother again and try to put their harsh words behind them.

Or so she hoped. She couldn't deny she was a little bit tempted by Heather's offer.

"I have to do this on my own." Amy had come back to Heartache to make peace with the past, but her rift had never really been with her siblings. Not if she was totally honest with herself. True, she'd felt abandoned by them. But they'd never hurt her the way her mother had. "She's the reason I stayed away. And she's the main reason I needed to come back."

Funny how revealing the details of The Incident had made that so clear to her. Being molested in the dark by a stranger had traumatized her—yes. But she'd dealt with it in therapy. And now she'd shared it with Sam, who'd played a role in that night without ever knowing.

She'd found closure there, but she'd still felt unsettled because she hadn't confronted what had hurt her most of all. Her mother's emotional abandonment when she'd needed her the most.

"She's much more level than she used to be, more regimented in staying on her meds and working with her doctor." Heather had a giant mug of tea on the table beside her small wooden porch swing. Everything about the bungalow remodel was as sweet and charming as Heather herself, and Amy found herself curious to see the inside. The fact that it was such a quaint home now was a testament to her sister's creativity.

"It's been a long time." Amy knew how much she'd grown and changed in ten years. She could only hope her mother had, too. "I just wanted to tell you I was over there in case—" she wasn't entirely sure what she thought might happen "—you hear arguing."

That was one reason she hadn't wanted Heather with her. No one except Amy and her mother knew what they'd fought about that day, and Amy would prefer to keep it that way.

Heather readjusted her lap blanket, an elegant cashmere throw folded over her legs. A legal pad rested on the swing cushion nearby, and Amy guessed that her sister had been working on song lyrics now that she was exploring more options with her music.

"I think Mom will be too happy to see you to argue with you today, but if I hear loud voices…am I allowed to intervene? Or call for reinforcements?" Heather tapped her ballpoint pen against the wooden swing's armrest, a small, nervous tap.

"Absolutely not." Amy wiped clammy hands on the pockets of her jeans, more nervous than ever. "Let us hash it out. I'll give you a debrief as soon as I recover from my visit." She pointed to the guitar resting in a wooden stand nearby. "I saw a flyer in the consignment-shop window advertising your performance at Mack and Nina's restaurant this weekend. I can't wait to hear you sing again."

"Thank you. I hope you bring Sam. And anyone else you can think of. I'll need help filling the seats."

"That's not what I hear." She'd learned from more than one source in town that Heather had the kind of voice and showmanship that would carry her as far as she wanted to go in country music. "But I'll make sure I fill at least one table."

She hoped it would include Sam Reyes. But would he understand her decision not to testify? He was having a hard time forgiving the mother of his own son for not informing him of her pregnancy. How harshly would he judge Amy for not being willing to testify against the man he desperately wanted to convict?

Taking her leave, Amy walked the short distance to their mother's home. The flagstones on the path were worn just the way she remembered. The big screened-in porch still had a latch that stuck. The decor on the porch was different, though. The colors were brighter and more modern. There was a cartoon drawing of the Tastee Freez over the outdoor fireplace, the Heartache haunt rendered in bright pinks, yellows and purples.

After she'd knocked on the door, she heard her mother's footsteps inside before the door opened. When she caught her first glimpse of Diana Finley in a gold-and-purple caftan, she was besieged by about a million impressions. Her mother seemed smaller. More fragile. Yet her face, while more lined around the eyes, seemed more relaxed around the mouth. Her dark hair had been lightened in places, probably to hide the grays. But it looked good on her.

"Amy Marie. You're home at last." Her mother opened her arms wide and hugged her, folding her in an unexpected embrace that made Amy's throat painfully tight with unspoken emotions.

The scent of lemon furniture polish and patchouli clung to her clothes and hair, the smell familiar and strange at the same time. A deep, shuddering sigh huffed past Amy's lips, and she knew already that no matter what came out of today's conversation with her mother, she'd already defeated one old personal demon.

Her mother still loved her. And as she hugged her back, Amy realized that had been what had scared her about this meeting more than anything. The fear that connection had been broken for good.

"It's nice to see you," Amy told her honestly as she pulled back to study the woman in front of her, so different from the one she remembered.

But then, Diana Finley had had a nervous breakdown since then. She'd been hospitalized. On different medical treatments. She'd lost a husband. Of course she'd changed. It occurred to Amy that she may have been too hard on her parent in the same way she'd accused Sam of being too hard on Cynthia. At least Sam had a running dialogue with the mother of his son. He hadn't closed a door between them for years on end.

The realization softened her heart toward him; that was for sure. It took a lot of emotional strength to forgive people who hurt you.

"I'm glad to hear that. I've wondered what you would have to say to me when you came home, and I have dreamed up a lot worse things over the years—I can tell you that much." She stood away from the door and waved Amy inside. "Come in now and have a seat so we can catch up. I've been making peace with my children, one by one, over the last few years. But I can't truly celebrate until you and I put to rest whatever it is I did to send you away."

She doesn't remember.

The knowledge shifted the ground under Amy's feet. That fight with her mother had spurred Amy to strike out on her own—to quit school and get her GED instead of graduating with friends. She'd scrimped on a waitress's meager salary for years to put herself through college. All because she'd been too furious with her family to take a cent of support from them.

Yet her mom didn't even recall what had happened. It felt like Amy's whole world had been just slightly out of focus all those years, and now, suddenly, it tilted back into clear view.

As they entered the living room, Amy noticed lots of other differences, including the addition of a hideous purple art-deco chair that her mother chose to sit in—a clear favorite flanked by books, a water glass and an open packet of mints. There were more cartoon drawings around the space, giving Amy the idea that her mother was the artist behind the local scenes depicted in vibrant colors.

Amy wondered how she'd ended up in accounting with so much creativity in her family.

"Oh crap. I should have offered you coffee or tea or something." Her mother moved to stand again.

"No. I can help myself. Should I bring you something?" She ducked into the kitchen they'd just passed through and peered into the brown refrigerator so old it must be an antique.

Seeing it—and some of the other ancient things in the Finley home—made Amy smile to remember how hard her father had worked to keep some of those older machines going long after other people might have dragged them to the dump. Amy might not have inherited much in the way of creativity, but she had her father's thriftiness and self-reliance.

"Maybe bring the whole pitcher of lemonade? I made it just yesterday. And there are gingersnaps, which I seem to recall—"

"Are my favorite." Amy still knew the cabinet where her mother kept the freshly baked cookies.

Because was there any happier memory associated with childhood than warm cookies?

Grabbing a serving plate, she balanced two paper cups on it along with the cookies, then lifted the lemonade pitcher in the other hand to rejoin her mom.

It was so strange to be here. And she was glad for the distraction of cookies and lemonade while wondering where to begin. If her mother didn't remember, was there even any point of hauling the past back up now?

"Thank you." Her mother had cleared a spot on the coffee table, shoving aside an open case of pencils and a stack of newspapers. "I'll serve us, and you can dive right into your story. And don't hold anything back, please. It helps me to process what happened better if I have the whole, unvarnished, ugly truth. My therapist is good at putting it all in perspective for me. The hope is one day I'll have my head on straight again." She passed Amy a cup of lemonade.

"I worked through a lot of what we argued about with my own counselor." Still, maybe she'd never have a relationship with her mother if they couldn't move past this. "But I can tell you that it took me a long time to share with anyone because I was..." *Flattened. Unhinged. Walking wounded.* "Deeply hurt."

"I have been asking myself for years what I could have said. I knew it must be worse than I could possibly imagine when you didn't come home for your father's funeral." Frowning, she shook her head. "It wasn't the skinny-dipping fight, was it?" Mom asked, taking a bite of a gingersnap. "Because I thought for sure we worked through that, even though I do remember screeching like a shrew about propriety. But that was *my* issue. My father once called me some very unflattering names for wearing a tank top around a young caretaker who worked for him."

Amy blinked, never having heard about arguments like that between her mother and grandfather. "Seriously? And, yes, we had worked through the skinny-dipping thing. But then we had another blowout that pulled all previous arguments into it."

Her mother pointed her cookie at Amy. "That, my daughter, is precisely how my mind was working at that time. A jittery, hopping, hot mess."

Amy's cookie caught in her throat at the unexpected characterization. Coughing, she couldn't reply, so her mother continued.

"I jumped from one thought to another and tied random bits together in a way that made my whole existence feel unstable. I was paranoid all the time, certain all the neighbors were judging me because I couldn't get my act together." Her mom set the rest of her cookie on her plate and folded her hands on her lap, studying Amy. "Tell me. What happened?"

This was her chance. An opportunity to explain her side. To finally air the hurt that had weighed on her for so long.

"I was molested in the woods." The words came out easier now. Unlike when she'd relived the nightmare as she recounted it to Sam, Amy now related the simple fact in the most straightforward way possible. "I was terrified, and I couldn't see the man's face. I was traumatized, Mom. And after walking my bike home for hours since I couldn't possibly get on the thing to ride it—" She'd hurt. Really hurt. She didn't remember those hours well at all, but she'd finally reached her front steps before dawn. "When I got here and told you what happened—" She'd wanted her mother's embrace and understanding. She'd needed a mother's tender compassion and willingness to fight for her child.

Her mother made a small sound. Amy met her gaze, seeing the tear slip down Diana Finley's cheek. "I'm so sorry, Amy."

Sorry she'd been molested? Or sorry because her mother had made it all worse with her reaction? Amy couldn't think about that now; the moment had come to finally get it all out in the open.

"You told me you weren't surprised. That it had been only a matter of time before something like that happened to me because I was teasing boys, sneaking out at night and skinny-dipping where anyone could see me—" Breaking off, she couldn't go on. Didn't want to share the worst of the names her mother had called her.

"I'm so sorry." Her mother's voice all but disappeared as she seemed to struggle to keep her own emotions in check. She swallowed hard. "That's so much worse than anything I imagined." She shook her head helplessly. "I sucked as a mother then, Amy. I should have demanded your father quit his job and be here to take care of you. But I was struggling so hard with my own issues, I couldn't see past them—"

"Even me telling you now—you don't remember that night?" Amy sipped her lemonade, trying to shift her perspective on her mother. All these years, she'd assumed her mother had truly been grateful to be rid of a troubled daughter.

"No. My God, *no*. But I was also taking some medications I probably shouldn't have been. I was seeing any doctor I could to try and find a new prescription that would help me. And your father had his own ideas."

"So no one else in the family knows what we fought about, either?" She'd wondered sometimes if her father had known about The Incident. If he'd been as judgmental and uncaring as her mother.

"Of course not." She bit her lip. "I probably

didn't remember what happened long enough to relate it to anyone. Furthermore, I think that would have been the straw that broke the back of my marriage. He would never have forgiven me."

There was an odd comfort in that, somehow. More than any of her mother's apologies, those words about Amy's father soothed the old wound a little. Even after all this time, it felt nice to imagine her father standing up for her, indignant and protective on her behalf.

It reminded her of Sam, actually. That was the kind of parent he would be.

"Then no one knows about that night, Mom. And I'd prefer it stays that way." Amy listened to the *tick-tick-tick* of an old grandfather clock in the hallway, the sound a soft connection to the life she'd lived under this roof. Saturday morning cartoons with her sisters. Making paper chains for the Christmas tree at the dining room table. Wrestling with algebra problems at the desk against one wall.

There were more good memories here than bad ones.

"If that's what you want. I lost the right to tell you how to lead your life a long time ago. But I do hope you pressed charges against whoever assaulted you. Or took your vengeance some other way." Her mother scowled.

"Vengeance? That doesn't sound like what the counselors would advise in therapy." Amy frowned, sipping more lemonade.

"My daughter was molested. I think vengeance would make me feel a lot better than any therapy."

Amy nearly choked on her lemonade, not expecting the dry bite of dark humor.

"I will keep that in mind," she replied once she cleared her throat.

"And I know I can't take back whatever putrid words shot from my mouth during those years. But I am more sorry than I can say. And if it helps, I'm trying to do a better job with my granddaughter." Her mom turned a gold-framed photo toward her. It was the high school graduation photo of Amy's niece.

Bethany and Scott's daughter, Ally, had also been diagnosed with bipolar disorder, but apparently her therapy of medication and counseling kept the condition in check, and she was thriving in college.

"Heather's letters have mentioned how much you've been a help to Ally." She owed her sister thanks for keeping her in the loop on the family, a task that must have been frustrating since Amy had often found it difficult to reply. "I've realized that I should have come back a long time ago to face all this but—" She'd been afraid that the man who lurked in those woods outside the Chances' house might still live in Heartache. "I just wasn't ready."

Not until she'd heard Jeremy Covington was in jail and suspected of other sexual crimes over the years. That had given her the confidence to come home. Coupled with the miscarriage, it had finally been time to make peace with her family.

"No one blames you. Especially after what you just said. But you're here now, and I've heard the cabin renovation is going well. Your father would have enjoyed seeing you tackle that project, you know. He always wanted to expand that little cabin one day and put on a second story." Her mother rose from her chair at the sound of scratching at the door. She opened a side entrance and her black Lab, Luce, came bounding in, tail wagging.

Setting aside her lemonade, Amy greeted the dog, who seemed to remember her. Actually, Luce seemed overjoyed to see her, tucking her head into Amy's lap and licking her chin until Amy had no choice but to share her seat with the dog.

"You've been missed," her mother announced, setting a hand on Amy's shoulder as she moved past her to return to her seat. "The dog is just better at showing it than the rest of us."

Her throat tightened again. And for the first time since she'd returned to Heartache, she wondered if it might be more difficult than she anticipated to leave town again. Her family hadn't stopped loving her just because she'd moved away. All but ignored them for years on end.

Her home and her family were still here. Missing her.

She'd spent years being lonely, losing her unborn baby and mourning all by herself. Did she even know how to be a part of a family anymore? Could she even call herself a loving family member when she was too scared to give testimony that might help send Heather's attacker to jail for good?

Sam sure wouldn't think so. He was a man who viewed the world in black and white, his choices simple because right and wrong were so clear to him. And Amy's decision to keep her secrets was, in his eyes, wrong.

Burying her face in Luce's soft, dark fur, she wiped the sudden moisture on her cheeks, knowing she couldn't stay in Heartache just for her family. She needed Sam more than she realized, and a life here without him would never be enough.

CHAPTER FIFTEEN

BAILEY CONSIDERED WHO to confide in. Her dad
was moody and quick to anger, so he wasn't on
Bailey's list. Her mother didn't live with them
anymore, and she'd phoned earlier to say she'd
turned over her cell phone to the cops after receiving a threat to Bailey. So getting in touch
with Mom wasn't an option, either.

That meant if she was going to come clean
with someone about what had truly happened
between her and J.D., her friend Megan ranked
as her best outlet.

She'd made the decision the night before
while lying in bed, unable to sleep. Torn between excitement over the news that Dawson
liked her and embarrassment over having to
confide in someone about J.D. hitting her, Bailey had finally decided she'd rather be honest
and have a chance to see what happened between her and Dawson.

Now, pulling into the driveway of the Hastings' house for their babysitting gig, she tried to

recapture some of last night's bravado. Megan was her best friend. She wouldn't judge her.

Except what if she did? Her stomach knotted as she parked the Volvo. Megan hadn't ridden with her today because she'd been out of school. Her protective dad had insisted she avoid any place she might run into J.D., and he'd been at Crestwood daily. Bailey hated seeing him too, but he'd ignored her completely, to the point where she stopped holding her breath every time they were in the same hallway or classroom.

The pile of brightly colored bikes outside the Hastings' house seemed smaller than normal, and she guessed the younger boys must have ridden to friends' houses after school. Dawson had already told her that he was meeting with the guidance office today, so he wouldn't be around. Stepping out of the Volvo onto the gravel driveway, she gave a small, awkward wave at the police officer on duty. He nodded back. He had his window rolled down, but even so it was tough to gauge the man's expression behind his dark aviator shades.

She hurried inside, hoping Megan's dad had already dropped her off. Now that Bailey had made the decision to tell her friend the truth about J.D., she wanted it done and over.

"Hello!" Lorelei Hasting appeared in the

doorway, her patchwork boho-style bag in one hand and car keys in the other. Her long, dark curls were scraped back into a pony-tail that trailed over one shoulder. "So glad you're here. I'm running late for my appoint-ment with Dawson and the guidance coun-selor over at the school. I let the boys go to a friend's house for a few hours, so you'll be on your own with the baby until I get back." Lo-relei brushed past her, her heavy leather shoes slapping the flagstones as she hurried by. "I told Officer Stallworth to keep an extrasharp eye on you."

"I'm sure I'll be fine." Her conversation with Megan would be all the easier without anyone around to overhear. "But where's Megan? She's not here yet?"

"You didn't hear?" Lorelei turned, her patch-work bag swinging out as she moved. "Her fa-ther took her up to Franklin to stay with his sister. He's going to homeschool her until the trial's done to keep her away from that boy who assaulted her."

That was what Megan had wanted to talk to her about on the phone, but Bailey hadn't called her back. Had she even checked her mes-sages? So much had happened since her mom and J.D. had gotten out of jail. Bailey felt her whole world tip sideways even more. Megan was her only friend. And while she'd been okay without her in school, she'd assumed she'd at least be able to see her at work or on the weekends. Now?

She'd have to keep her silence about J.D. a little longer. And somehow, she'd have to get through the days without her bestie. Hard to imagine when she'd been hanging on by her fingernails as it was. Someone had threatened her life this week, for crying out loud.

"I'm surprised she didn't text me." She went to check her phone before remembering that was rude to do in the middle of a conversation. She let the phone fall back in her leather purse. "She must have been busy packing."

"I think it was very spur-of-the-moment." Dawson's foster mom continued toward her car with a wave. "The baby monitor is on the kitchen table, but I doubt Aiden will sleep much longer."

Pulling herself together, Bailey returned the wave and rushed inside, locking the front door behind her. She couldn't believe Megan would be out of town for weeks. And who knew how long the trial could stretch on?

Chewing her bottom lip, she slid her backpack to the floor and grabbed the nursery monitor off the kitchen table, wondering if it would be totally tacky to sneak a peek at Dawson's room.

Yes. Absolutely.

Her feet wandered that way anyhow, curiosity getting the better of her since she'd been thinking about him a lot. They'd texted a few times after his visit to her house, but she hadn't seen him in person.

And he liked her.

A really genuine, good guy liked her. Amazing how, in spite of her mom moving out, her father ranting about her constantly, her best friend abandoning her and her own life being threatened, the thought of Dawson still made her feel like twirling in circles and singing.

Reaching the top of the stairs, she peeked into Aiden's nursery. He was still sleeping under a mobile of brightly colored circus animals, so she continued past the room the younger boys shared toward Dawson's door at the end of the hall.

Bang.

A sound like the screen door slamming made her pause.

Had Lorelei forgotten something? Bailey stepped into a small bathroom on the front side of the house to peer out the window overlooking the driveway. There were no cars out front except for her own and the police cruiser. She could see Officer Stallworth's head drooped forward like he was sleeping.

Which, while not impossible, seemed unlikely.

A chill skittered up the back of her neck.

What if whoever had threatened Aiden—and her—was ready to carry out the job? She remained very still in the bathroom, listening for any sounds downstairs. She debated calling out to ask if anyone was there.

She hoped it was one of the boys. Except kids made noise. Lots of it. And it seemed frighteningly quiet in the house after the screen door had slammed.

Another soft creak sounded from downstairs, as if someone was trying hard to be quiet.

Fear clutched her belly in a tight fist. She knew how fast life could smack her on her ass.

What if it was J.D., looking for her?

Her mind running at warp speed, Bailey stepped silently back into the hallway and tiptoed down to Aiden's room. She was getting out of here.

And she was taking Aiden with her.

SAM WASN'T HAVING any luck finding the women he wanted to see.

Rapping his knuckles on the door of apartment B in a duplex building just off the interstate, he waited for some sign of life inside the residence of the Wilkerson sisters. Faith hadn't shown up the day before to give her promised testimony. Patience hadn't been at home yesterday when he'd stopped by after questioning Tiffany McCord. Then Amy—the woman he wanted to see more than anyone else—had been avoiding him.

And she hadn't even been subtle about it, surrounding herself with her family at the hunting cabin and working on renovations late into the night. Scott and Erin, the two Finleys with the most hands-on construction experience, had been there when he'd dropped in last night. And he'd heard the table saw working well past midnight, a sound that had carried on the still autumn breeze.

Reminding him that, with each new improvement at the cabin, his time with her dwindled.

She had to stay through the trial at least. She might not be offering any testimony herself, but she'd come back to town to support her sister Heather as she faced Jeremy Covington in court.

He was about to abandon apartment B when he heard someone unbolt the thin, red-painted door.

"Patience Wilkerson?" he asked, voice raised.

There was no answer, but her sister Faith's

face appeared in the narrow crack as the door opened. Short brown hair curled around the older sister's face, and a yellow cap with the name of a fast-food joint sat on her head. A television blared in the background.

"She's not here, Sheriff." Faith's voice was low and hoarse, like she'd been yelling. Or crying.

Sam stepped closer, peering at a dark shadow along the top of the young woman's cheek.

"Is that a bruise?" He moved to tilt her chin up for a better view, but she jerked away, retreating deeper behind the red door.

"Please. My sister is not here. It's just me and I'm really tired—"

"Faith. Let me see your face," he demanded, tired of women in his life keeping secrets.

He'd kept Gabriella Chance's secrets from the rest of the world for years, costing him time with Amy, someone he'd really cared about even as a teen. Then Cynthia hid the news of his child from him. And now Amy refused to reveal her encounter with a predator. He'd had enough.

Slowly, the door opened. He didn't step inside, instead waiting for her to come closer. When she moved into the light so he could see her more clearly, the outline of a bruise around her eye became visible, darker near the temple.

"Who did this to you?" His cop instincts twitched with new urgency. After long, slow days of getting nowhere on this case, he was making progress, and he couldn't follow up on the leads fast enough.

She debated lying. He could read it in her eyes.

"My sister." She whispered the words, almost as if that might lessen the impact.

"Patience." The woman rocketed from person of interest to danger to society. "Jeremy Covington's new girlfriend." He made the connection to test Faith's reaction to it.

"I guess I'm the last to know." Shaking her head, she ran an impatient swipe through her hair while the television played in the background—an ad ran for his foster parents' pizza shop. "The guy who I believe assaulted me is behind bars and also happens to be nearly twenty years older than her. I don't get it."

Sam did, though. He was beginning to expand his understanding of Covington. The guy wasn't the first sexual predator with a keen understanding of how to lure his victims. He'd pretended to be someone else—a local teen she knew—when he'd convinced Gabriella to meet him in the woods ten years ago. Now the guy had upped his game. He could woo a young woman into doing his bidding while he was behind bars.

Including intimidating a witness. Had he also told Patience to send threats to Sam and Tiffany McCord?

"Was your sister upset you were going to offer testimony against Jeremy? Is that why she hit you?"

"Yes. But she's just confused. She ran out of here after we argued, and I didn't have a chance to talk to her. But I'm sure once I sat her down and told her—"

"Where do you think she might go if she needed to hide?" Sam asked impatiently, concerned that Patience Wilkerson might be running scared and feeling desperate. What if that desperation drove her to even more witness intimidation? Or to carry out the threats she'd made against Aiden or Bailey?

Not on his watch.

He needed to check on his son and Bailey McCord. And he should alert Zach and Clayton to keep a close eye on Heather Finley, too.

And Amy. Damn, but he had to keep Amy safe. What if Covington was worried about some of his old victims coming forward? She could be at risk, too. More so than the others since she wasn't under police protection.

"I have no idea where she would go." Faith

held her arms wide, gesturing to the cramped apartment full of furniture and disarray. "Our mom took off a long time ago. I've been taking care of Patience since she was in high school." Almost as an afterthought, she added, "She has no money. Neither of us do."

Which made her even more desperate. Sam wondered if Jeremy had any way to float funds to her.

Certainly not through his wife. If Tiffany's read of the situation was correct, Kate Covington would be livid to learn her husband's new mistress wasn't much older than his son.

With Kate out of the question as a resource for Patience, that left J.D., who'd helped his father before. Unless Patience was operating alone.

"There are family services that can help you," he told Faith gently, fishing in his jacket pocket for a business card to hand her. As much as he hated to leave when Faith Wilkerson seemed to be near her personal breaking point, what choice did he have? "I want you to call them. But right now, I'm worried that your sister is in trouble, and I need to locate her as soon as possible." He passed her a second card. "Call me if you hear from her or think of anything that might help."

The young woman stood taller, her eyes

full of concern as she tucked the cards in her pocket.

"Please find her before she does anything stupid." She gripped his arm with both hands. "Now that I know what she's been doing, I can help her see this scumbag for what he really is. She's not a bad person, Sheriff. Just misguided."

If she'd threatened an infant and a young girl, she was more than misguided. But this wasn't the time or place to mention that distinction. So Sam placed his hat on his head and took his leave, returning to his truck to find Patience Wilkerson.

Where would a young woman go who was desperate, alone and at odds with her family? A woman with no money to her name?

His jaw clenched tight as he withdrew his phone and dialed a number. He knew someone who would have some ideas. Another woman who'd been in that same position once.

Amy.

Then again, maybe he just needed to hear her voice and know she was safe. He had a cop watching over his son and Bailey McCord. But Amy was working at her house on top of that remote hill, probably all by herself.

"Hello?" Her voice soothed some of the agitation inside him.

She was safe. In the background of the call, he could hear a loud mechanical whine suddenly quieting—a power tool being shut off.

"Amy, it's Sam." He wanted to see her. Wanted to speak with her about more than just this damned investigation that had taken over his life. "Are you by yourself right now?"

It took her a moment to answer.

"Yes. Why?" There was a guardedness in her voice. A caution he'd put there, damn it.

Flooring the gas, he shoved the blue police light onto the dashboard for safety's sake. His gut told him Patience Wilkerson was on the move, and Amy was the most vulnerable of Covington's potential enemies.

"Covington has a girlfriend intimidating witnesses for him. I don't want you alone up there." He exited the highway and wound through Heartache. He avoided Main Street since it was slower than taking the road past the Hastings' house toward Partridge Hill.

"What girlfriend? You mean Tiffany McCord?" She sounded hoarse, and he found himself wondering if he was the first person she'd spoken to all day.

It occurred to him that as much as he admired her independence, it was also sad that she'd lived for so long away from any help or support. Would she even be willing to let him in her life if he could convince her he cared about more than just her testimony?

"No. Patience Wilkerson. You met her older sister at Erin's consignment shop."

"Faith's sister is Jeremy Covington's girlfriend?" Her voice grew louder, her surprise evident. "How old is she? Twelve?"

"Twenty." He took his foot off the gas as he neared the Hasting house, just to take a quick peek in the driveway.

The police cruiser was there, of course, as was Bailey's vintage Volvo. But where was his foster mother's vehicle? Slowing down even more, he knew everything was probably fine. Lorelei ran bank errands sometimes in the afternoons or stopped over at the pizza parlor.

But then he noticed Stallworth's window was rolled down, and the officer's head was hanging forward at an awkward angle.

What the hell? A low hiss of suspicion—of dread—slid between his clenched teeth.

"Is something the matter?" Amy's voice was instantly alert.

He must have said something out loud.

"Aiden." The bottom dropped out of his world. "Something's wrong at my mother's place."

Yanking hard on the steering wheel, he

pulled into the driveway fast and flipped on the police camera.

"What can I do?" The steeliness in her voice pierced through the fear for his child.

"Get to one of your brothers' houses." Vaulting out of the truck, he still hoped Stallworth had just fallen asleep. But he knew damn well that wasn't the case. "Be safe."

Disconnecting the call, he alerted dispatch even as he sprinted across the lawn toward his officer. Stallworth was breathing but unconscious. A minor head wound.

But Sam's son was inside that house. Unprotected except for a teenage girl who was also a target for Covington.

Drawing his weapon, he charged inside, ignoring police protocol because this was his family. His home. Adrenaline fueled every step as he shouted his way through the eerily silent house.

He'd never been in this place before when it was empty.

Ever. And the quiet had him fearing the worst. It was something of a relief when he found each room vacant. His throat grew tighter, but he forced his hands to stay steady, his training never more important than now.

Still, when he reached the nursery and his son's crib stood empty, his knees damn near gave out. He had to hold the crib rail for a second to pull it together.

Aiden was gone. And Bailey McCord had disappeared, too.

CHAPTER SIXTEEN

HOLDING AIDEN AS tightly to her as she dared, Bailey sprinted through the woods, channeling her inner huntress. She prayed she made it out of the woods alive so she could tell Megan that one.

She kept picturing one of the video-game Ts that Megan wore, the one with an iron-on patch of a fleet-footed archer queen in a green felt hat. Had she crossed the line into total hysteria that she wanted to laugh out loud about that as she zipped between trees and avoided patches of crunchy leaves that might give her away?

Definitely. But it was either laugh or vomit from fear.

Peering behind her, she couldn't see any signs of movement through the trees behind her. If it had been dark, she might be able to hide better. She hadn't gotten a good look at the person who'd entered the Hasting home, but she was sure it was a woman. Bailey had heard a female voice shrieking at her to "get back here" when she'd first sped into the forest.

After that, she'd thought she'd heard footsteps pounding the ground behind her, but it could have been her own. Her heart had been beating too loud to tell for certain, her blood rushing in her ears. She'd been too afraid to look back until just now.

Seeing a pile of rotting wooden pallets up ahead, Bailey sprinted—fast and quiet—never letting go of Aiden. She'd ducked into a baby sling on the way out the door and placed him inside, but she didn't trust the cloth to keep him secure as she ran. A baby's tiny neck was so thin. She used her forearm as reinforcement up his spine, cradling his head in her palm through the sling.

So far, he hadn't cried. But if he did?

She didn't have anything else with her. No purse. No cell phone. No pacifier or bottle for Aiden.

She swallowed hard, practically choking from lack of air as she slid behind the pile of pallets.

"Shh. Shh. We're okay," she whispered to Aiden, wishing she had the smallest sense of direction to know where to go next.

Dawson had ridden his bicycle through the woods to her house earlier in the week. Maybe if she ran long enough, she'd arrive in her own backyard. She'd let her father take care of the psycho following her.

But she had no idea where she was or in which direction she'd run.

"Gah!" The baby's sudden noise startled her.

She fell back from her crouch, landing on her butt on the cold ground.

"Shh," she urged, terrified that whoever had followed them would hear.

What had the psycho woman done to Officer Stallworth? Had she shot him? Bailey hadn't really taken it seriously when her mother had warned her that someone had threatened her. Who would want to hurt her besides her cruel ex-boyfriend?

"Bah!" The baby made another little noise that might as well have been a cannon shot for the way it carried through the quiet woods.

Bailey pressed her knuckle gently to Aiden's lips, where he gummed it happily for a moment. Squeezing her eyes tight shut for a moment, she prayed for a clue of what to do. It wasn't just her at risk here.

What if that crazy woman hurt Aiden? Her heart hurt at the thought. Who could hurt a helpless little baby?

Dawson's words from the other night echoed

in her ears…about how much it sucked to watch someone else be hurt and not be able to do anything about it. She couldn't imagine that kind of pain—so different from being the target of someone's abuse. Awful in a whole different way.

Her stomach curdled around the granola bar she'd eaten after school. She swallowed hard. She couldn't throw up now; it would make too much noise.

Another good one to share with Meg. She'd write her next descriptive essay for AP English on why puking was too loud when a homicidal maniac was chasing you.

She looked down at Aiden in her arms. Were they better off running to put more distance between them and whoever chased them? Or was it safer to hide?

She decided to listen a while longer. See if she could catch her breath, get her bearings and come up with a plan. But already she had one small part of her plan set.

If she was lucky enough to get both her and Aiden out of here alive, she wasn't going to be keeping her secret about J. D. Covington anymore. Dawson had said telling the truth would keep her safe. And never in her life had she wanted to feel safe more than she did right now.

She'd go to the sheriff and file a complaint. That might also help ensure J.D. didn't hurt another girl down the road.

The fierceness of that new realization straightened her spine as she looked out over the forest. Maybe she really had channeled some of that damn archer queen after all.

GET TO ONE of her brothers' houses?

Not happening.

Amy might not want to make her teenage encounter with a sexual predator public, but that didn't mean she was going to cower in fear every time trouble lurked. She was already in her car on her way to the Hasting home. She'd listened to the police scanner long enough to find out Aiden and Bailey were missing from the home. While Amy had been gathering that bit of information, she'd double-checked the contents of her purse for her pepper spray and her baton.

She'd drop-kicked a post beam she'd installed in the kitchen, testing her fighting skills. It made her feel strong, though she doubted she'd be able to drop-kick anyone who dared to hurt Aiden Reyes. Although she might.

It amazed her how much stronger she felt when she focused on protecting a child she cared about as opposed to protecting herself. There was no comparison. She'd already lost her own baby. She wouldn't let anything happen to Sam's.

And if that sounded like a maternal thought...

It was. She acknowledged, even as she turned her beat-up old car into the Hasting driveway along with what must be every emergency vehicle in town, that she already loved his son as much as if the boy were her own. He'd captured her heart the moment she'd seen him cradled in Sam's strong arms.

She might not be ready to think about what that meant for her feelings for the sheriff himself. But with Aiden missing, her love for his child was a clear, shining, immutable thing, filling her with a sense of purpose.

She wasn't sure what she could contribute at the scene, so she parked her car out of the way of the emergency vehicles. She just knew she couldn't sit around and do nothing. A couple of uniformed officers were working at the front of the house, searching the bushes by the windows and examining the flower beds. Another officer sat in the back of the ambulance with a couple of EMTs working on him. She didn't see Sam as she shut off the ignition.

Her aging vehicle backfired, making every head swivel her way. Two of the cops straightened, hands moving for their weapons, perhaps thinking a gun had discharged. Amy held very still, just in case, silently cursing her car.

"She's cleared." Sam's voice boomed over the yard, and the man himself suddenly stood in the front doorway.

The rest of the first responders quickly went back to whatever they'd been doing. She raced toward Sam, her feet taking off before she even thought about what she was doing. She knew without question, no matter how stern and serious he looked looming over the site, that he felt the same strangling fear inside that she did. Maybe that was the only reason she was here. To hold on to him just long enough to share that panic for his child and somehow give it less power by facing it together.

"I told you to go somewhere safe." He opened his arms to her and squeezed her hard. Fast.

No matter what else happened between them—no matter if he couldn't forgive her for not testifying against a man who'd cost them both so much—she was glad she'd been in Heartache for this. To lend Sam her faith in him right now.

"He's fine. I know it." She said it softly as he released her. "What have you found out so far?"

"No sign of forced entry." He drew her into the big, rambling house she remembered from

their youth. It echoed now with brusque conversation between officers through open doors
and windows that chilled the rooms. "The front
door was probably unlocked since Stallworth
was posted out front. He was hit on the temple
with a rock—possibly by slingshot through the
open car window."

"Slingshot?" She frowned, surprised a twenty-
year-old woman would be carrying around
something like that.

"We found one on the ground nearby, probably a kids' toy, and the attacker put it to good
use." Sam brought her into the kitchen, though
his focus was on his phone that was buzzing
nonstop with messages and alerts. "Lorelei has
her phone off, but we spoke to a neighbor who
is watching the younger boys. She said Lorelei had a meeting with the guidance office for
Dawson's school admission."

Amy took in the scene in the kitchen, where
another officer was looking through a leather
handbag that, she guessed, must belong to Bailey McCord based on all the purple accessories
and the white feather fringe on the bag. The officer used gloves to check the girl's phone. It
was in a purple case that said "I love my Irish
setter" and showed a picture of a dog's profile.

"Bailey didn't take her purse with her." Her

unease grew seeing the cop handling the girl's personal belongings with those gloves on.

"We're still trying to determine if she left with the intruder or not. We haven't found any signs of a vehicle parked in the driveway, and none of the neighbors saw anything. But then, the closest house is three-tenths of a mile up the road." Sam's jaw flexed, his whole body radiating tension and frustration.

"We got a fresh print out here, sir," a young man wearing jeans and a sweater shouted through a back window.

Sam didn't invite her to join him, but then again, he didn't duct-tape her to the kitchen chair, so Amy rushed out into the yard with him.

"Did you call Cynthia?" she asked, her brain firing off a hundred thoughts at once as her sneakers crunched through dead leaves from a nearby tree.

"I'm calling in five minutes." He picked up his pace toward a young woman bent over something in the grass behind a metal shed. "Maybe we'll know something by then."

She prayed so. As worried as Amy was about Aiden, what would the news do to the boy's mother, who was already suffering from postpartum depression?

"We have a clear Nike imprint," the blonde

crouched on the ground said, waving Sam closer. "It's size seven, heavy on the toe like she was running."

"Good. That's Bailey." Sam shoved his phone into a leather strap at his waist. "Linda, I need you to organize the search parties. Groups of two, canvass the woods in a mile of each direction from here."

The younger woman stood. In her uniform and with her hair tightly pulled back, she had that all-business look of someone who could marshal the troops.

"I'll have them rolling in five. With your permission, I'll also ask some of the neighbors to take the outer flanks. Everyone wants to help."

"However you want to handle it. You're in charge until I'm back." Sam took Amy's hand and pulled her forward with the momentum of his hope.

"How do you know the print is Bailey's?"

"I'm pretty sure the person after her is Patience Wilkerson. Her sister informed us that she wears a size-nine shoe."

"Oh no! Poor Faith. Should we call out to Bailey, then? Or do you think Patience is with her?"

"Patience left a boot print outside a front window. We think she exited that way and is heading in a different direction." Sam jogged deeper into the woods, his phone still buzzing with messages while they searched the area. "So I don't think they're together. But the question is—which one of them has Aiden?"

Her stomach churned with the sick feeling of not knowing. This had to be killing Sam.

"After meeting Faith, I find it hard to believe her sister would be such a monster as to…hurt them." Her eyes roamed the trees and low undergrowth, searching for any sign of someone having been through the area. A dropped baby toy. A piece of torn clothing or a broken branch.

"She could have killed Stallworth with the rock to the head." The steel in Sam's voice only chilled Amy more.

In her adrenaline-fueled rush to leave the house, she'd forgotten her jacket, and now with the sun going down and the trees shading her completely, she felt the full impact of the cold.

"If she truly found the slingshot on the lawn, she probably didn't realize it could be lethal." Amy, on the other hand, would have known. How often had she studied ways to hurt an attacker in her self-defense classes?

They'd taught her to use any means at her disposal to incapacitate someone. Her pepper spray was in easy reach and so was the baton as they rushed through the dense brush, past rotten logs and a discarded, rusted washing machine someone had been too lazy to haul to the dump.

Her chest ached to the point of pain as Sam stopped to open the washer and look inside it. She thanked God it was empty except for a chipmunk that scurried out.

"Criminal intent or stupidity doesn't matter to me if she hurts my son." The words were so evenly spaced, so deliberately articulated, that they revealed a wealth of emotion seething just beneath the surface.

She reached out to run a hand over his tense arm, never taking her eyes off the ground as they searched.

His radio crackled with static and a sharp tone, making her realize he had more communication equipment on him than just the phone.

"Sheriff, we have a reported sighting of Patience Wilkerson on Partridge Hill Road, near your house." The voice belonged to Linda.

"No word about an infant accompanying her?" Sam asked, his voice sharp.

"No, sir."

"Then send a car over there with whoever you can spare, but keep the bulk of the resources focused on the woods." Sam's gray eyes met Amy's over the black handheld device as he released the button. To her alone, he asked, "What in the hell do you think she's doing on the street where we live?"

"Maybe when she didn't find Aiden, she started to doubt Aiden was at Lorelei's?" Amy couldn't make sense of any of it, still not believing Faith Wilkerson's sister could be so evil. "She might still be searching for Aiden if Bailey has him."

"Either that or she already has Aiden and she's looking for you."

"Me? No one else knows what happened to me that night," she reminded him, unwilling to consider the idea that Patience Wilkerson might have Aiden.

Or worse.

"No one but your attacker. Jeremy Covington." Sam walked with slower deliberation, his gaze sweeping the terrain with methodical care. "He could have told his new girlfriend to silence anyone who might speak out against him. Jeremy wouldn't know you aren't planning to testify. He might have simply heard you were back in town and assumed that you would come forward."

Anger simmered. At herself for letting shame and fear keep her silent for so long. At Sam for reminding her of it now, when she needed all her strength focused on the search for Aiden.

But at least that was better than the icy grip of fear.

"Right. Because he doesn't know that I'm too weak willed to help you with a case that means everything to you," she fumed, her emotions getting the best of her as she bit out the ugly words.

"You know that's not what I meant." He kept his own emotions in check, but she could see the tension in his body. Focused. Immovable.

Lifting his hands to his mouth, he shouted Bailey's name into the dim forest ahead.

"It's been five minutes," she informed him, because it was past time he notify Aiden's mother. "Cynthia should learn about this from you before she hears it on the news."

He paused, his body going still for the first time since her car had backfired and she'd seen him across the Hastings' front yard.

"I didn't want to call until I found him." The tortured look in his eyes was obvious to her even in the growing darkness. Or maybe she heard it in his voice.

She could feel his hurt and regret. She understood it, even as she had to wonder what it meant.

Cynthia was still the mother of his son. They shared something Amy could never fully be a part of, no matter how much she loved

Aiden. The pang in her chest now was different from her fears for Aiden. It was smaller, because it was her own hurt. But she knew it would ache long afterward since it was the dawning of a new realization that would affect her future. Her forever.

She needed to give Sam and Cynthia a chance to heal. To be a family. Cynthia shouldn't have to suffer and miss Sam for ten years before she had the chance to patch things up with him, the way Amy had. Maybe if Amy was out of the way, the two of them could put their rocky start behind them.

"You should call her." She pushed the statement past dry lips. "I'll...keep looking."

Turning, she stalked deeper into the forest, giving Sam a moment of privacy while her heart broke. Only now, with everything else stripped away from her—the attack, the fight with her mother, her own miscarriage—could she truly make sense of what she'd been feeling these past few days with Sam.

What a horrible time to fully appreciate how much she loved him. But that truth was as clear to her as what she'd realized she felt for his son earlier. Love like that made a person strong.

Love like that could make a person better. Help them do the right, noble thing.

Even, she feared, walk away.

"Aiden, where are you?" she said quietly into the fast-darkening woods, shivering at the wind, which was growing colder by the minute. "Please be safe."

A rustling sound nearby made her pause. She looked back, seeing only the glow of Sam's cell phone by his ear now that the sun had set.

"Bailey?" She said it tentatively, hoping it wasn't just another chipmunk or squirrel. "Are you out there?"

Holding her breath at another rustle of leaves, she spotted movement near a pile of logs. A glint of blond hair reflecting a patch of moonlight.

"Who are you?" a girl's voice came back.

"Sam!" Amy shouted, relief almost taking her knees out from under her. "Bailey, I'm Amy Finley. The music teacher's sister." She babbled words, not sure how this teenage girl would know her. "I have the sheriff with me. Do you have Aiden?"

A baby's cry was her miraculous answer.

Behind her, Sam's footsteps vibrated the ground, a welcome sound even if it might be the last time those feet headed her way. Amy had to hold a hand out to a tree to steady herself, not realizing how dizzy the swell of relief could make a person.

"Bailey." Sam's form took shape in front of her, his broad arms wrapping around both the girl and, Amy could now see, the small bundle that must be his son. "Cynthia?" Sam barked into the blue glow of a cell phone. "We have him. He's safe."

Amy swallowed hard and stepped closer, sliding an arm around the girl's shoulders. She remembered the feeling of being alone and terrified in strange woods at night. The confusion and shock that came with the aftermath of a traumatic event. She recalled wanting someone's arm around her, to lead her out of the dark, so she offered what she could to this brave girl who had sheltered a defenseless infant.

Sam held his son now, ignoring his phone and the police radio for a moment longer to cradle the child to his chest.

"Are you okay?" Bailey McCord asked Amy suddenly, her pretty young face close to Amy's in the dark.

"Am *I* okay?" A crazy sort of laugh bubbled free. "Of course. I'm so relieved you're both okay."

"You're crying so much." Bailey pulled her shirtsleeve over the palm of her hand and swiped Amy's right cheek, then her left. "I'm fine. We're both fine," she assured her, crooning to Amy as if she still cared for an infant and not a grown woman.

Wordless in the face of her strength, Amy could only nod.

"Here." Sam turned to her then, his powerful presence affecting her deeply. "Can you take him while I call in?"

"He's really hungry," Bailey explained, patting the wailing boy's back while Amy settled him against her chest. "I didn't have time to get the diaper bag. I just ran when I heard someone in the house."

Amy swiped more tears aside, focusing on the people who needed her. "Hunger is a welcome problem after what we've been fearing."

Following the outline of Sam's broad shoulders on their way out of the woods, Bailey chattered about trying to keep Aiden quiet and worrying someone was following them. Amy listened with half an ear as Aiden's cries grew more frantic.

She kissed his downy head and knew Sam would take care of everything else tonight. She could go home since she didn't really have a place here anyhow.

It was time to finish the cabin renovation. Because Sam was going to have a lot of evidence against Jeremy Covington very soon. Once he picked up Patience, Amy had the feeling things would start to fall into place. Her sister would be okay to testify whether or not Amy was in town.

Now that she'd made peace with her family, she needed to leave Heartache and let Sam move on with his life with his family.

CHAPTER SEVENTEEN

BAILEY SAT AT the dining room table at Mrs. Hasting's house, a cooling cup of cocoa beside her. Wrapped in a warm blanket that Dawson's foster mother had given her, she was flanked by her father on one side and her mother on the other—a minor miracle she would have never anticipated.

But it seemed no matter how angry they remained with each other, they'd both been equally worried about her tonight. They'd arrived within minutes of one another, greeting her with hugs and tears. Yes, *her father* had shed tears for her safety. It was a moment Bailey would never forget.

And during her debriefing about what had happened tonight, she'd also told the officer—and her parents—everything that had happened between her and J.D. The shoving. The shouting. The wrestling that had turned painful on two different occasions.

When she was alone in those woods tonight, the need to share the truth seemed so simple and clear. Now a police report would be filed. A temporary restraining order was already in effect. And she felt like a boulder had been rolled off her back.

"Mr. and Mrs. McCord, I will never be able to thank your daughter enough," Sheriff Reyes told Bailey's dad after the lady police officer finished taking Bailey's statement. "She showed an incredible amount of presence of mind to keep my son safe today."

Bailey sipped from the mug of hot chocolate, letting the sweet warmth settle her nerves. The second wind she'd felt after the sheriff had found her was starting to fade, making her realize—and really, deeply appreciate—how very lucky she was to be safe right now. How lucky that tiny baby was, too. How would she have ever slept again if Aiden Reyes had been kidnapped on her watch?

"I couldn't be more proud," her father was saying while her mother stroked a hand over Bailey's hair in the middle of her back.

"Bailey." Her mom leaned closer to whisper in her ear. "Officer Marquette said we're free to go. But I think someone else would like to speak to you."

Just outside the dining room, she noticed Dawson straddling a kitchen chair at the breakfast bar, scrolling through screens on his phone.

His gaze darted toward her, long enough to make her heart skip a beat.

"Is that okay?" She shouldered her way out of the blanket as she stood. "I mean, I don't need to do anything else?"

"We can leave anytime." Her mom rose to her feet, too, slipping her arms into a heavy cardigan sweater. "And I'm so sorry if I pushed you to be with J.D.—"

Bailey shook her head, unwilling to walk down the path of "what if" anymore. "It's not your fault. It's no one's fault but his." She kissed her mom's cheek and lowered her voice. "I like this boy, Dawson. And I trust him."

"I'm glad for you, sweetheart. And so proud of the woman you are becoming." She tugged lightly on the strings of Bailey's hoodie. "Will you be okay to drive home, or do you want me to wait and give you a ride?"

"I'll be fine." Saying good-night to both her parents, Bailey picked up her mug and walked out of the dining room to where Dawson sat.

He shoved his phone aside on the butcher-block countertop while Mrs. Hasting led the two younger boys—Tucker and Nate—up the stairs for bath time.

Leaving her and Dawson sort of alone. A few people from the sheriff's department were still going in and out of the house through the backyard, loading equipment and talking on phones. But things were definitely winding down. Ms. Finley had left a long time ago and the sheriff had followed Bailey's parents out the door with Aiden sleeping in his baby carrier.

Dawson spun the counter stool beside him so that the seat faced her.

He looked a little rumpled and still so handsome in a white T and jeans. His feet were bare where he rested them on the rung beneath the seat. She set her cocoa on the bar and lowered herself to the spot near him.

"I told everyone," she blurted. In a day that had seemed to last forever, she didn't want to waste any time telling him what she needed him to know. "About J.D., that is. I told both my parents and the officer took a statement about it."

"That's great, Bailey." Dawson nodded slowly, his hazel eyes serious.

They were both quiet for a long moment. The only sounds around them were the quiet swoosh of the dishwasher and the muted sound of conversation between the police officers in the backyard.

"I thought you'd be...happier, somehow," she said finally. "When we talked about this at my house you said—well, I thought—you liked me."

Well said, Bailey, she chided herself wryly. But her skill with words had dried up. She was all awkwardness and jitters.

He tipped his head just slightly to one side. For a moment, it made her think of the way Hazel looked at her when she didn't understand something. He studied her intently as he closed the distance between them.

Making her realize…

He's going to kiss me.

The realization warmed her faster than the hot chocolate. And when his fingers brushed her cheek to tilt her chin toward him, it was the sweetest touch she could have ever imagined. Gentle. Caring. Sincere.

His lips brushed hers, melting her insides until she thought she might slide right off the seat.

When he eased back, it took her a moment to pull her eyelids open again. He still stared at her intently, but the serious expression on his face had eased. His fingers were still curved around her cheek, his thumb stroking her jaw.

"I do like you, Bailey. So much that I was really scared today." His words raked along a dry throat. "When Lorelei said you were missing—" He closed his eyes for a second. "I was ready to tear apart the woods myself to find you. But by the time Lorelei and I got back here, Sheriff Reyes had found you and Aiden."

Her thoughts still stuck on the kiss and what it had done to her insides, Bailey leaned into his touch, liking everything about this boy.

"I figured I'd be safer in the woods than in the house."

"You're smart and brave." One side of his mouth curved in a half smile. "But I really hope you never scare me like that again."

"Maybe you should start babysitting with me," she suggested. "Then you could be sure I was...you know, safe."

"You think the sheriff would mind?" He smoothed a hand down her hair, and she wondered how the worst day of her life could have the nicest ending imaginable.

"We probably couldn't kiss on the job." That would be okay, though. She liked just talking to him. Looking at him was also really nice. Everything about Dawson made her smile.

"We can save the kissing for afterward," he suggested. "I would be okay with that."

"Me, too." Bailey leaned closer to him, so grateful he had come into her life when he did. So grateful he was staying. "But lucky for us, I'm not working right now."

SAM HAD WORKED almost straight through the night after Aiden was found, putting in a twenty-two-hour day before he fell into bed. Alone.

Now, behind the wheel of his pickup and on his way into work again just a few hours later, he debated calling Amy again but decided against it for the same reasons as the night before. She might be sleeping. And after the way she'd had his back in that two-hour window that Aiden had been missing, he didn't want to drag her away from well-deserved rest.

She'd looked exhausted and upset when she'd told him she was heading home after they'd returned to the Hasting house yesterday. She'd offered to watch Aiden for him, but Sam had made new arrangements with Zach. Heather and Zach had promised to look after Aiden, and Clayton had said he'd make sure they were all safe. That gave Sam the chance to close the case.

And he was so damn near to nailing every last crime on Jeremy Covington. Sam rolled down the window to let the cold fall air into the truck, hoping it would help revive him before the caffeine started working.

Patience Wilkerson had been picked up for trying to break into his house. Between the arresting officers' statement and—he hoped—fingerprints on the slingshot, she'd be in enough trouble to possibly give evidence against her boyfriend. If not—at least she was behind bars. Assaulting a cop would keep her away from Aiden for a long time.

But Sam's case against Covington had really tightened up when Tiffany McCord had called late last evening and promised to deliver both Kate Covington's and Jeremy's family computer files to the sheriff's office today. Kate had confirmed that those records contained messages he'd sent to at least six known victims on a computer that previous police searches hadn't unearthed.

With those elements in place, he wouldn't have to torment Covington's victims by making them testify in court. He had a handful of depositions that established a pattern of crimes. And now he'd be able to prove solicitation. The evidence was solid. The conviction would help Heartache heal after the nightmare this case had brought into their midst.

And Amy's secrets could remain her own. But not just because Sam had more evidence now. He understood that the decision to testify or not was hers alone. Now that he'd gotten his own taste of soul-crushing fear, he no longer saw victim testimony as black-and-white. And he hoped that would make him a better, more empathetic cop.

More important, he hoped it would make him a better man.

As he drove down Main Street, he waved at Erin Finley, already at work on her storefront, sweeping off her walkway with a cup of coffee in hand. Lucky's Grocer was quiet as he turned the corner, but a boy on a bicycle refilled the newspaper dispenser with the day's stories.

Parking the truck in the lot outside the town-hall building, he planned to review Bailey's statement and make sure the restraining order against J.D. was extended for a long time.

"Back already?" The town clerk smiled at him as he shoved open the outside door.

The woman tended to put in her hours early, too.

"Can't stay away." He looked forward to quieter months in Heartache soon.

"I saw Kate Covington come in here earlier. She had a big box of files. She said she was going to be in later to give you a statement?"

"Yes. After what happened yesterday, she's been very helpful." It was a relief to hear Kate had delivered on her promises. He had Jeremy Covington now; he could feel it.

"Has it been noisy at your house with all the construction up the hill from you?" the woman—Delta—asked him. She was filing some papers and listening to the morning news on the radio, but she turned it down now as he got closer.

"Not really." He was curious how she knew about Amy's renovations. "There's a good bit of road between the Finley place and mine."

Although he had noticed a lot of trucks in and out of there lately. Between her own work and what she hired out, the cabin had probably come along quite a bit since he'd seen it last.

After closing the filing cabinet, Delta rearranged photos of her grandchildren on her desk, and one of a baby caught his eye. He had that same snuggly seat for Aiden. Damn, but that made him smile. He'd nearly gone out of his mind when he'd found that empty crib the day before.

"I wondered because Ms. Finley left me a phone message last night, asking if I could get the property inspectors over there as soon as possible. She must be making good progress."

It took a moment for the words to click into place. Amy wanted her inspection dates moved up.

And she'd called about it last night. After the ordeal with Aiden and Bailey.

Why would she do that? She'd been tired and a bit shaken when she'd left the Hastings', but she'd said she was fine to go home alone.

Why the sudden rush to be done with the renovation?

He could think of only one reason. Amy was getting ready to leave town.

"When did she want the inspections?" Sam rested a shoulder on the glass window looking into Delta's office, trying to tell himself that Amy couldn't just up and leave town with a big project under way.

Delta shrugged, running a feather duster over a plastic plant as part of her morning tidying. "As soon as possible. But she has to know it takes time to arrange all that. She needs approval on the electric, the new roof she raised…a lot of things."

Amy wanted to get out of town as soon as possible.

That was the only explanation. And it was happening over his dead body.

"Delta, I just remembered some paperwork I forgot at home." Plowing right back out the town-hall doors, he charged toward his truck. He was going to settle the Amy Finley business once and for all.

"THANK YOU FOR letting me come over so early." Gabriella Chance settled onto one of the new counter stools. Amy had bought them to go around the new kitchen island that had taken the place of a former wall in the expanded hunting cabin.

She was happy with the way the kitchen had come together. The creamy speckled granite and stainless-steel cooktop brought a sleek, industrial look to the home. The whole cabin now mingled rustic and modern in a way that pleased Amy's aesthetic. She just hoped a new homeowner would love the way the place was coming together as much as she did.

She flipped the switch on the coffeepot to brew some more and then settled into the molded leather seat next to the high school friend she hadn't seen in a decade. Not since that night. She'd been surprised to get the text from Gabriella that morning—a message the other woman had sent the night before when she'd boarded a red-eye flight to Tennessee—asking if she could see her first thing in the morning.

"You look great," Amy told her honestly, trying to work up enthusiasm for the visit that would have made her happy any other time. But with the events of the day before still leaving her raw, she had to work at the conversation all the more. "West Coast life must agree with you."

"Getting my head on straight agreed with me is more like it. And it took a long time—I can tell you that much." She gave Amy a crooked smile and smoothed her long, fine blond hair—

the same hair that had been the envy of their whole class at Crestwood.

Gabby was a lovely woman, but delicate in the way of fine china or a Victorian painting. She'd always had that kind of beauty—ethereal and otherworldly, her lashes so blond they were almost colorless. But Amy found after a decadelong struggle with her own self-esteem that she didn't envy that brand of beauty so much anymore. She was okay with her blunt-cut copper hair and her average, ordinary features.

She had other qualities that made her stand out.

"Cheers to that." Amy understood the sentiment perfectly. "It took me a while to get myself together, too, and I'm the happier for it."

Or she would be, once her heart understood that Sam had a life apart from her.

"So you must think it's strange of me to be in such a hurry to see you after all these years." Gabriella played with a stack of bangles around one thin wrist, letting them clank gently against the new countertop. "But the truth is I would have visited sooner if I'd known where to find you."

"We both pulled a disappearing act, didn't we?" Amy stood to retrieve mugs from the cabinet, glad she'd stocked the revamped kitchen with at least a few basics before going to bed the night before. The house was still in a state of dust and disrepair, but the kitchen and the new upstairs rooms were in good shape.

"Yes. And I need to apologize for mine since I took Sam with me." Gabriella stared at her across the kitchen. Did that unflinching gaze see how much just his name hurt her today?

"Um." Amy took her time pouring the coffee into two gray stoneware mugs. "That's certainly nothing you need to apologize for. And it was years ago."

"I always felt bad about it, though. He adored you, and he dropped his whole life to rescue me and help Zach—to keep me safe." She licked her pale lips. "I took a self-help seminar recently that demanded we own up to people we'd wronged, and I just— I wanted to say I'm sorry for that."

Any other day, Gabby's words would have been easy to shrug off. But today she was having a hard time talking about Sam when she'd have to leave him soon. Again. She carried over the drinks and set them down in front of the stools.

"Then I accept your apology, Gabriella, but I assure you it's not necessary. Sam made his own choices." The last few words stuck in her throat, but that had more to do with the present than the past.

"But I had a crush on him." Gabriella slid aside her coffee and turned to face Amy. Woman-to-woman. "Or at least I told myself I did in order to forget about someone else. Because Sam was the guy who saved me, so he was safe for me to crush on because I knew—my God, I always knew—you were the one he really cared about."

The open refrigerator door smacked Amy in the butt as she stood there with the creamer in her hand, confused. None of this even mattered now, did it? Except Gabriella seemed determined to get it off her chest. And Amy couldn't help but be interested. It'd been years since she'd let herself think about that long-ago summer, and now—in the last two weeks—she'd seen it from so many new angles it made her head spin.

"Sam and I have talked about that summer. I hope you don't mind, but he told me what happened to you, Gabby." The old nickname rolled off her lips without thought, but the conversation had definitely ventured into highly personal terrain. "What happened wasn't your fault. You can't feel guilty about something that you didn't do."

Listen to her. *Doctor, heal thyself, right?*

She'd been giving herself the same pep talk for years.

"But I don't—" The other woman cut herself off. Straightened. "You're right. I know you're right. I've dealt with a lot of the facets of what happened that summer—my father went to jail, I tried to kill myself, I got attacked, we ran away..." She shook her head. "It was all such huge stuff, and I've battled it. But now it's the smaller things that come back to bite me. Like the fact that I took your guy out of town and I really freaked anytime him or Zach mentioned calling anyone from home."

"You were scared." Amy poured sugar in her coffee and passed the plastic container to Gabriella, surprised how much easier it was to talk to her about huge life-and-death events than it was to talk to regular people about little things. But Gabby was a survivor, like her. She understood how that felt. "Sometimes being scared is what keeps you safe. And that's not a bad thing."

"Yes. Yes. And hell yes." Gabby added sugar to her own drink and stirred.

"Can I ask you a personal question?" Amy tipped her head sideways to reassess the delicate blonde, seeing the strength beneath that pretty exterior.

"Anything. You made a weird and difficult confession easy on me, so I owe you a freebie." She lifted her mug to her lips, her stack of bangles tinkling.

"Who were you trying to forget about when you talked yourself into a crush on Sam?" She was curious. They'd gone to school together. Maybe she knew the guy.

"He hadn't lived here long when I left, so maybe you wouldn't remember the boy who moved into the Hasting house after Sam. Clayton Travers?"

Amy's mug slipped in her grip, sloshing coffee forward before she got a better hold on it.

"Has Zach mentioned to you Clayton is in town?" Amy tried to remember what Sam had told her about him.

Gabriella's expression froze. She looked like a photo image of herself, unmoving.

"Gabby? He's not a bad guy, is he? He's working for your brother, at least until the trial. Zach hired him to be my sister Heather's bodyguard." Amy hadn't met him, but Heather liked him well enough. "He's a PI in Memphis, but he came back for a reunion of the Hasting foster kids."

"Clayton?" Gabriella's voice sounded off. "Travers?"

Okay, then. Definitely a past there.

"Yes. I'm surprised Zach didn't mention it to you."

"I haven't spoken to him in a few days. I was out of town for that seminar, and then I decided to fly straight here for the trial." She stood, seeming to forget all about her coffee.

Amy rose, too, but before she could try to convince Gabby to sit back down, a flash of metallic black paint passed her front window, and the shadow of a big pickup truck slid by.

Sam was here.

"I've got to go, Amy." Gabriella picked up her sweater. "I'm so sorry to leave awkwardly. I just— I need to go."

She darted out so fast, she barely acknowledged Sam in the driveway. Amy's heart was racing now for completely different reasons anyhow. What was Sam doing here?

She couldn't seem to pull her eyes off him as he stepped out of the truck and said hello to Gabby.

Struggling to catch her breath, Amy ran nervous fingers over her hair. She'd expected him to be busy with work while she finished up on the house and quietly left town. But the way his stormy gray eyes zeroed in on her, she had the feeling he wasn't here for any quiet goodbyes. There was a tense set to his shoulders. A determined jut of his chin.

And, yes, she could read the man that well, a skill she had probably developed long ago because he simply didn't say much. He expressed himself in other ways. Like now, when he wore that fearsome expression.

What on earth had set him off this morning?

"I wasn't expecting you." She folded her arms across her chest to ward off the morning chill as she stood in the doorway.

"And I sure as hell wasn't expecting you to turn tail and disappear right out from under my nose. Not after everything that's happened between us." He didn't stop until he stood a hand's span from her, so close she could feel the heat of his frustration and his raw, masculine appeal. So close she could almost forget her nobler instincts that told her he deserved a chance to be a real family with Aiden and Cynthia.

"I wasn't going to disappear." She fought the urge to touch him. Or to step back so she didn't touch him. Either option would send the wrong message and reveal how very much he affected her.

"Can you deny you're leaving town again?" His hands seemed just as restless as hers when he rapped the back of his knuckles against a porch post in a quick, anxious rhythm.

"I never planned to stay." It was the truth, although she might have entertained the thought briefly after she'd spent the night with Sam. So many things in her life had started coming together—her relationship with her mother, her siblings...herself. "I have a life in Atlanta."

"Oh? Tell me about it." He sidestepped her to sit on the porch swing, keeping his feet planted on the plank flooring, his elbows on his knees. "I want to hear about this life in Atlanta that you want to return to so damn badly that you moved up the time frame of your renovation project just to get out of here faster."

Ah. That explained why he was on edge. He must have heard something from the woman who worked in the permit office. No surprise in a small town.

"I have my own business. Doing accounting for people. Some consulting. Some tax preparation. Whatever it takes to stay afloat." She shifted to stand near the porch post farthest from him, needing that distance to keep perspective. To prevent herself from throwing herself at him and losing herself in the chemistry that had always sparked between them.

"A job you could do anywhere, if you chose to." He templed his fingers together, never taking his eyes off her as she moved.

"I guess. Although Atlanta is a bigger city where I could hopefully find more clients."

Though suddenly she didn't want to return

to her tiny apartment, where she'd scrimped and saved every penny for years.

She'd been too proud to ask her family for any kind of support, needing to prove to herself she could be strong. Independent. She actually had solid savings and a few good clients. Plus the profit from her share of the cabin would help her expand the business. She'd planned it all carefully.

"Maybe, but a bigger city means far more competition," he pointed out, as if this conversation would have any bearing on what she chose to do with her future. "Here, the Finley name is trusted, respected and well-known."

"True." But it didn't matter that he made reasonable arguments. Or that he was the best thing that had ever happened to her. That she loved him and wanted to be with him.

She loved him too much to think about herself.

"Your family has missed you, Amy. I've missed you." The sincerity in his voice was reflected in his eyes.

He was a man of few words, but she knew he meant what he said.

Her throat tightened up.

"It's been really good seeing you again." She owed him that much, didn't she? She couldn't just pretend this time with him hadn't affected her, even if she was still going to leave.

"So why the rush to go?" He rose to his feet again, stalking across the planks toward her, not stopping until he was close enough to touch her.

And he did.

His hands cupped her elbows, and his fingers gently stroked the backs of her upper arms through the heavy knit of the long sweater she wore over leggings.

"I know you think there's nothing left between you and Cynthia. But you share Aiden, and he's the most important thing in your life. You told me yourself that no one can take a mother's place." He'd always said how important family was to him as a foster child. "The two of you will share that bond for a lifetime. And I won't ruin your chance of having the family you always wanted."

His hands stilled, but he didn't move away.

"You weren't going to ask me about the family I always wanted? You just decided who belonged in it and who didn't?" His eyes searched hers.

"She's the mother of your son." She stepped back, unable to think when he touched her and looked at her like that. "That gives her a pretty strong claim. You said you didn't want

Aiden to go through the pain that you did, losing a mother."

"She will always be his mother, Amy. But I still get to choose who I want in my family. You should know that blood doesn't dictate that for me." He didn't move to follow her, allowing her to pace the small porch, dodging a roll of leftover insulation from the roofing project earlier in the week. "Lorelei is the only woman I'll ever call my mother. That's a bond we chose, not one biology pinned on us."

"I understand. But I know how it feels to be shut out of your world." She'd been so hurt when Sam had left town ten years ago. She'd been adrift for years, and it had owed as much to his defection as any rift with her family or even that awful night in the woods. "I remember how awful it was to be on the outside looking in, powerless to have a relationship with you. I don't want to do that with her when she loves Aiden and maybe she could love you, too."

She wrapped her arms around her midsection, suddenly unbearably chilled. A breeze ruffled her hair, sending strands across her cheek and neck to tickle her skin.

"But I'm in love with you."

Even without his hands on her, the words

cracked through her defenses to touch the softest, most vulnerable part of her.

Because Sam Reyes was not the kind of man who said things lightly.

She forgot all about the cold.

"Sam." She couldn't breathe. "I never thought— That is, I didn't—" Stopping herself, she wasn't even sure what to say. She hadn't counted on this.

"You can't deny that being back together... It's as if we were never apart. That day we went to the bridge and you came back to my house, those hours made me happier than I've been in a long time." He stepped close so he was toe to toe with her again, bringing all that strength and raw male appeal with him. "And that was all while I was wrapped up in a huge case. Can you imagine what our days might be like when the only crime I'm stopping is public nudity from teenage skinny-dippers?"

A surprise laugh escaped her even as her heart urged her to accept what he was suggesting. "We might have been the only kids crazy enough to try that."

"Let's find a little of that crazy again and take a chance on each other. On a future. I want you in my life, Amy, however I can have you. You leaving isn't going to change that."

He did touch her then, his hand sifting through her hair to curl a strand around one finger.

"I do love you, Sam." She had kept enough secrets to last a lifetime. This was one truth she needed to share. "So much. I want you in my life, too. But while I'm getting closer to being ready to testify, I'm not sure I'm quite there yet. Can you ever understand that?"

His arm snaked around her waist, his lips brushing hers as his breath warmed her mouth. "Yesterday made a lot of things clear to me, Amy. And one of those was that things aren't always black-and-white. I'll support you whatever decision you make."

He drew her body to his, fitting her curves to his hard planes in a way that made her light-headed.

Almost as much as his words did.

"I want all the things you talked about. A life here. With you and Aiden." She confessed the deepest needs of her heart, knowing they would be safe with him.

She didn't have to give him up so he could have a family. He wanted *her* for his family.

"I believe I can make you happy here. But if you want to move—"

"I'm excited to be a real Finley again. Family first."

"Except I'm going to work on making you a

Reyes." He kissed her so softly her toes curled inside her boots, her whole body responding.

"Remember when we first met?" Opening her eyes, she looked into the ones she wanted to see for the rest of her life.

"The teacher asked us to carry the archery boards." His lips found a vulnerable spot on her neck, and she had to wrap her arms around him to keep from melting at his feet.

"And I told you not to bother helping me because I could manage on my own?" She'd tell that story to Aiden one day when he was old enough to have his first girlfriend.

"So surly when I'm not kissing you." He swept aside her hair to nip her ear.

"I'm glad you didn't listen." She cradled his face in her hands, hardly believing her path had brought her back here, to this man.

The one who'd been so right for her all along.

"Just because you can manage on your own doesn't mean you should." He lifted her up in his arms, sliding her body against his as he tugged her off her feet to kiss her thoroughly. "I don't suppose you have any of the bedrooms finished inside this place?"

He paused to open the front door of the re-modeled cabin. Warmth drifted out to envelop them along with the scent of sawdust and pine.

"There is one." Now that she didn't have to move up the renovation, she had hours to love this man.

"Good." He carried her across the threshold and locked the front door behind them. "I want you to show me because I'm in the market for a house. I'm tired of renting. And I have a family to think about."

Her heart swelled at the possibility they could stay right here in this place she'd come to love deeply. "Really?"

"Only if it can feel like home to you." He wrapped a hand around each of her thighs and levered her legs up around his waist, striding through the kitchen with her toward the new staircase. "I want a house you'll never want to leave."

"This is going to be perfect." Heat flooded her skin at the intimate brush of their bodies. Her fingers worked the buttons on his shirt as he climbed the stairs to the all-new second story.

He took them sideways through the open door at the top, the one bedroom she'd set up. The bed waited at the center of an otherwise empty room, a new white duvet rumpled on top of the sheets where she'd slept for the first time the night before.

"You know what makes a house a real

home?" he asked, tunneling strong hands under her sweater to caress her hips. Her waist.

"Love." She edged back to look him in the eye.

"That's right." A grin lifted one side of his mouth as he lowered her to the bed. "Let's make some."

* * * * *

LARGER-PRINT BOOKS!
GET 2 FREE LARGER-PRINT NOVELS PLUS
2 FREE GIFTS!

◆ HARLEQUIN®

Romance

From the Heart, For the Heart

YES! Please send me 2 FREE LARGER-PRINT Harlequin® Romance novels and my 2 FREE gifts (gifts are worth about $10). After receiving them, if I don't wish to receive any more books, I can return the shipping statement marked "cancel." If I don't cancel, I will receive 4 brand-new novels every month and be billed just $5.09 per book in the U.S. or $5.49 per book in Canada. That's a savings of at least 15% off the cover price! It's quite a bargain! Shipping and handling is just 50¢ per book in the U.S. and 75¢ per book in Canada.* I understand that accepting the 2 free books and gifts places me under no obligation to buy anything. I can always return a shipment and cancel at any time. Even if I never buy another book, the two free books and gifts are mine to keep forever.

119/319 HDN GHWC

Name	(PLEASE PRINT)	

Address		Apt. #

City	State/Prov.	Zip/Postal Code

Signature (if under 18, a parent or guardian must sign)

Mail to the **Reader Service:**
IN U.S.A.: P.O. Box 1867, Buffalo, NY 14240-1867
IN CANADA: P.O. Box 609, Fort Erie, Ontario L2A 5X3
Want to try two free books from another line?
Call 1-800-873-8635 or visit www.ReaderService.com.

* Terms and prices subject to change without notice. Prices do not include applicable taxes. Sales tax applicable in N.Y. Canadian residents will be charged applicable taxes. Offer not valid in Quebec. This offer is limited to one order per household. Not valid for current subscribers to Harlequin Romance Larger-Print books. All orders subject to credit approval. Credit or debit balances in a customer's account(s) may be offset by any other outstanding balance owed by or to the customer. Please allow 4 to 6 weeks for delivery. Offer available while quantities last.

Your Privacy—The Reader Service is committed to protecting your privacy. Our Privacy Policy is available online at www.ReaderService.com or upon request from the Reader Service.

We make a portion of our mailing list available to reputable third parties that offer products we believe may interest you. If you prefer that we not exchange your name with third parties, or if you wish to clarify or modify your communication preferences, please visit us at www.ReaderService.com/consumerchoice or write to us at Reader Service Preference Service, P.O. Box 9062, Buffalo, NY 14240-9062. Include your complete name and address.

HRLP15

LARGER-PRINT BOOKS!

HARLEQUIN

Presents®

GET 2 FREE LARGER-PRINT NOVELS PLUS 2 FREE GIFTS!

PASSION
GUARANTEED
SEDUCTION